HARD
VENGEANCE

J. B. TURNER

HARD VENGEANCE

THOMAS & MERCER

Text copyright © 2021 by J. B. Turner
All rights reserved.

Published by Thomas & Mercer, Seattle

www.apub.com

Amazon, the Amazon logo, and Thomas & Mercer are trademarks of Amazon.com, Inc., or its affiliates.

ISBN-13: 9781542025348
ISBN-10: 1542025346

Cover design by blacksheep-uk.com

Printed in the United States of America

To my sons

One

The target would soon be dead.

The two women sat on a luxury yacht, sipping rosé, unaware they were being watched. The sun dipped low in the sky, bathing the teak deck in an ethereal orange glow. The water was like blue glass, barely a ripple on the surface. But a mile away as the crow flies, a man crouched in the back of an RV, watching them.

He was parked on an overlook high on the cliffs of the Spanish island of Mallorca, training his powerful binoculars on the forty-something woman and her friend. He turned up the volume on his headphones as he listened in to the conversation.

The man smiled. He was patient. He had been tracking the target for months. Logging her movements. She occasionally changed her route from her home to her office in DC. Then this vacation had come up, on a yacht owned by the Spanish husband of her college friend. Her friend's cell phone had been surprisingly easy to hack. And from that moment, the target's inner thoughts, plans, and any desires she confided were his.

He'd been planning this moment for months. But his reasons for it—those had been years in the making.

The target curled her hair behind her ear. He had watched her do that before, as she talked to her hairdresser in Bethesda or waited in line at a supermarket. It was a charming mannerism. He had grown to be rather intrigued by the woman. He'd followed her when she headed back to her hometown of Chicago for Thanksgiving.

The more he'd gotten to know her, the more he admired her. The work ethic. The 5:00 a.m. starts. Gym at six. Pilates, occasionally, at the end of the day. He watched her jogging in her Cubs vest around tree-lined streets. He watched her get into her car in the morning, cell phone pressed to her ear.

The man scanned the rest of the deck, focusing on the college friend. She looked younger than her years. Good genes. High cheekbones. He adjusted his headphones, listening to the conversation flow.

He trained the binoculars away from the yacht to a position just over a mile up the coast. A frogman wearing a wet suit and mask, oxygen tank on his back, emerged from the water onto a sandy cove.

The frogman pulled off the wet suit, mask, flippers, and oxygen tank, burying it all in the sand. The mysterious figure looked around for a few moments, then disappeared into the twilight, like a ghost.

The man in the RV afforded himself a wry smile as he trained his binoculars on the yacht for one last time.

Not long now.

Two

FBI Assistant Director Martha Meyerstein lounged on a cream sofa on the sundeck of the luxury yacht, gazing out across the water. In the distance, the lights of Cala San Vicente twinkled. The white-washed houses and villas built into the rugged mountain shielded the quiet town. The early evening sun splashed the distant cliffs in a tangerine glow.

She closed her eyes for a moment, glass of wine resting on her lap. She felt like she was truly unwinding. "I could get used to this life," she said.

Ann McCaul, her closest friend from college, laughed. "I love the Mediterranean in the summer. It's the best."

"I seem to have lost all track of time."

"That's a good thing, right?"

Martha nodded. "A very good thing."

"I'm glad you joined me for this trip. Feels like old times."

"Doesn't Sergio mind you taking off for a full month on his yacht?"

Ann laughed. "My second husband is more chill than my first, let me tell you."

Martha smiled. "I hear you."

"Besides, he's working on some highly leveraged deal of some sort in Singapore. Place of the future, he keeps saying."

"This is more my speed," Martha said. "Time standing still. Time to breathe."

"My mother-in-law, God bless her, wants us to go and live with her in Madrid. But I like having my own space."

"I know what you mean. That said, you're lucky to have an understanding husband in your life."

"What about you?"

"What about me?" Martha said.

"You're happily divorced now, right?"

"I wouldn't say *happily* divorced, Ann. Gimme a break."

"You know what I mean."

Martha rolled her eyes. "No, I don't know what you mean."

Ann topped off their glasses. "What I'm saying is, why on earth haven't you gotten together with that guy you told me about?"

"Jon?"

"Yeah, Jon. Don't act so coy."

"Listen, it's strictly professional."

"Is that all you want it to be? For the rest of your life?"

"Probably not."

"So why don't you give him a call?"

"And say what?"

"Jeez, I don't know. Maybe, *Jon, you want to go out to dinner next week and then back to my place?* That kind of thing."

Martha winced at the idea of being so forward. "That's not me."

"Isn't it? Well, maybe it needs to be. Come on, Martha, you're not getting any younger."

Martha laughed. "Yeah, thanks for reminding me. Besides, you don't know what Jon is like."

"Neither do you. Maybe you need to find out."

"He's . . . emotionally detached at times. He's complicated." She grinned. "Which I like."

Ann rolled her eyes. "Give him a goddamn call."

Meyerstein shook her head and took a sip of her wine. "Maybe when I get back home."

"He's the one, Martha. You talk about him. All. The. Time. Don't forget, I know you. You need a little nudge now and then. Otherwise you'll be stuck working your tail off, year in, year out."

Martha knew what her friend was saying was true. She was reticent about taking the first step. She had thought about it at length. But she didn't want to cross the line, believing it could be construed as unprofessional. How would those she worked with at the FBI react? She worried about the optics of it. She was, by nature, very cautious. She didn't like being rushed.

"Is he a womanizer? Is that what's stopping you from taking the first step?"

"A womanizer? On the contrary, Jon hasn't been with—or at least I don't think he's been with—a woman since his wife died. That was nearly twenty years ago."

"I'm sorry, that was insensitive."

"Forget it. Listen, I care about him, that's true. And I like him. And his daughter. She's sweet."

"Do you think you could love him?"

Martha closed her eyes. She had often posed herself that same question. "Actually . . . I do think I could love him. OK, there, I've said it!"

"So give him a call!"

"And say what?"

"I don't know . . . reach out to him. Stop being that buttoned-up FBI woman. Take a chance."

"What if he rejects me?"

"What are you talking about? You need to tell him how you feel." Ann's wine sloshed a little in her glass. Martha felt like she was back in college, the two of them drinking at an off-campus party, gossiping about the boys across the room. "You've known him for years, and you've only gone out for a drink. Dinner. You need to pick up the pace."

The idea of just going for it was exhilarating, and yet Martha wondered why on earth she was listening to her friend about this. Martha was more comfortable dealing with things in her own way and in her own time. But the fact of the matter was, her relationship with Jon Reznick had already spanned years. Maybe the problem was that she'd been stuck in a rut since her divorce. She was reluctant to open up her emotions again. Her husband's adultery had hurt her deeply.

Ann leaned forward. "Give him a call. It's early afternoon on the East Coast." She winked. "I'll give you a few minutes of privacy." She got up and headed toward her starboard cabin on the lower level.

Martha knew Ann was right. Perhaps emboldened by the wine, she took out her cell phone and dialed Jon's number. It rang five times before she was diverted to voice mail. "Hi, Jon, it's Martha. I'm on vacation in Spain. On a yacht, believe it or not. The water here is so clear, and I was wondering if it's like that in Maine. You always promised to give me a VIP tour of your hometown. I was wondering if you'd want to meet up in Rockland when I get back? Maybe take me out for a nice dinner. Just the two of us. I'd like that. I . . . I guess what I'm trying to say, in a roundabout way, is I've been thinking about you a lot. About our friendship and whether it's time to let it develop further. I hope you understand what I'm trying to say. Anyway, gimme a call. My cell phone is on. I . . . miss you."

Meyerstein felt giddy when she ended the call. It was so out of character. She watched the last remnants of the evening sun sink over the horizon. She thought of Reznick thousands of miles away. She wondered what he was up to. She imagined he would be hanging out in Rockland. Maybe in a bar. Maybe quietly at home. She'd always had a little trouble reconciling his ruthless black-ops expertise with the quiet life he claimed to live when he wasn't consulting with the FBI. Then again, maybe he had business to attend to overseas. He might be working as a consultant to a foreign government. Perhaps he still had connections in the CIA. Maybe he was doing a job for them. He didn't solely work for the FBI. Maybe he was in New York with his daughter. She wondered if he was treating her to a pizza. Maybe taking her for a beer. She thought of herself and Reznick walking down Fifth Avenue. Walking in Central Park. Sitting on a bench in Bryant Park, drinking coffee. Taking in a concert at night. Staying out drinking late. Just hanging out.

She closed her eyes and began to imagine a new future.

Three

The phone call had been rather touching.

The man adjusted his headphones as he listened to the conversation on the yacht from the back of the RV. He picked up the long-range telephoto lens at his feet and focused on the target. He gazed at her long and hard. A striped blue-and-white summer dress. Auburn hair blowing in her face. Sun-kissed cheeks. She'd been picking at a Greek salad since her friend joined her again on deck.

He snapped close-up shots of both women. He knew which was which. But he had to be forensically certain.

He took out the camera's memory card and inserted it into the side of his MacBook Pro. He uploaded the photos to an encrypted facial recognition database of 117 million Americans, set up by a disgruntled former State Department cybersecurity consultant.

Three minutes later, his cell phone pinged. *We have a perfect match. The woman in the striped dress is Martha Meyerstein, Bethesda, Maryland.*

The man took off his headphones. He picked up the binoculars with one hand, cell phone in the other. He controlled his breathing. He looked at the woman's beautiful features, natural and completely at ease. A woman at peace with the world.

He smiled as the adrenaline began to flow through his body. He began to feel alive. For the first time in a long, long while. The anticipation was the thing. The euphoria that would follow.

"Sweet dreams," he whispered to the woman.

He scrolled through his cell phone contacts and tapped a number. It rang three times. He set the phone down and waited.

An almighty explosion ripped through the yacht. Flames engulfed the boat and licked the Mediterranean sky, inky black smoke filling the air.

The man afforded himself a smile. Martha Meyerstein was dead.

Four

Jon Reznick picked up the voice mail when his plane landed at JFK after a grueling flight from Dubai. Thirteen hours after attending the wedding of a former Delta operator, Teddy Fredericks. He was due to meet his daughter, Lauren, that night for dinner in Manhattan. His grouchy mood dissipated when he listened to the forty-five-second voice mail message.

Reznick checked his watch. It was not even 6:00 a.m. in New York. But that would be around noon in Spain, where Martha was calling from. He decided to call and maybe catch her having lunch, but there was no answer.

He caught a cab to the Mercer in Soho and checked into his room, exhausted.

Reznick slept most of the day and woke up midafternoon. He showered, feeling refreshed. He walked around the streets of Soho for an hour or so, glad to be back on American soil. It felt good to be stretching his legs, clearing his head. He headed back to the hotel and to the bar, wondering what he was going to say to Martha when he called.

He tried her number again. But still no answer. *Strange,* he thought. He wondered if she was having second thoughts. Maybe she regretted making that call. It had been, on reflection, out of character. She had shown a rare side of herself that Reznick hadn't often seen—the woman, not the senior role she occupied. She had dropped her guard, albeit briefly. But perhaps she'd had time to reflect on the ramifications of starting a relationship with Reznick. Had it suddenly dawned on her? How could she, an FBI assistant director, start a relationship with a guy like him? A man who lived in the shadows. A man who killed people for a living.

Reznick pushed those thoughts to one side as Lauren arrived. She wore dark jeans and a black T-shirt, blond hair shoulder length, shiny. His girl was all grown up. Her eyes were clear and sparkling. He kissed her on the cheek, and they hugged tight.

"You look tired, Dad," she said.

"Long, long flight. Dubai. Thought it was never going to end."

"What was it like?"

"Hot. Very nice hotel. And great wedding. You're not going to believe what I'm going to tell you."

"What?"

A waiter escorted them to their table.

Lauren sat down, Reznick opposite. He ordered a bottle of Rioja and a bottle of sparkling water. "So are you going to tell me or not?" Lauren said.

"Listen to this," Reznick said. "Martha called me from Spain."

"What's she there for?"

"Vacation, what do you think? Anyway, she called when I was in the air. I got the message when I landed. And this may interest you."

"Dad!"

Reznick leaned closer to his daughter and whispered, "She wants to meet up. Not business."

"Oh my God. That's great, Dad!"

Reznick shrugged. "It's nice. Unexpected, but nice."

"It's time. You need to move on. Jeez, how long has it been since Mom died?"

He smiled sadly. "A long, long time." Another life, it sometimes felt like. Elisabeth had died on 9/11, sending Reznick, who was already a Delta operator, plunging into a spiral of depression and binge drinking, leaving him struggling to raise their baby girl alone. He had briefly, for a couple of years, handed over the responsibility to Elisabeth's parents in Manhattan. That was his lowest point. But he pulled himself together. He thought Elisabeth would be proud of the job he'd done, of who Lauren had become. And now that she had recently graduated and begun to forge her own life, he thought Elisabeth would want him to move on with his.

"She's the one, Dad."

Reznick nodded and smiled. "I hope so." He paused for the waiter to pour the wine and water before he resumed the conversation with Lauren. "I like her. A lot. So, we'll see."

"What does that mean? She's fantastic. What's not to like? She's supersmart, tough, highly intelligent, and she clearly loves you."

"Well, let's not get ahead of ourselves. She never said that."

"So, what did she say?"

"She wanted to meet up in Rockland, get to know each other better. That kind of thing."

"That's really fantastic news."

"I tried calling her back, but she's not answering."

"She will, believe me."

Reznick looked into his daughter's eyes as she took a large gulp of the wine. "What about you?" he said. "You're all grown up and back in the big city."

"FBI field office, lower Manhattan. Only a few months in. But I'm loving it."

Reznick leaned forward, grinning. "I know you are. I can tell just by looking at you. So, how does New York compare to Quantico?"

Lauren looked thoughtful. "Quantico was the basics. Twenty tough weeks. New York is . . . It never stops moving. And there's so much to learn. It's fantastic."

"You've got to work hard to get the rewards."

She raised her glass and clinked it with his. "To family. And hard work. And love."

"Gimme a break, will you? It could be nothing."

"It could be everything."

Just after midnight, Reznick hailed a passing taxi to take his daughter back to her Midtown apartment. He kissed her on the cheek. "Take care, honey."

"So good to see you, Dad."

Reznick shut the cab door, rapped on the window. Lauren smiled and waved back. He felt much better after seeing his daughter. He headed inside for a nightcap before bed.

The barman poured him a Talisker single malt, neat. He took a sip as his stomach warmed. He checked his messages again. No message or voice mail from Martha. He called her number again. But it just rang and rang.

He wondered if poor cell phone reception at sea was affecting things. He figured it probably was. Perhaps she had access to a satellite phone on the yacht. But he knew her FBI-encrypted cell phone was typically all she would use.

He thought back to the evening with Lauren. She looked great. And her career was taking off. Most of all, she was happy.

He felt at peace. There had been times when he'd wondered if he'd ever feel like that again. But his daughter was in a good place. She was thriving. And Martha wanted to talk about them. Together. About spending time with him.

The more he thought about it, the more he considered that it was the sort of future he could embrace. He began to imagine a life with Martha. He had cut himself off emotionally for too long. It was like he had endured an endless night since his wife's shocking death. The pain of the past was always going to be there. But he needed to heal. And to be healed.

Reznick got up from his barstool. He left a generous tip and headed up to his room. He watched *The Late Late Show*—a clip of a Hollywood celebrity who appeared in musicals, a guy he had never heard of, singing a Beatles song in a car with the English host.

He flipped between the cable news stations, which were focusing on the President's upcoming speech at the United Nations.

Reznick felt his eyes getting heavier as the anchor droned on. He felt himself falling deeper into a bottomless pit. He sensed he was swimming in darkness.

His cell phone buzzed, rousing him from sleep.

Reznick squinted at the TV. The news was still on. It was the dead of night. Who the hell was calling? He wondered for a split second if it was Martha. But when he checked his cell phone, he didn't recognize the caller ID.

"Jon, is that you?" The man's voice was shaking with emotion.

Reznick sat upright, picked up the remote, and turned off the TV. He switched on a bedside lamp. "Who's this?"

"Is this Jon Reznick?"

The voice sounded familiar.

"Who is this?"

"It's Jerry Meyerstein. Martha's father."

"Jerry? What's going on? It's real late. Are you OK?"

"No, I'm not OK. I'm sorry to bother you at this ungodly hour. It's just that I don't know who to talk to. I don't know who to turn to."

"Jerry, what's happened?"

"You're the only person I thought of to call. I don't know what else to do."

"Jerry, tell me, what's wrong?"

"There's been an explosion. Martha's dead."

Five

The sky was slate gray on a sultry Chicago day. Reznick's plane touched down at O'Hare, and he took a half-hour cab ride to the affluent North Shore suburb of Winnetka. The Meyerstein family home was situated on a quiet, tree-lined street.

Jerry Meyerstein was standing at the front door of the beautiful colonial. He wore a maroon wool sweater, plaid shirt underneath, navy cords, and brown brogues. His eyes were bloodshot as if he had been crying. "Good of you to come, Jon," he said. "My wife is in bed; her doctor prescribed her some medication. She collapsed shortly after being told the news."

Reznick nodded as he took Jerry's firm grip. "I'm so very, very sorry for your loss. It's devastating news."

Jerry wiped the tears from his eyes. "Goddamn." He stepped forward and hugged Reznick tight. "She talked fondly of you, Jon. Trusted you. As do I."

Reznick was shocked at the display of raw emotion. He knew Jerry Meyerstein as a tough, uncompromising figure. One of the most feared litigators in the city. A man who put the fear of God into opposing law teams. The guy was a bruiser. Old school. But here he was, as if his soul had been ripped out.

"Thanks for coming on such short notice."

"Of course."

Reznick shut the front door behind him and followed Jerry across the highly polished hardwood floors into a living room that overlooked a sprawling manicured garden.

Tears filled Jerry's eyes. "I don't know where to start. I would never have imagined this happening." He pointed to the sofa. "Take the weight off, Jon. Can I get you anything? Sandwich. Coffee?"

"I'm good."

Jerry slumped down in a brown leather armchair and shook his head. "You're a father, aren't you? A child should never go before a father. It's unbearable."

Reznick's stomach tightened. He knew only too well the fear of losing his child. It didn't bear thinking about.

"I don't know what to do. I don't know what to goddamn do! I've usually got answers. The truth is, I don't know how to deal with all this. I feel like I'm drowning."

"Tell me what happened."

"I will. But first I need you to know something." Jerry glanced toward the ceiling, no doubt thinking about his wife lying upstairs. "My wife doesn't know this yet, but I'm sick. The doctors don't think I'll see out the year."

Reznick felt as if he'd been hit hard in the guts. The wind was knocked out of him. "Christ, I'm so sorry."

"It comes to us all, Jon. I hope you don't mind. Maybe this is presumptuous on my part. But I want to ask a favor."

"Name it."

"I knew from the moment I met you that you were a man of integrity. I don't know much about what you do or have done. But I know enough about people to know that you're someone I can trust. A man of character."

"Tell me about this favor."

"I knew my daughter's mind. She confided in me. I know she was very fond of you. She valued your judgment. That's why I'm going to tell you what I know."

Reznick nodded.

"I got a call from the State Department."

"Interesting."

"I didn't catch the man's name. I think I went into shock or something. Anyway, he said there had been a gas explosion on a yacht. That Martha and her friend Ann had been on board. He expressed his condolences. It was all very flat. Strange." He tilted his head. "Almost . . . rehearsed."

"Why didn't this call come from the FBI?"

Jerry snapped his fingers, and Reznick could see the legendary prosecutor in front of him. "Why indeed?"

"But they specifically said an explosion? A gas explosion on board?"

Jerry nodded.

Reznick felt an emptiness open up inside him. He imagined Martha's final few moments. Consumed by flames. Thousands of miles from home.

"I said I wanted to fly out."

"What did they say?"

"Not an option. And that was that."

Reznick frowned. "How do they know for sure?" he said. "That it was a gas explosion? An accident? It must've only just happened."

The sharpness in Jerry's rheumy eyes said he wondered how Reznick knew that he had been asking the exact same questions. "They just know. The guy said they were presumed dead."

"And you're sure it was the State Department that called you?"

Jerry nodded slowly, head bowed. "You know, I never in my darkest days imagined my beautiful daughter ever going before me. And in such awful circumstances. Never. That's the thing that's eating me up. But to be told I can't even travel to see her final resting place?"

Reznick stared at the feared Chicago lawyer. He had read his profile in the *New York Times*. About his tough upbringing on the South Side. Going up against corrupt city hall politicians. And then heading into private practice, setting up one of the city's most respected law firms. "I don't know what to say. Martha meant a lot to me."

"I know she did. Jon, you're probably wondering why I invited you here. I could've told you all this on the phone."

"It crossed my mind."

"I needed to speak to you face-to-face. I know what Martha thought of you. What she talked to me about. Private talks. You were more than a colleague to her."

"Jerry, I got a short voice mail message from her."

"You did? From Europe?"

"She was on the yacht in Spain at the time."

"Do you mind if I listen?"

"Not at all." Reznick took out his cell phone and placed it on the coffee table. The message began to play.

Jerry listened, tears streaming down his face, to his daughter talking about the future, unaware of what was about to happen.

"I was on a plane and didn't pick up until I landed in New York yesterday morning. The message was probably left very shortly before the explosion."

"She had the most beautiful voice. Just like her mother's. Can you give me a copy of that?"

Reznick sent the voice mail attached to an email. "It's yours. Jerry, it goes without saying that I'll do anything I can to help. So tell me why you called me out here?"

Jerry nodded. "The State Department guy told me, in no uncertain terms, that the media couldn't know about this—that it was a national security issue. They said the information was classified. And they couldn't allow me to fly out there. That's the rationale."

"I understand that rationale."

"So do I. The problem is, I asked them why the FBI hadn't contacted me, and he said as far as he was aware, the State Department was leading on this."

Reznick kept silent, content to listen.

"Here's the kicker. I asked him if the FBI had been informed of what had happened, and he said, 'I don't believe so.'"

"'I don't believe so'? What a strange thing to say."

"That's what he said. He said something along the lines of 'We believe it's best that this information is not shared with them at this stage, as this accident is outside their jurisdiction. I hope you understand and respect that, Mr. Meyerstein.'"

"Now, that is strange."

"It's more than strange. It's an insult to my intelligence. An accidental explosion, and the FBI, at least according to this guy, should not have this information, at least at this stage? It's bizarre. And I'm not buying it."

"That doesn't make sense. Did they say what exactly caused the gas explosion?"

"They say it's too early to say, but they pointed to a maintenance issue with the yacht, an electrical wire linked to the gas canisters, which may have been responsible. But it was all very vague."

Reznick sat in silent contemplation. He thought again of Martha's voice on the message.

"They say she's dead. But I don't have a body. Nothing. I can't grieve for her—we don't have a goddamn body. We can't lay her to rest."

"What about the body of her friend?"

"Nothing."

"What do you want me to do, Jerry?"

Jerry stared at him long and hard. "I believe the State Department knows more than they're letting on. A helluva lot more. If it was a terrible accident, why shouldn't the FBI know this? And why not the goddamn public? What is there to hide?"

Reznick said nothing.

"They're being economical with the truth. I know, I'm a lawyer. I can spot liars a mile off."

"You don't believe this was an accident, do you?"

"No, I do not."

"That's why you asked me to come, isn't it? You want me to find out how she died."

Jerry's gaze burrowed into him as if delving into his soul. "I believe she was murdered. And the State Department is covering it up."

"You know as well as I do, Jerry, there is no evidence pointing to that scenario."

"I have reasonable suspicion, a legal standard of proof under US law. This was murder, not some goddamn accident."

"You seem very sure."

"What they're telling me is a crock of shit. You know it, I know it. And I'm not going to sit around waiting until I die. I want answers."

Jerry sat forward in his chair. "I want you to head over there. I'm not physically strong enough. And my wife needs me. Besides, it's likely that the State Department has flagged my passport. If I were to be pulled aside and stopped at the airport, it would make things even harder. So I want you to find out what really happened."

"You really believe Martha was murdered?"

"I believe she was assassinated."

Reznick said nothing. He didn't know enough at this stage to come to such a conclusion. He wondered if Jerry's emotions were overshadowing his rational thoughts. "You want me to find the person responsible?"

Jerry nodded. "That's why I had to speak to you face-to-face, and not on the phone. Do you understand? I know what you can do. I know I can trust you. And I know Martha loved you."

Reznick nodded. "Are you sure this is what you want? What you really want?"

"More than anything. Kill the son of a bitch who killed my daughter. Can you do that for a dying man?"

Six

A cotton candy dawn greeted Reznick when he finally arrived in Mallorca, the largest of the Balearic Islands. It had been another long, arduous flight. First, a layover in New York. Then Madrid, before the final leg of the journey to the capital of the island, Palma. He had wondered if he should tell Lauren before he headed out of the country. But since she worked for the FBI now, he didn't think it was wise to tell her—either about Martha or about his trip. At least not for the time being.

Reznick rented a car, then drove north to the town nearest to where the accident happened, Cala Sant Vicenç, or Cala San Vicente, as it was known to tourists. He felt drained as he checked into an attractive beachfront hotel. He unpacked his belongings, then charged up his cell phone.

He located the smoke detector on the ceiling, removed it, and replaced it with his own—a surveillance device hidden inside a fake smoke detector.

Reznick often did that when he was checking into a strange hotel abroad. He took a long shower, which felt good, helping to revive him. He pulled on a fresh navy shirt over dark jeans with black sneakers.

He opened the gun case he had kept in his checked luggage during the flight. He took out a 9mm Beretta and tucked the gun into the back of his waistband, putting the spare one in the room safe. The cold steel felt good on his skin. He picked up his backpack with his military-grade binoculars and ammo inside. He always came prepared. He didn't know who or what he'd encounter. But it was always best to be ready for anything.

That was his motto.

He headed out of the hotel and into the dazzling, broiling sunshine. The nearest bar was just across the street from the beach. It was populated by a few Mallorcan locals, a sprinkling of British and German tourists drinking coffee and beer, and a couple of sweat-drenched cyclists enjoying a refreshing drink.

Reznick ordered a coffee, a glass of sparkling water, and an omelet and toast. He sipped his coffee as he pondered what the hell he was doing there. He had flown all the way across the Atlantic. And for what? Was he letting his emotions cloud his judgment? He wondered if he had been hasty in agreeing to what Jerry Meyerstein had asked of him.

It was a gut reaction to the tragedy of losing Martha. He felt obligated. He needed to be here. If not here, where? Was he going to just cut himself off from the outside world again because he'd lost her? Just like he had when Elisabeth died? Numb his senses with booze until he couldn't think? That wasn't an option. Not again. It was better to be here, doing something, even if it was only to quiet the rage that would surely consume him if he sat in isolation. Better to use his skills to find out the full story of what had happened on that yacht than spiral into an inevitable depression. He needed to keep the demons at bay.

Reznick knew all about lows. Bad, bad lows. Unable-to-get-out-of-bed lows. And he knew, just knew, that a black-dog depression would engulf him if he didn't keep busy.

Jerry Meyerstein might have done him a favor. Now he had a purpose. Sure, Jerry had crossed the line with what he'd said. Maybe he had made those comments in the heat of the moment. When his blood was up. Surely he didn't want Reznick to kill the person who was behind this? Jerry would have known Reznick was ex-Delta. He also, Reznick suspected, knew something about the black ops and assassinations he had been involved in. Perhaps Martha had told Jerry that he had avenged his ex-Delta buddy Charles "Tiny" Burns, after a Quds assassination team tracked down and targeted the American Special Forces team involved in taking out a group of Iranian nuclear scientists. He had to assume Jerry knew all that.

Reznick didn't kill lightly. Nevertheless, he wanted to honor Martha's memory and find out what really happened. At the very least.

He looked across the street, beyond the beach, and stared out at the sparkling blue waters glistening like a million diamonds. A place of tranquility. It was hard to believe the carnage that had happened in the waters around this sleepy little tourist town.

Reznick sighed. He had nothing to go on. He didn't have an inside track with the FBI. Not now, with Martha gone. Her boss, Bill O'Donoghue, had always felt uncomfortable with a man like Reznick working in the shadows with the FBI. Reznick understood perfectly well that O'Donoghue and the senior executive team within the FBI had long wanted to cut the cord with him. And Martha's death, assuming the Feds already knew about it, would give them the perfect opportunity. So that avenue of logistical backup had been blocked off. He didn't have a scrap of hard information. He didn't even have the GPS coordinates of where the yacht had exploded.

The bar owner returned with his food.

Reznick thanked him and wolfed down the food, washed down with his chilled water. It was the sort of place he had once imagined visiting with Martha. The kind of place where they could disappear. Be themselves.

The guy picked up his empty plate. "You enjoy?"

"Very nice, thank you."

"You American? I can detect your accent, I think."

Reznick nodded.

"Nice to have you here, my friend. You here on holiday?"

The guy was asking more questions than Reznick was comfortable with. His senses switched on. "It's a bit of business and vacation."

"You want anything, you just let me know."

"Thank you." Reznick sipped his cold water and surveyed the cliffs in the distance. He shielded his eyes from the glare of the sun. He saw kids jumping off the rocks into the water. Tombstoning. He finished his drink, left a tip, picked up his backpack, and slung it over his shoulder.

He got up and headed across the street to a sidewalk. He strolled along and up a winding cliffside road. It opened out to reveal dramatic views over another bay at the far side of the small town. More kids tombstoning from the cliffs.

He climbed up a rocky outcrop and looked out over the water.

Reznick scanned the sea and spotted three red buoys in the distance. A Civil Guard patrol boat was sweeping the area beyond that, as if keeping sightseers at bay.

He wondered if that was where Martha and her friend had met their terrible fate.

Reznick sat down on the rocky outcrop beside a metal weather vane that creaked in the balmy offshore breeze. He'd seen his share of gruesome deaths during his time as an operator with Delta Force. He thought about Martha being blasted out of the yacht, perhaps losing a limb. Catching fire. Screaming. Then throwing herself in the water for respite. But there would be no respite. Whatever had happened, she'd died in agony.

The burns and shrapnel from the explosion would have been too extensive to survive.

Gas explosions were not uncommon. But they usually only happened in badly maintained or very old yachts or boats. Virtually unheard of in the high-end yachts, which would be serviced and repaired frequently. Cost wouldn't be a barrier to the owners of such vessels.

And where was the wreckage? There had to be wreckage. And from that wreckage, the investigators could glean numerous clues. And the bodies. Where were they?

Reznick's mind was seared with images from Iraq. Twisted, bloody, burning limbs, screaming soldiers, roadside bombs, flames, booby-trapped dogs, abandoned cars detonated remotely.

He turned the phrase *detonated remotely* over and over again in his mind. He wondered if that's what had happened here. If the explosion hadn't been an accident. That was the most likely scenario. A device could be rigged to trigger with a simple call from a cell phone. But that would have required planning. Perhaps military expertise. And inside knowledge of the yacht's movements and operation.

Reznick's mind flipped back to a terrifying night in Iraq. He'd been all alone. In Fallujah. An alley. Radio not working. Backup on the way. These dark whispers from his past were never far. They echoed down the years. He'd still sometimes wake up screaming. In a cold sweat.

He forced the memories to one side and reached into his backpack.

Reznick took out his binoculars and trained them on the Civil Guard patrol boat. He could see two divers on deck, putting on wet suits and oxygen tanks, preparing to dive. He watched as they sat down and pulled on their flippers. Then they carefully walked to the side and stepped off the boat, splashing down into the water.

The divers surfaced thirty minutes later. Pieces of metal and wood were hauled onto the boat. Was this wreckage from the yacht? Perhaps the Civil Guard was taking it in for closer forensic examination, looking for clues. Other bits of the wreckage might have washed ashore with the tide. Maybe farther up the coast.

Reznick felt bereft. He was certain now that this was the spot where Martha had met her end. In the beautiful, clear blue waters half a mile, maybe more, from dry land. Slowly, he began to imagine a scenario.

He realized that the rocky overlook, beside a rusting weather vane, jutting out above the sea, provided a perfect line of sight to the area where the yacht had been. It would make sense for someone to set up here to get a visual of Martha on the yacht. But was it really a remote detonation that had caused the explosion?

He looked around. No security cameras in sight as far as he could see. Tourists huffed and puffed in the blistering morning sun as they walked up the winding, steep incline, and cars and buses negotiated the narrow, twisting road. The road had likely been carved out of the mountainside decades earlier to open up the town as mass tourism grew in the 1960s and 1970s.

Reznick put the binoculars away and slung the backpack over his shoulders. He watched the kids on the rocks a little ways below, some jumping into the water, some just watching. They looked like local kids with Mediterranean complexions.

He climbed down the rocky outcrop beside the weather vane to the jumping-off point. "Any of you guys speak English?"

The group turned around and shrugged. Apart from one kid.

The muscular teenage boy walked up to him and shook his hand. "Yeah, I speak English. You American?"

Reznick nodded. He pointed to the Civil Guard patrol boat. "Can you tell me what's going on there?"

"Big explosion. Expensive yacht."

"Were any of you guys here when it happened?"

The boy shook his head. "Friend of mine, he was here."

"Where is he?"

"I don't know. He was interviewed by police."

"Your friend was interviewed by the police?"

The boy nodded.

"And you don't know where he is?"

The boy shrugged. "I asked his parents, but they just said the police are still speaking to him. That's all."

Reznick took a twenty-euro bill out of his pocket, along with a scrap of paper on which he scribbled his cell phone number. "I'm a friend of one of the two American women who died." The longer he thought about the circumstances, the more convinced he became that Martha had been targeted—not her friend or the friend's husband. He thought about the friend's distraught family. A family who'd likely been told a lie, who would be oblivious to the fact that their loved one had probably become collateral damage in the assassination of Martha Meyerstein. "I'd like to speak to your friend. Do you understand?"

The boy took the money and number. "I don't want your money."

"Keep it."

The boy shrugged. "Whatever, señor. So you want me to call you when I see my friend?"

"I'd appreciate that, thanks."

"So, who was the person who died?"

"Just a friend. A close friend."

Reznick walked back into town and headed to the small beach. He found an empty beach hut, changed into some trunks, and swam in the sea to cool off. The cliffs loomed all around. He swam out farther. A lot farther than anyone else.

The police boat was circling and spotted him. A cop on board shook his head, pointing back to the shore. *"No mas, señor."*

Reznick recognized from his rudimentary Spanish that the cop had said, *No farther, sir.* He turned around and swam all the way back to shore. He lay on the beach, drying off in the blazing midday sun. He felt himself drifting off in the heat, the jet lag and exhaustion kicking in.

He sensed he was floating. On the water. The sound of soft whispers in his ear.

The sound of a child crying roused him from a nap.

Reznick turned and saw a boy being scolded by his parents. Reznick picked up his things and headed back to his room. He shut the blinds and showered again, glad to get all the sand and sunscreen off his skin. He lay down on the bed and slept in the cool, air-conditioned room until six.

He had been drained. Exhausted.

The sleep had revived him.

Reznick felt like himself again. He put on a fresh linen shirt, jeans, and sneakers and headed back to the bar overlooking the beach.

"You back again, my friend?" the bar owner said.

"Best view in town."

The bar owner smiled. "You know, my father bought this bar thirty years ago. I'm continuing the family business. He said it was a little slice of paradise."

"It's a lovely spot."

"What can I get you this evening?"

"Cold beer, steak, and fries. Lots of them."

"Wow, you're hungry, right?"

Reznick nodded. "You have no idea."

"You got it."

The guy returned with a cold beer as Reznick surveyed the locals and tourists still occupying the sand or swimming in the sea. He handed the owner a fifty-euro bill. It was amazing what hard cash could do when you needed to pry information out of someone. He'd seen it in Afghanistan. Afghan lawmakers, tribal elders, local power brokers, *maliks*, and Taliban commanders were on the payroll. It bought support. Some were given hundreds, maybe thousands, of dollars. Some a lot more. Some passed on information. Tidbits, sometimes. Scraps. Maybe a favor. But occasionally, it was enough to find out the whereabouts of a high-value target.

"Thank you, señor."

Reznick felt the sweat stick to his shirt. He stared out at the picture-perfect scene. The sun was dipping lower in the sky, long shadows slowly forming. It provided much-needed shade from the oppressive heat.

He took a long gulp of the chilled Spanish beer. It certainly quenched his thirst. Reznick's gaze was drawn to a tattooed white guy, shirtless, shaven head, running hard up the hill.

The guy was clearly superfit. Lean. Not an ounce of fat.

The bar owner returned with the plate of food. "Hope you enjoy this," he said.

Reznick glanced at the food. "Looks great."

"I hope you don't mind me asking, señor, but you said you were American, right?"

Reznick picked up his napkin. "That's right."

The owner leaned closer, hands on the table. "You're not FBI or working with the local police, are you?"

Reznick's senses sparked for the second time with this guy. The specificity of the question meant he knew something. "What do you mean?"

"It's just that we've had a few Americans in. Since we had an accident out there. I was wondering if you were with them."

"No. But one of the people in the accident? She was a friend of mine. One of the people on board."

The color drained from the guy's face. "I'm so sorry, señor. I had no idea."

"Relax, you couldn't have known. So, you're saying some FBI were in here?" Interesting that they were in the loop despite what the State Department had told Jerry Meyerstein. At least the team over here was. It was common for the FBI to have legal attachés on foreign soil to help coordinate investigations that were of interest to both countries.

"Yes, wanting to know things. A lot of questions for a lot of people. They were here in town the morning after the accident, asking questions."

"What kind of questions?"

The bar owner shrugged. "Let me think . . . Did I see anything suspicious on the day of the accident? Any unusual activity in my bar or people in the bar? But there was nothing. This is a peaceful, beautiful place. I heard it was an accident. A tragic accident."

"Did you hear how the accident happened?"

"I heard a spark from a stove ignited gas in the galley on the yacht, down below. That's what I heard. But who knows, right?"

"Who told you that's what happened?"

"That's what people are saying. That's all I know."

Reznick looked at the bar owner and smiled. "Well, just so you know, I'm not with the FBI or anyone. Like I said, one of the people who died was a friend of mine."

"Sincere condolences. If there is anything I can do, just ask. I'm a father as well as a husband. I love my family."

"I appreciate that, thank you. Look, I'm just trying to piece together how such a tragic accident happened. Maybe hoping to speak to someone who saw it happen. Maybe knows something. That kind of thing."

The bar owner's gaze was drawn to a family signaling to be served. "Nice talking to you, señor. I'll be back in a few minutes. Excuse me just now."

Reznick sipped some beer and dug into his steak and fries. He finished the rest of the San Miguel and ordered another from a young waiter. His table was cleared, and he was handed another cold beer. "Gracias, señor," he said. He stared out over the waters, families and tourists leaving the beach. Towels over their shoulders, children in their arms. A place to unwind. That should have been what Martha was doing right now.

He watched the people drift away from the beach as the light began to fade. Some headed to their cars in the parking lot behind the bar. Some headed to the bars and the restaurant overlooking the cove. Some headed into the same beachfront hotel Reznick was staying at. Others sat on a small stone wall, watching the world go by. Some just sat, doing what he was doing, staring at the waters as if transfixed by the beauty of the place. It was that kind of scene.

Reznick closed his eyes, but it seemed like every time he did, he began to imagine Martha's final moments. The split second before she was killed. He hoped and prayed that she'd felt no pain. He'd had so much to talk to her about. A lot between them had gone unsaid. His regrets clawed away at him. A terrible reminder of what might have been.

He grew more morose the more he thought about it.

Reznick snapped back to the present. He gulped some more beer, hoping to numb the pain. He felt it deep. Gnawing the darkest recesses of his soul. A place where he tried to push all the terrible things he had seen and done. The deaths. The suffering. The bullets. The firepower. The endless screaming. The ghostly whispers in his head as he tried to fall asleep. Haunted by the spectral figures, nebulous in form. Ghosts of the past. And now, it was almost too much to stomach, to bear. Not Martha. Anyone but her.

The bar owner approached his table. He looked over and smiled at Reznick as he busied himself wiping down an adjacent table. "I was just speaking to my son," he said softly. "He works in the kitchen. He says there is someone who might be able to help. With trying to find out what happened to your friend. The man, he is, how do you like to say . . . a tough nut."

Reznick took a long sip of his beer. "You have any idea where this guy is?"

The bar owner pointed across the street to the sidewalk beside the beach.

Reznick saw the tattooed, shaven guy was doing another grueling lap in the boiling heat. "The guy without the shirt?"

"That's him."

"Who is he?"

"He comes in here most nights. Usually when it's dark. A word of warning: you don't want to mess with him, huh?"

"Why?"

"It's best to stay clear of him. He's always very respectful and quiet. But not the sort of guy you want to cross."

"Why does your son think this guy might help me?"

The bar owner crouched down beside Reznick. "They arrested him the day after the explosion," he whispered. "They arrested him here at this bar. Right here. I wasn't here at the time."

"And he comes in here for a drink?"

"Every night. When it's dark, you might see him."

Reznick tipped the guy another fifty euros. "Thank you. And your son."

The bar owner leaned in close. "Be careful. That's all I say."

Seven

The line of sight from the sprawling modern villa, perched high up in the hills overlooking the village of Cala San Vicente, was comforting for Adam Ford. It was one of the prime reasons he'd rented the property from a billionaire Spanish real estate tycoon. It had everything he desired. Privacy. Secrecy. Seclusion. And most important of all, that crucial line of sight.

The 4,500-square-foot rental house, shrouded in trees, could not be seen from the nearest road, half a mile away. But the small gap he had carved out by chainsaw, carefully cutting down a young olive tree, allowed him to observe what was going on in the town.

Ford peered through the telescope, out the floor-to-ceiling windows of the living room as he scanned the town's beachside bar, adjacent to the Cala Molins cove. A sheltered haven. He felt his pulse quicken. The profile of the man nursing a beer was unmistakable. He was looking at none other than Jon Reznick.

Ford smiled. His gamble had paid off. Just as he'd known it would. He had calculated that Reznick would show up. He knew the type of man Reznick was. A guy like that couldn't just sit by the phone at home and accept that the explosion had been an accident. He wouldn't trust his own country's intelligence organizations to figure it out—or if they did, not to cover it up in their own interests.

Ford could have drawn Reznick here by broadcasting that he was involved. But it was much more fun to conceal that he was pulling the strings.

He looked long and hard at Reznick. Lean, handsome face, crumpled shirt, sunglasses, jeans.

Reznick looked like any tourist. He just blended in. Very astute. No loud clothes. No Day-Glo colors. No loud Hawaiian shirts or sartorial mishaps like that. Nothing memorable. He wondered what exactly Reznick knew already. The basics—an explosion, a tragic accident? How had he learned the news?

Ford had known it wouldn't take long for Reznick to turn up. And sure enough, here he was. Sniffing around. No doubt asking questions. Trying to figure out how his dear friend, the fragrant but sadly deceased Martha Meyerstein, had met her untimely death. It would take him a long time. And that was good. Very good. It meant Ford had all the time in the world to deal with Reznick.

The thought made him feel giddy.

Reznick, for all his street smarts, was no match for Ford. It felt gratifying to acknowledge it. Intellectually, Reznick was his inferior. Ford was on a whole other level. The truth was, Ford couldn't abide average citizens. They enraged him. When he saw the average Joe—what he read, how he behaved, what interested him—he had nothing but contempt. He wanted to wipe the fuckers out. He was disgusted by them. He'd seen them every day at the hospital in DC. Porters. Nurses. Fat-assed fuckwits. Low-IQ burger-chomping nobodies. Dumb morons. Subnormal. Their subservience. Their herd mentality. The whole human gene pool seemed to be regressing.

Reznick's one saving grace, at least as far as Ford was concerned, was that he had never been part of the herd. Reznick had something those nobodies would never have: raw courage. He did his own thing. He didn't answer to anyone. Ford admired that. The average Joes were cowards. Weaklings. The sort of people who were walked over, day in, day out. Reznick was many things, but weak was not one of them. He wasn't feckless. He wasn't a spineless son of a bitch who simply endured his life. He put himself out there. Sure, the bastard operated in the shadows. But Reznick wasn't the type to hide when the shit hit the fan.

Ford was going to have fun. He had Reznick where he wanted him. Right here. In his sights. Just like Meyerstein had been. This day had been a long time coming. Too long. He'd been planning this for years. Vengeance, retribution—call it what you will. How sweet it would be. He closed his eyes for a moment.

Vengeance is in my heart, death in my hand / Blood and revenge are hammering in my head.

The words, spoken by a character in *Titus Andronicus*, had seeped into his soul. His very being. Reznick wouldn't have read Shakespeare. A guy like that wasn't well read. He imagined Reznick would read military history. He could imagine him poring over biographies of military leaders. That kind of thing. But Ford's brain was far, far superior. He read Nietzsche. He liked that special brand of philosophy. It appealed to him. The mind and order on the one hand, passion and chaos on the other. Ford needed stimulation. Constant mental stimulation to make everything he had endured bearable. He didn't believe in boundaries. A man didn't need boundaries. Conformity led to only one place: mediocrity.

Ford believed a man should lead life on his terms. Answerable to no one. What was right and what was wrong? It was all a matter of interpretation. Perspective.

He stared through the telescope at Reznick. God, he had prayed that this day would arrive.

How often he'd fantasized about how he was going to kill Meyerstein, about ensnaring Reznick. Toying with him. Then killing him. Ford had many options available. A man always needed a backup plan. He had a plan A. But he also had a plan B and a plan C. His Special Forces training came in handy. The need for an operation to be flexible, changing tactics and strategies as and when the occasion required. Modifying existing plans. Refining plans. But always willing to change course and deploy unorthodox methods to achieve the mission's goal. The end result was all that mattered.

Ford also understood human psychology. He knew what made a man like Jon Reznick tick. He had paid a hacker on the dark web fifty thousand dollars to find out everything there was to know about Reznick. He had seen his medical reports. The psychological profile. Reznick was a formidable operator. He was a killing machine. He had concealed his shadowy role from his private life well. But what Ford had also unearthed during his surveillance was Reznick's close relationship to Martha Meyerstein.

Ford had been watching from afar. Sometimes near her home in the affluent DC suburb of Bethesda. Sometimes in New York, if she and Reznick were working together. He had studied Meyerstein's demeanor. The way she walked. The way she talked. The way she interacted. She played tough. But she never played tough with Reznick. She tried to. But it was all surface. She seemed more relaxed around him. Natural.

Ford couldn't understand what a smart woman like Meyerstein saw in a cold-blooded assassin like Jon Reznick. Granted, he was ruggedly handsome, if you liked that kind of thing. But she should have been way out of Reznick's league. She was classy.

Reznick was uneducated. Wild. Untamed. His father was a Vietnam veteran. Reznick himself was an ex-Delta operator. A warrior. He could kill with his bare hands. And he had done so.

Many times. Hand-to-hand fighting in Basra. Stabbing jihadists at close quarters during search-and-destroy missions. He seemed to excel in the hellish environment. Not to be fazed by it. He could compartmentalize. But like most men who had seen real fighting, death up close, he never bragged or boasted or even talked about it. That wasn't Reznick. He kept those things to himself. He didn't do emotion.

Ford tried to push the thoughts of Meyerstein and Reznick's relationship to one side. But still it niggled at him. Why the hell had she been smitten with him? She was highly educated. Her father a wealthy lawyer. She liked opera. She and her college friend, Ann McCaul, went to the Met when McCaul was in New York. Reznick, by contrast, was more at home in dive bars. Playing pool with guys he knew from high school. Blue-collar guys. Guys like his father. A father who had fought for his country in Laos and Vietnam and returned to the grinding poverty of the good old United States. Unloved. No hero's return for him or his veteran buddies. Just scorched memories and scars.

Ford had delved deep into Reznick's background. Spent countless hours reading the military reports of both father and son. Anti-authoritarian traits ran in both. Run-ins with superiors were a common thread. Reznick's father had been incarcerated at the notorious Long Binh jail on the outskirts of Saigon for brawling with sailors on leave. Reznick senior was eventually released after three weeks' solitary confinement in a military-rehabbed shipping container. It was noted by guards that the temperature often climbed above one hundred degrees and that inmates were left naked. Reznick's father survived that. He survived Vietnam. Reznick himself had knocked out an officer in Fallujah who had squared up to him, screaming in his face. They had the same trait. Nonconformists, both.

The father's spirit could not be crushed. Even when he returned to the low wages and humiliation of working in the sardine packing plant, foremen riding him all the time, he didn't break. He took it. That same unbreakable spirit was part of Reznick. These were tough, tough people.

Ford focused on Reznick again as he sat at the bar. A shaven-headed man came into view. The guy ordered a beer and sat down at a table adjacent to Reznick.

Ford's gaze was drawn to the man's forearms. Thick like lamb shanks and covered in tattoos. He watched as Reznick signaled the bar owner. A short while later the owner came over with two beers. One for Reznick, one for the shaven-headed man.

Ford was intrigued. "Well, well, well, Jon. Who is your new friend?"

Eight

Reznick gulped cold beer as he stared out at the sea, bathed in an orange glow from the setting sun.

The tattooed guy at the next table was glaring at him. "Do I know you?" The words sounded extra threatening in his gruff Scottish accent. More than a hint of menace.

"I don't think so."

"You don't think so. People don't as a rule buy me a drink unless I know them. What's this all about?"

Reznick shrugged. "I was told you might be able to help me."

The guy glowered, giving off icy vibes.

"Maybe you can, maybe you can't, I don't know," Reznick said.

"Thanks for the beer. But you must have me mixed up with someone else."

Reznick picked up his beer and took a long gulp. "I don't think so."

The guy got up and sat down in the seat beside Reznick. "You mind telling me exactly who the fuck you are?"

Reznick looked straight at the guy's piercing blue eyes. "I'm looking for some information. I was told you might be able to help."

"I asked you a simple question. Who are you?"

"Name's Reznick. Jon Reznick."

"Is that supposed to mean anything to me?"

"A friend of mine, a close friend, died in an explosion on the water not far from here, a few days ago."

The tattooed guy said nothing.

"She was on a yacht. She was a mother. She had two children who are now facing a life without their mom. A woman who provided for them. They'll need to know what happened to their mother. What I can't understand is how exactly this happened. Some people are saying it was an accident."

"You've come all this way to find out what happened to your friend?"

"I heard you might know what transpired."

The guy was staring long and hard at Reznick as if trying to unnerve him. "I heard it was a gas explosion."

Reznick sighed. "Maybe it was."

"You don't seem too sure."

"I have my doubts."

The man scrutinized Reznick's face. He picked up the beer Reznick bought him and downed the contents in one swallow. He leaned forward and, without asking, frisked under Reznick's arm and the back of his collar. "You wearing a wire? You recording this? You FBI?"

"No, I'm not. Listen, I want to talk to you. Nothing more. I want to talk in confidence. Just me and you."

The guy turned and stared out over the water.

"Talk to me, man," Reznick said. "What do you know?"

"Listen, I don't have anything against you. But you don't want to get involved in this. Just leave it."

"Why?"

"You don't have any idea what the hell is going on."

"Listen to me. My friend died. She meant a lot to me. To a lot of people. She had a family. Can you understand that?"

The guy was quiet.

"If you know something, and I believe you do, I'd appreciate a heads-up."

"I don't know exactly what the hell is going on. What I do know is that there are troubling elements to this. Very troubling."

"What do you mean?"

"It's all fucked up. My advice? Head back to the States."

"Listen, pal, maybe I didn't make myself clear. I'm not going anywhere. And I won't be until I get some answers. A friend of mine is dead. And I believe there's more to her death than meets the eye. What is so difficult to understand?"

The man sighed. "What the hell is wrong with you? Trust me on this, you don't want to get involved."

"Tough shit. I'm already involved. So are you going to help me or not? One way or the other, I will find out what happened. Either from you or from someone more obliging."

The man sat in silent contemplation for a few moments.

"Listen," Reznick said. "I've played nice so far, but my patience is going to wear thin if you're going to jerk me around. Now, can you help me or not?"

Finally, the man cocked his head in the direction of the narrow street adjacent to the bar. "Follow me."

Reznick and the guy headed down the street toward a parking lot at the rear of the bar.

"You ask a lot of fucking questions, my friend," the guy said. "So I'm going to start asking you a few."

"Fire away."

"You working for the Agency? Feds? And I want straight answers."

"You sound like you know what you're talking about."

"I'm waiting."

"I have worked for the FBI in the past. And I have some history with the CIA, but that was a little while ago."

The man stopped as they passed the parking lot. He looked around, as if making sure they weren't being watched. "You have no formal connection to the FBI or the Agency or the State Department?"

"One hundred percent correct."

"Who've you been speaking to about me?"

"It's a small town. People talk."

The guy stepped forward, eyeballing Reznick, who didn't back down. "You don't get intimidated. I like that."

"Are you going to ask me out on a fucking date?"

The man's whole demeanor changed. He roared with laughter, tilting back his head. "I like that too. What's your name?"

"I already told you."

"I know you did. I'm just checking."

"Jon Reznick."

"You're military. I can tell. Special Forces, right?"

"A few years back."

"Why didn't you say?"

"You didn't ask."

"Who were you with? US Rangers?"

"Delta."

The guy whistled. "I knew a few of those guys. Nasty fuckers, if I remember."

"We have our moments."

The guy laughed uproariously again. "I hope you don't mind me grilling you like that."

"Forget it."

The guy smiled. "So who're you working for? I mean really working for."

"I'm working for me."

"You flew all this way? You expect me to believe that?"

"Believe what you want. I want to know what you know. This is a personal thing for me."

The man nodded, shaven head perspiring. "I like an honest man. Now that we've cleared the air, let's go get another beer and we can talk."

Reznick liked the guy. He reminded him of himself.

The man picked a quiet table this time, no one within earshot. After ordering two more beers, the man said, "My name is David, by the way. David McCafferty."

"Nice to meet you, David."

"Let's get a few basics out of the way. I used to be in the Parachute Regiment and then the SAS. You might've heard of them."

Reznick nodded. It was Britain's elite Special Forces.

"People call me Mac." Mac leaned back in his seat and sighed. "That's got that sorted. Now I want to know more about that friend of yours. The one who died on the yacht. Who was she?"

"She was someone I worked with professionally."

"Was she your boss? How did you work with her? In what capacity?"

"I don't know if I can reveal that, Mac."

"Jon, we need to be clear. If I give you something, I need to know who she was."

"I don't think you do."

Mac leaned in close. "I'll decide what I need to know."

"What do you know about her?"

"Not much. But I figure, from the conversations I've had, that she was FBI. Very senior."

"The conversations you had?"

45

Mac nodded. "Two FBI special agents have spoken to me, face-to-face. At a police station not far from here. And as the Feds don't operate outside the States, I figured the woman who died was someone very important or worked for them."

Reznick was satisfied that Mac already had enough knowledge of Martha's background that it wouldn't hurt to divulge more details. He nodded. "She did work for them. And I worked with her at one time."

"Meyerstein, right?" he asked. "Position?"

"You seem to know all this already."

"I do."

"Her name was Martha Meyerstein. FBI assistant director."

Mac whistled and gulped down some beer. "Fucking hell. That's what I heard too."

"You said you spoke to a couple of Feds. When?"

"A couple of Civil Guard guys picked me up the morning after the explosion. They took me to the station. Strip-searched me and interrogated me."

"You look like an interrogation wouldn't bother you too much."

"It didn't. A bit irritating, that's all. But I know how to deal with that. Anyway, it was four guys from the counterterrorism branch of the Civil Guard who were asking the questions. A few slaps. The usual."

"Why did they bring you in?"

"Purely circumstantial. Think about it. I live here. I kayak and dive around this coast, near where the explosion was. I'm a foreigner. And I have military training. I'm ex-SAS. They asked hours and hours of questions about British military intelligence. Did I work for them? Was I working for a foreign government? Have I ever worked as a mercenary? Do I work for MI6? Do I know any British intelligence operatives in Mallorca? Do I know any American operatives in Mallorca?"

"And do you?"

Mac shook his head. "That's in the past. I came here to get away from everything. I've started a new life here."

"Tell me more about this interrogation. Who was there?"

"The Americans, unsurprisingly, were there."

"Where? Actually in the room?"

"No, but they were watching. I heard their voices when I was brought in. State Department and CIA, almost certainly. And the two men who identified themselves as FBI turned up the following day. So what does that tell you, Jon?"

Reznick nursed his beer before taking a large gulp. "All this tells me is that they don't think this was an accident. This was a targeted killing. An assassination."

Mac snapped his fingers. "Exactly what I thought! I'm telling you, from the way they were speaking, it was clear they were working on the premise that this was a targeted attack. They asked constantly about not only my background but my understanding of the waters around here. They really zeroed in on that."

"I'm sorry, I don't follow."

Mac grinned. "Am I talking too fast for you?"

"No, I didn't follow what you meant by your understanding of the waters around here."

"Alright, I see. Well, I know the tides, the rip currents, undertows; I need to know all these things in my line of work. I speak to fishermen, locals, and I see the ebbs and flows."

"What line of work is that?"

"I teach scuba for tourists. And locals, though not so much."

Reznick's mind was racing ahead. "So you're a scuba expert, and you're a former Special Forces soldier from the UK. And you live here?"

Mac nodded.

"So they're putting this all together, all these factors. A yacht blown out of the water, one of the locals is a Special Forces guy who knows the waters, and they're thinking you might have been involved, am I right?"

"You've got it in one."

"I need to know more."

Mac turned and stared toward the beach. A Civil Guard vehicle slowed down in front of the bar. "Think we've got company."

Reznick turned. The cop in the front passenger seat was looking at them, talking into his cell phone. "They really have a thing for you."

Mac said nothing.

"I think you know more than you're letting on, Mac."

"I do."

"What do you know, Mac? Tell me the whole story."

"This was definitely, one hundred percent, not an accident. It was a clear, targeted attack."

"Why so confident?"

"They're already working on the assumption that this was an attack. They know it was no accident. And I know it too."

"How can you be so goddamn sure? All I've heard so far is just pure conjecture."

Mac sipped some more beer and leaned in close. He quickly glanced at the Civil Guard vehicle still idling across the street. "I scuba dive, like I said. And when I was released, later that day, I returned here. I knew I was a suspect. But this is my home. I wanted to help. I volunteered to help the Spanish frogmen from the Civil Guard launch. They told me it wasn't my business. Anyway, I dived well away from the launch, into an isolated cave about a mile from the explosion. Remember, tides move stuff around. And I discovered parts of a device. Small parts. I handed it over to the Civil Guard frogmen."

The cop in the passenger seat got out and walked over to their table. "Señor Mac," he said, "my boss wants you to answer a few more questions. Some paperwork, nothing big."

Mac gulped the rest of his beer and looked up. "I'm busy."

The Spanish cop placed his hands on the table, face in Mac's space. "It won't take long."

Mac looked at his watch before he glared at the cop. "I said I'm busy. Now piss off."

"We are instructed to bring you to speak to some people."

"Some people? What kind of people?"

"Señor, we can play this the easy way. Or we can play this the hard way. Which one do you want us to take?"

"Listen, my sister is flying in to see me tomorrow. And I need to be up and about early to pick her up from Palma. So, I'm sorry, I'm not going to risk being late for her."

The cop shook his head. "It won't take long. Maybe fifteen minutes. A form to sign. Some questions. I promise. It's routine. One form."

"A form to sign." Mac sighed and looked at Reznick as he reluctantly got to his feet. "Never a fucking break."

"Where are they taking you?"

"Sa Pobla, at least that's where they took me before."

Reznick could see Mac was distracted, as if he knew that he wasn't going to be released in fifteen minutes. "You going to be OK?"

Mac grinned. "Relax, I got this. It's just a twenty-minute trip up the road. I'll be back in time for a nightcap."

Nine

The hours dragged beyond midnight as Reznick waited until it was clear Mac wouldn't be back. He finally called it a night at three o'clock. He gave his cell phone number to the bar owner for Mac to call if he got back.

Reznick headed to his room, but he wasn't going to sleep. Quite the contrary. His mind was racing. He wondered what the hell had happened to Mac. He wondered if the Civil Guard had kept him overnight. He could see why Mac's background would make him a person of interest. But what if there was something more sinister planned for Mac? What if he was about to be disappeared?

Reznick began to contemplate what he should do. What he *could* do. He wondered if this was something worth pursuing. After all, his focus should be on determining how Martha had been killed and by whom. And if necessary, to take them out. It wasn't really his place to go down a rabbit hole trying to figure out what had happened to a character who had a walk-on part in the whole episode. Who was peripheral at best. But maybe Mac wasn't peripheral. Maybe he knew more than he'd let on. Maybe what he knew could help Reznick understand who was behind the explosion.

The more he thought about the figure of David McCafferty, the more Reznick wondered if that was the case. Was that why the cops had a thing for the shaven-headed Scot? Were they going to be bringing in interrogation experts to make him talk? To loosen his tongue?

Reznick knew from what he had seen of Mac that he could handle himself. But every man also had a breaking point, and Spain was not America. Things were done differently on this side of the Atlantic. Sure, Spain was part of the European Union and would have signed on to the European Convention of Human Rights. In particular Article 3. Human rights were enshrined in their laws. But Reznick wasn't naive.

Spain, despite being a democracy, was still haunted in some senses by ghosts from the Franco era. The era of fascism. The era of torture. Disappearances. State control. State torture. The Civil Guard was quasi-militaristic.

Reznick pushed those thoughts to one side. He checked his cell phone. No messages, battery running low. He plugged it into the charger. Slowly, he began to formulate a plan. He couldn't just sit around. He needed to try and find out where Mac was—what had happened to him, where he had been taken. But more than anything, Reznick needed to make sure he was OK.

The ideas were bouncing around his head as he took a shower. He put on some fresh clothes and popped a couple of Dexedrine. He slid his gun into the back of his waistband, cool linen shirt over his jeans. He pulled on the backpack after adding two bottles of water from the minibar.

Reznick locked up his room, left the hotel, and headed back to the bar. Still no sign of Mac.

It would soon be dawn.

He ordered a black coffee and a fresh-squeezed orange juice. He felt better, the amphetamines kicking in with the sugar and caffeine rush.

"Mac hasn't shown?"

51

The bar owner yawned, shaking his head. "Nothing, señor."

"You hear anything, let me know."

He hung around for a little while. Watching and waiting.

A short while later, the sun peeked over the mountains in the distance, bathing the water in a golden glow. Reznick's gaze was drawn to a taxi that pulled up across the street. He half expected a disheveled Mac to get out. But it was only an elderly couple.

He took a few moments to consider whether he should make a move. He couldn't sit around all day watching and waiting. He got up, left money for the check, and walked across to the taxi.

Reznick looked in the passenger window, which was down. "Guardia Civil, señor, Sa Pobla?"

The cabdriver shrugged as he scratched his unshaven face.

Reznick hopped in the back. It was a twenty-minute drive south to a bleak sun-scorched town in the island's interior. The modernist Civil Guard building was located on the outskirts of town.

He asked to be dropped off half a block away. All the time, a plan was forming in his head. A game plan. Preparation and planning were important in his line of work.

He got out of the cab and walked up to the building, which was enclosed by a high concrete wall. He spotted the pinhole camera embedded in the video intercom adjacent to a sturdy wooden door. He pressed the intercom button twice.

The sound of a man clearing his throat. *"Sí. Quién es usted?"*

Reznick thought the guy had said, *Yes, who are you?* He didn't know much beyond rudimentary Spanish. *"Habla usted inglés, señor?"*

"A bit. What do you want?"

"I'm looking to speak to the man in charge."

"Señor," the voice boomed back, "we don't open until nine in the morning. Did you hear what I said? Do you know what time it is?"

Reznick looked at his watch. It was only 7:45 a.m. "I'm looking for a friend of mine."

"Come back later."

"Not until I see my friend."

"Señor, please, we are busy people."

"Can you help me?"

A deep sigh. "What is your friend's name?"

"David. He's known as Mac. David McCafferty. UK citizen. Scottish."

A silence opened up for a few moments. "You mean he's British?"

"Yeah, he's a British citizen."

"What is your name, sir?"

"Jon Reznick. I'm an American. And I want to see Mr. McCafferty."

"You are American. Are you his lawyer?"

"No, I'm not."

"Then I can't help you. He's not here."

"So, where is he? When did he leave?"

"I don't have that information. I just came on duty, sir. Good day."

Reznick buzzed again and again. He got no answer. He buzzed again, still no answer. He stood on the sidewalk and shook his head. He felt a growing sense of unease about Mac. It was true he hardly knew the man. But he felt a kinship. The man was a fellow warrior. One who didn't suffer fools. He felt a bond with the guy. Some might have been put off by Mac's brusque exterior. But underneath the hard-man persona was integrity. Reznick had sensed it from the way Mac had opened up to him. There was no angle. But he also realized Mac knew more than he'd had a chance to reveal. Quite a bit more.

But what?

He wondered if the Civil Guard officer he'd spoken to through the intercom was telling the truth. Maybe Mac wasn't inside. Then again, maybe the guy didn't know. The reality for Reznick was that he was an American in a foreign country, thousands of miles from home. English use was widespread here but hardly universal.

Reznick sensed he was getting involved in some murky shit. But truth be told, that didn't bother him. In fact, the more doors that were slammed in his face, the more he would kick them down. It was just his way. He would find out what he needed to know, no matter what it took.

Reznick glanced along the perimeter of the premises. He could try and climb over the high concrete wall. But there was no guarantee he could gain access to the inside. At least not without knowing the plans of the building.

He walked farther down the street, trying to clear his head. Mac was either inside, getting interrogated over what he knew one more time, or he might have already been taken somewhere else— to another police station or even out of the country. But there was a third option. Maybe Mac had been released. Which posed the question: Why hadn't he made it back to Cala San Vicente?

Reznick was frustrated. He needed answers.

He paced the concrete sidewalk, glad to have the shade from some large trees. Video surveillance cameras were watching him. He sat on a bench in the shade of a lemon tree, unzipped his backpack, and took out a bottle of water. He drank a few welcome gulps, quenching his thirst. He put the half-empty bottle in the backpack and zipped it up again as his gaze wandered around the perimeter wall. He looked at the entrance again.

He watched and waited for over an hour. He watched cops come and go. He waited until nine before he slung his backpack over his shoulder and buzzed again.

"What is it now, señor?" The voice belonged to the same cop as before.

"I'm not going away until I see David McCafferty or get an explanation as to what's happened to him. You want me to call up the British consulate in Palma? Maybe even the American consulate? You want me to do that?"

"Señor, please go away. We've been watching you just hanging around. You'll end up being arrested. We'll have no choice. You need to go home, back to your hotel."

"Not until you tell me where McCafferty is. I ain't going anywhere until I find out where he is. Now, do you want me to call the American embassy and ask them to make a call to your superiors in Madrid?"

Another long silence. "You say you're an American?"

"Jon Reznick. American."

There was a long silence, as if the man was checking with a superior about what he should do. "One moment, sir. OK, you've got five minutes." The external door was buzzed open.

Reznick pushed open the door and headed inside, down a cool, tiled hallway, and into the lobby of the building. He was greeted by a small plainclothes man sporting a scraggly goatee. He wore a faded navy polo shirt and cargo pants, an ID lanyard hanging around his neck.

"Javier Sanchez. I work for Servicio de Informacion de la Guardia Civil."

Reznick nodded. He knew it meant the intelligence-gathering unit of the Civil Guard.

Sanchez cocked his head. "Follow me."

Reznick followed him down a long corridor to a windowless room. A desk and a chair sat on either side. A huge map of Mallorca hung on the wall. A photo of the King of Spain on another wall.

Sanchez sat down behind his desk and pointed to the seat opposite. "Please, relax."

Reznick pulled up the seat and sat down. "Nice place you've got here."

"Don't play games with me. You say your name is Jon Reznick. Who are you? What do you want? How do you know Mr. McCafferty? And what is this obsession with him?"

"I'm an American tourist. A friend of mine was killed in the explosion."

Sanchez leafed through some papers in front of him. "You say a friend was killed in an explosion?"

"You know who I'm talking about. Let's cut the bull."

"You are an unusually persistent man, Mr. Reznick. And you ask a lot of questions for a tourist."

"Tell me about McCafferty. Where is he now? Is he here? Has he been detained?"

Sanchez leaned back in his seat and smiled. "I don't think you understand how it works here in Spain. I ask the questions, sir. Do you understand that?"

Reznick nodded. "Not a problem."

"Good. So, how do you know Mr. McCafferty?"

Reznick sighed. "I met him in a bar."

"So you met a Scottish man who lives on this island in a bar." Sanchez shrugged. "Why are you so interested in him?"

"Why? Because a couple of your guys picked him up last night, said it wasn't going to take long. You arrested him before, but he was released, apparently. So this is the second time you've hauled him in for questioning."

Sanchez gave a thin smile as he leaned forward, elbows on his desk, hands clasped tight as if he were a priest at confession. "I think I've said enough."

"You've said nothing. I want to know where McCafferty is. Tell me about the explosion. I want to know about that."

"I'm rapidly running out of patience, Mr. Reznick. I don't know what you're talking about. What explosion?"

Reznick took a few moments to compose himself as he realized what he was going to have to do.

Sanchez seemed to take his silence as defeat. "So, Jon Reznick, why don't you go back to America, and I can get back to doing my job."

Reznick felt a switch flick in his head. He got up from his seat, pulling his gun from his waistband. He pressed it tight to Sanchez's forehead. "Here's how it's going to work. I don't give a shit who you are or what you do. But I want answers. Where's McCafferty?"

Sanchez closed his eyes. "Sir, you're making a major mistake."

"Answer me!"

"Please . . . I don't have any idea what you're talking about."

"I will leave your brains exploded all over the walls of this shitty fucking office if I don't get answers. Do you *comprendi*?"

Sanchez nodded.

"Good, we're getting somewhere. I want the truth. Right fucking now! Where is McCafferty?"

"Please . . . McCafferty is no longer here."

"OK. So where the fuck is he?"

"We held him until five. He was taken by Americans."

"What Americans? What agencies?"

Sanchez scrunched up his eyes.

"One last time! What agencies?"

"State Department. FBI. CIA. Three vehicles. That's all I know."

Reznick disarmed Sanchez and grabbed him by the neck. "Now, that wasn't so difficult, was it?"

Sanchez shook his head, eyes closed.

"Relax. So this is what I need you to do. You're going to escort me off the premises, smiling, leading the way, confidently, and I'm going to walk out of here. You or any of your goons follow me, and I'll kill them. Bang! Bang! *Comprendi?*"

Sanchez had real fear in his eyes.

Reznick tucked his gun into his waistband. "Nice and easy, and we can all go back home. What do you say?"

Sanchez took a few moments to compose himself.

"Flick any switches or any panic buttons, and me and you have a problem. And trust me, it won't end well."

"Don't shoot me. That's all I ask. I have a family."

Reznick nodded. "Don't do anything stupid and they'll see you later. It'll be fine. Can you do that?"

Sanchez took a deep breath and escorted Reznick out of the windowless room and through the station to the front door. He buzzed him out.

Reznick brushed past him and into the sunshine. He headed sharply down a side street. He crossed the road and ran after a bus that was just leaving its stop.

The driver stopped, the door opened, and Reznick hopped on. He sat down in the seat, ignoring the curious looks from the other passengers as the bus picked up speed. It accelerated out of the town, headed back to the coast.

Ten

It was late morning when Reznick jumped off the bus on the out-skirts of Cala San Vicente. His mind was racing after the encounter at the Civil Guard station. It would only be a matter of time before they caught up with him. But that was fine.

He would deal with that as and when required. Besides, Reznick knew that sometimes you had to let them know you were there. What you were all about. It would result in the other side, in this case the Civil Guard, having a firm choice. Do nothing, or apprehend Reznick. If they chose the latter, the move might open things up in unexpected ways. Provoke a response. Did the American consulate want Reznick to get dragged into whatever was going on here? What if local media got wind of an American being arrested after an explosion on a yacht where two American women had died?

Sometimes creating ripples could work in your favor. Helping the truth work its way out from the center.

Reznick walked through the town and headed along a minor road, taking the sidewalk, skirting the town's small Civil Guard outpost. Behind a fence he saw a couple of cops drinking coffee in the shade of the tree.

He returned to the bar.

"Señor," the owner said, handing him a note. It had a cell phone number on it.

"What's this?"

The bar owner put a fresh jug of water on the table along with a glass that had a slice of lemon in it. "A message."

Reznick slumped in the seat and poured himself a large glass of chilled water. He gulped it down. It felt good.

"I can see that. But who gave you this?"

"A señorita, very pretty lady, wants to talk to you."

"What's her name?"

"I don't know her name. She's Mac's sister. That's all she said."

Reznick looked at the number scribbled in black ink on the scrap of paper. "Appreciate that, thanks." He remembered Mac had said his sister was flying into Palma that morning. He took out his phone and called the number. A woman's crisp voice answered. He said, "I was asked to call this number."

"I believe you know my brother." She also had a distinctive Scottish accent, slightly more refined than her brother's.

Reznick shielded his eyes from the glare of the sun. "Who are you?"

"Catherine McCafferty. We need to talk. I hope you can help me."

"Quid pro quo?"

"Maybe."

Reznick was intrigued. "Where are you?"

"Right now?"

"Yeah."

"Watching you."

Reznick turned and looked across the street. Sitting in the back of a cab, wearing sunglasses, was a woman speaking into a cell phone.

"So, what are you waiting for?" she asked.

Reznick got up and walked across the street and slid into the back seat beside her. She wore a pale yellow summer dress and white sneakers and had long chestnut-brown hair.

She took off her shades and shook his hand. "Jon, pleased to meet you."

"Likewise."

Catherine tapped the driver's shoulder. "Take me on to the villa, señor," she said.

The driver nodded and pulled away.

"You have any idea where my brother is?"

Reznick shook his head.

"I just got off the plane at Palma. Had expected to see my brother. The bar owner suggested I get in touch with you. Said you were looking for my brother. He gave me your number. I hope you don't mind."

"Not at all."

"I hope you don't think I'm too forward. Just . . . I'm just hoping you can help."

"You're not being too forward. I was with Mac last night."

Catherine sighed. "Something's wrong. I knew it when he wasn't there when I landed. David is solid. Dependable."

Reznick nodded.

"Something is wrong, isn't it? I can tell."

"Damn right there's something wrong."

"What's happened?"

"Wait till we've got more privacy. I'll try and explain."

The cab pulled up at a modern villa on the other side of town. The house was on a quiet side street, three blocks from a small beach.

Reznick helped Catherine with her bags and followed her inside.

"Where do you want these?" he said.

"Just put them down in the hall," she said. "Thanks."

She went into the kitchen and took out a large bottle of spring water from the refrigerator and poured two glasses. She drank one and sighed. "Just so we're clear, I don't usually invite men back to my villa the first time I see them."

"Relax."

"OK, what's the story? Something's wrong. I know my brother. He wouldn't not turn up like that."

Reznick took a gulp of the water and nodded, putting the glass down on the black granite countertop.

"How do you know David?" Catherine asked. "I'm worried about him."

"I'd seen him running through town earlier."

"Yeah, he's a fitness nut."

"You can say that again. Anyway, I was asking the bar owner about an explosion earlier this week, offshore. Was told your brother might be able to help."

Catherine nodded slowly as if she was aware of what had happened to the yacht.

"So, he came into the bar. We spoke. Had a beer. He told me he'd been taken in for questioning the day after the explosion."

"You don't mind me asking, I hope, but why are you interested in the explosion?"

"Friend of mine was killed on that yacht. So, it's personal."

"God, I'm sorry."

"What's done is done. Anyway, the last I saw of your brother was when the Civil Guard pulled up at the bar and picked him up for the second time, to answer a few questions, they said. I went up to the police station this morning. But he wasn't there."

Catherine dropped her head. "Christ, this is not good."

"You sound like you know what happened."

She sighed. "I know a fair bit. I'm worried."

Reznick nodded for her to continue.

"I'm worried that they think David is involved."

"With the explosion?"

"He said that within a few hours of the incident, the place was swarming with the Civil Guard as well as Americans. Scores of them. That's not normally what happens if there's an accidental gas explosion on a boat."

Reznick said nothing, letting her talk. She was smart. No one was going to pull the wool over her eyes.

"I think they thought David was involved in some way, what with his . . ."

"Military background?"

"Yes. And his skill set . . . He told you about that?"

Reznick nodded.

"Look, Jon, do you understand the risks you've taken by getting involved with this?"

"I know all about the risks."

Catherine took another swig of water. "You don't seem too fazed by all this."

He smiled. "I used to be in Delta. And I don't mean the airline."

Catherine smiled too. "Got it. David mentioned working alongside Delta Force a few years back in Libya."

"I've also advised the FBI on a few cases. One of the women who was killed was an assistant director. But that didn't come from me."

"That's a lot of information you're sharing."

"Well, hopefully you can share what you know in return. I'm trying to be as upfront as I can. I want to find out who did this."

"You mean find out who blew up the yacht and killed this FBI woman?"

Reznick nodded. He looked around the kitchen and out to the pool at the back. "This all yours?"

"The villa is mine. I rent it out for ten months of the year. I usually visit in August and September to see my brother, get some much-needed sunshine, and recharge the batteries."

"What exactly do you do for a living, if you don't mind me asking?"

"I don't mind at all. I'm a criminal defense lawyer back in Glasgow."

"Interesting."

"It has its moments."

"And it keeps you busy?"

Catherine smiled. "Oh yeah. So you went to the Civil Guard station looking for my brother. That's above and beyond what I'd expect a stranger to do."

"Perhaps. Anyway, not surprisingly, they didn't let me in. At least not at first. But when they did, I was told that some Americans had taken him away."

"Americans? Did they identify who?"

"The CIA, Feds, and the State Department."

"And they told you that willingly?"

Reznick smiled. "I gave them a bit of encouragement. It's amazing how persuasive a 9mm can be when pressed to the forehead."

"Jesus Christ, seriously?"

Reznick shrugged. "So, sue me."

Catherine shook her head. "You're worse than my bloody brother. Don't get me wrong, I love him, but he can be a bit scary. And that's coming from someone who knows him. Knows what he's capable of."

"I liked him a lot."

"Thank you. He's not an easy guy to like. But he has a heart of gold."

Reznick nodded. "So, now I've told you what I know. But what do you know about this explosion? I got the impression your brother knows more than he was letting on."

Catherine tapped her fingers on the countertop. "I don't know if I should be telling you what I know."

Reznick leaned in. "If you know something that's going to help me understand exactly what happened, I would very much appreciate it. And so would the family of the woman who died."

"Sure, of course. You're right, David does know more."

"Take me back to the beginning. You had heard about the explosion. How?"

"David called a few hours after he was released. Told me he had been arrested. Mentioned the explosion the previous evening."

Reznick nodded.

"I sensed he wasn't himself when he called me, which is why I headed out here today. A week earlier than I was going to. He sounded worried. And he sounded stressed. Which wasn't like him."

Reznick thought about that. "He said he had discovered pieces of the yacht that had blown up. And he had passed them on to the Spanish police."

"I know, he told me."

"Did he give you any details? I really need to know, Catherine."

"David said he handed over all the fragments he found, in particular one larger metal piece, to a Spanish police diver. David thought at least one of the other divers might be FBI."

"FBI diver . . . Did he give you any details about what he found? Was the metal part of the boat's deck, galley, kitchen, engine?"

"It looked to him like, and I'm quoting here, an electronic circuit board. He said it was like an electronic motherboard. Like a control panel."

Reznick nodded. "What else?"

"The fragment he found, according to David, contained writing. A serial number as well."

"What sort of writing?"

Catherine grimaced. "He told me not to say a word."

"Catherine, listen to me. Your brother has been taken by Americans—maybe State Department, maybe CIA—God knows where. Something is wrong. My friend, an FBI assistant director, has been blown out of the damn water. It's sounding more and more like it was a bomb, not a gas explosion. So, if you know anything, you need to tell me."

"I feel conflicted. He's my brother. You understand, right?"

"Catherine . . . I need to know."

She sighed and closed her eyes for a moment, reluctant to divulge what she knew. "David said it was a national security issue. I agree."

"Tell me what your brother saw."

"This didn't come from me."

"I'll keep it in confidence."

"David told me that one of the fragments contained writing. Very distinctive writing."

"Catherine, spit it out. What kind of writing? What did it say? Was there a country of origin?"

"Yes, there was."

"What was it? For the love of God, tell me, what did it say?"

"I don't know."

"What do you mean you don't know?"

"The writing was in Arabic."

Eleven

A blood-red sky was spreading slowly like a cancer as far as the eye could see, enveloping the Serra de Tramuntana mountains in its crimson grip.

Adam Ford stood outside his villa, hands on hips, drenched in sweat after a run. He surveyed the scene around him. The olive trees. The smell of bone-dry earth. The hint of lemons from a nearby grove. The scent of wild fennel. It was idyllic. The sort of place a man could grow accustomed to. A place to love. A place to retire to. A place to meditate. A place to sit back and read for hours, undisturbed. A place to think. A place to forget.

Ford thought the island, in all its intoxicating beauty, was a perfect, almost poetic, place for a warrior like Reznick to be slain. Ford had plans. Boy, did he have plans. So many ideas. He felt crazier than he had for a while. He had a lot on his mind. Ideas. Projects. Money. Property. And killing, obviously. All these things were whirring around his head, unable to switch off. He was *on*. All the time. Every waking hour.

He approached the front of the house and pressed his sweaty right index finger against the biometric reader. He had paid a security company in Palma a small fortune to upgrade the security and technology in the house. He had also had the basement reconfigured two months earlier to meet his exacting requirements. A green light came on, and the door clicked open.

Ford headed inside, the three-inch-thick solid wood door closing firmly behind him. The cool air felt good on his skin. The marble all around. The whitewashed walls soothing. Calming. But he had work to do.

He headed through to his kitchen and finished his bottle of isotonic juice. His thirst had been sated. He felt his sugar levels return to normal after being depleted in the ninety-degree heat.

Ford cranked up the air-conditioning further. He felt cold blasts on his skin. Icy cold. Good. His body temperature was getting back in sync. He dimmed the lights. A chilly blue glow bathed the whitewashed walls, creating a serene atmosphere.

He took a bottle of water out of the fridge and gulped down half of it.

Ford began to pace the room as he thought ahead. He had work to do. And it would require energy. Mental as well as physical.

He quickly fixed himself a large cheese sandwich. He wolfed it down, ravenous. He opened the finest half bottle of red wine from the cellar. He sat down in the living room with the wine and a plastic Ziploc bag of cocaine.

Ford shook out a small pile and used his platinum credit card to chop up the cocaine into six thick lines. He snorted line after line, sniffing hard. The chemicals were rushing around his bloodstream. His head felt as if it was on fire. His mood was rocketing. The natural dopamine high, coupled with the chemical high, was kicking in. Tearing through him. Wow!

Ford was reaching peak crazy. His favorite position. He loved these fleeting moments. When he knew what lay ahead. The thrill of it, of knowing what was about to happen, was intoxicating. He had work to do. Loose ends to tie up, so to speak. He began whistling a song from *The Wizard of Oz*. A film he had watched a hundred times with his mother as a child. He'd loved it. It always reminded him of a time of pure innocence. A time when his whole world and the possibilities within it seemed endless. Before he became a different person. The man he was today.

"Coming, ready or not!" he said shrilly, before laughing out loud at his black humor.

Ford skipped down the marble stairs to the basement. He pressed his thumb against the biometric reader. The steel door clicked open. He headed inside, the door slamming shut behind him. Inside the room, the light was soft. He had rented the house via a shell company in Grand Cayman, but he could have bought it outright many times over. Unfortunately, he had no intention of staying around.

It felt good knowing he never had to work again. Never had to endure another shift at some goddamn awful hospital. The grind. The banality of work. Listening to the nurses try and engage with him. Instead, he was free. And it was wonderful. He could do whatever he wanted to do. And he intended to. The reality was he was a superior individual. He had risen above the herd. He was smarter, higher, and brighter. He was living life unperturbed by fear. Fear of what had gone before. Fear of self. Fear of social conditioning. He was free.

Money might not buy happiness. It might not even buy love. But it sure as hell felt good to have some.

Ford counted his blessings. His fortunes had accumulated when he hit the jackpot with Bitcoin. Big-time. He'd bought ten thousand Bitcoin in 2010 at six cents. And he'd sold when it hit fifteen thousand dollars.

He'd raked in a cool hundred and fifty million dollars.

That was what had given him the resources and time to plan the operation to get Reznick. And what better way to get him than through the ravishing Martha Meyerstein?

Just a few loose ends I still have to deal with.

Ford felt his breathing quicken. Heart racing just a bit. *Let's get on with it, Adam.* He passed through a glass door into an anteroom, where he put on forensic goggles, a mask, and a lab coat. Ford had rented this property once he learned Meyerstein was going to be sailing around the coast. The line of sight from the property to the town had been the clincher. But when he'd seen the plans for the building, half of it buried into the hills, deep underground, where he was headed now, he started to get excited.

The place was so fucking perfect it was unreal.

He pulled on the latex gloves and Bose wireless headphones. Then he turned on one of his several cell phones and opened the music app.

The sound of Johann Sebastian Bach's soaring organ masterpiece filled the space. Toccata and Fugue in D Minor. Full volume, ahead of the task at hand.

Ford's head was swimming. The music sounded like it was being played by a madman. Composed by a madman. It was perfect. He caught a glance in a mirror. His mind flashed back to his days as a medical student. The first autopsy he'd witnessed. He'd watched the other students. Two had puked. One had passed out. He just stood there, amazed. It was a privilege to observe up close a medical examiner opening up the human body. Most people found it difficult to watch. Traumatic, even. The smell of death lingered in their nostrils. But to Ford, it was no different from carving up a turkey for Thanksgiving dinner.

The process was fascinating. He'd watched like a hawk. The body was photographed. Then the clothes before they were removed. Then any residue—say, flakes of paint—on the skin was sampled for separate testing. Then came the Y-shaped incision. The removal of the vital organs. And most fascinating of all, the brain. Ford had always been fascinated by the brain. Everyone's brain was the same size, more or less. But while some, like him, were high-functioning, top-grade intellectuals, the vast majority of people didn't even have the brainpower to try and figure out a better life for themselves. It was pitiful.

Ford's gaze lingered on his reflection for a few moments longer. He was staring back at a monster. A twenty-first-century monster. It was wild. He took a deep breath and strode down the hallway. He took the elevator to the subbasement, three stories underground. The doors opened, and his breathing quickened even further.

The music was strident. Forceful. Crazed.

Ford stepped out of the elevator and turned right. The room was illuminated by blue recessed lighting, giving a strange ethereal glow to the Italian marble. A set of metal lockers stood at one end. He opened the last one and pulled out the bone saw and his black forensic bag.

And still that fucking organ music filled his head.

Ford sniffed hard. He shut the locker door and paused, gathering his thoughts. The music was soaring, his pulse was racing. He needed to calm down. A job needed to be done. A job he'd imagined from the early days of planning Meyerstein's assassination.

Ford took off the goggles for a second and pressed his face against the biometric eye reader. Another set of doors opened. He put his goggles back on. Then he took a deep breath and headed into the darkened room. The lighting was low; cameras filmed his every move for posterity.

He stared at the figure strapped down on the gurney. Just a kid, really. A brilliant Moroccan swimmer he had headhunted for the job of planting the explosive device on the yacht. The poor fuck was crying. His muffled screams could be heard even through Ford's headphones, through the Bach swirling around his mind.

Ford stood over the boy and smiled. The terror in the boy's eyes was a sight to behold. It was lovely how fear worked. The physiological reactions. The dilated pupils. Blood pressure going through the roof. The sweating. The heightened senses. The flooding of epinephrine and adrenaline through a person's body when they feared for their life. It was almost sensual.

"Don't be afraid, little one," he shouted, barely able to hear himself with the music blaring. "I'm a doctor. A very, very good doctor. I know what I'm doing."

The kid's screams blended perfectly with the staccato music.

"Don't you like Bach? That's ridiculous!" Ford howled at the macabre fun he was having. "I understand he's not to everyone's taste. Me? I love the guy."

The boy wet himself.

"Never mind. It'll all be over very soon. And trust me, you don't want to be awake when I get going. Don't get me wrong, you did great."

The boy was screaming for his mom. Reciting lines from the Koran.

"Beautiful words," Ford shouted. "Beautiful, beautiful words. I dig it. But here's the thing: God is dead. Night, night, little one."

Ford took an anesthetic spray from the pocket of his lab coat and sprayed it into the boy's right ear. Then up the right nostril as the boy struggled, eyes wide, chest trying to burst through the leather straps.

Ford watched for a few sad moments. Then he closed his eyes and counted to ten.

When he opened his eyes, the boy was unconscious, his central nervous system suitably suppressed. Bach was in full flow.

Ford picked up the saw, grabbed the boy's hair, and began sawing his neck, blood spurting over Ford's white lab coat.

Twelve

Shards of golden sunlight pierced the blinds in his hotel room and roused Reznick from a troubled sleep. He had only managed a couple of hours after he got back from meeting with Catherine. The revelation of the Arabic writing on the metal fragment her brother had found was stunning. His mind had been racing since he'd heard the news. Unable to sleep half the night, he had lain awake, staring at the ceiling, until 5:00 a.m. He wondered if this was the killer piece of evidence pointing to Islamist terrorism. And if it did, Reznick could see why intelligence agencies would want to conceal such information. If the public knew, all hell would break loose.

Reznick got out of bed and went to the bathroom and splashed cold water on his face. He checked his reflection in the mirror. Dark shadows under his bloodshot eyes. Not enough sleep. But he wasn't interested in that. He was interested in what had happened to Mac and if there had been any news of his whereabouts.

He picked up his cell phone and called Catherine.

"Morning, Jon."

"Sorry to bother you," he said. "Any word on your brother?"

"Not a thing. I was just about to contact you to find out if you had heard anything. I'm worried. I don't like it. He's been gone too long."

"I'd report it to the British consulate," he said. "They'll have a place in Palma."

"Already done that."

"What did they say?"

"*Very sorry to hear that.* That kind of thing. They took a note of his name. I asked what they were going to do about it. The consul, who was very posh, said they would try *everything possible.* But we know what that means, right?"

"Diplomatic niceties. Means they'll ignore it, or at best ask a few discreet questions. That sort of shit."

Catherine sighed. "I'm so worried, Jon. It will end my mother if something happens to David. He made it back from Iraq and God-knows-where. To lose him now, it would be too much to bear."

Reznick opened the blinds, pushed open the French doors, and stepped outside onto his balcony. He stared out over the beautiful blue waters. At the families enjoying an early-morning dip in the sea. The peace and calm of it all. To think that in those same waters, not far from shore, Martha had perished.

"Jon?"

He wondered, not for the first time, what the hell he was doing chasing ghosts of the past. Shadows. Was he in Mallorca only out of obligation to Jerry Meyerstein?

He knew there was more to it than that. Far, far more than that. He had felt a connection to Martha. A real connection to her. And that connection, to something good—true and unyielding and kind—was gone. He felt her loss deep within him. Gnawing away at him. And he knew that it would all catch up with him, further on down the road. It would floor him. He would hit a wall.

And when it had finally sunk in that he would never see or touch her again, he feared a descent into a darkness of his own making. That was what awaited him.

"Are you still there, Jon?" Catherine's voice snapped him back to reality.

"Yeah, I'm still here. Listen, Catherine, I know a few people. Let me make a call. I don't want to promise anything."

"What kind of people?"

"Just let me handle it."

"I'd really appreciate that. We need to try every avenue."

"How about I call you back later today?"

"Thanks, Jon."

Reznick ended the call. He had a direct number for the FBI's SIOC—Strategic Information and Operations Center—on the highly secure fifth floor of the HQ in Washington, DC. A number Martha had given him to be used in emergency situations. He pulled up the number on his cell phone.

"Identify yourself," a woman's voice said.

"Jon Reznick." He knew they would be doing voice analysis to ensure they were speaking to the right person.

"I'm sorry, Jon, but you are not on the authorized list anymore. I can't help you."

"I just need one minute of your time. I want you to be aware of a situation."

"I'll repeat that, Jon. You are not authorized. Do you copy?"

"I copy. Listen to me. This is a critical situation. It concerns the disappearance of David McCafferty, known as Mac, a British citizen, believed to be ex-SAS."

The line went quiet for a few moments. "Go on."

Reznick gave a summary of events since he'd arrived in Mallorca, including a description of the fragment allegedly found by Mac after the explosion of the yacht Martha Meyerstein was traveling on. "Do you copy that?"

"Yes, copy that."

"David McCafferty's whereabouts are unknown. It's possible he has been taken to a secure location by Americans, perhaps State Department or the Agency. Now I don't know what the hell is going on or what fucking games are being played, but I want to talk to O'Donoghue."

A silence stretched on for what seemed like minutes but was in all likelihood ten or fifteen seconds. "You are no longer authorized. I believe you have already had a discussion with the Director about this?"

"Get him to call me as soon as he's able. It's critical."

But the line went dead.

Thirteen

Reznick was becoming preoccupied, perhaps sidetracked, thinking of Mac's whereabouts. It wasn't a blind alley, though—he was convinced pursuing it would open up his investigation into Martha's death and perhaps lead to understanding the motivation behind the attack.

His stomach rumbled. He hadn't eaten in more than twelve hours. He ordered room service and ate it on his balcony, feeling the heat of the morning sun on his face and arms. Waves crashed onto the rocky coastline. His gaze was drawn farther along the coast. Kids were already tombstoning from the cliffs. The same cliffs he had visited when he had arrived. The same place with the perfect line of sight. The police boat was still there in the distance. The buoys marking where the yacht had been.

Reznick's mind flashed back to his meeting with Jerry Meyerstein. As far as he knew, the bodies of Martha and her friend still hadn't been found. But then again, with the secrecy surrounding the events, perhaps the bodies had washed up and been taken, at the behest of the State Department, to a military hospital in Madrid. Perhaps even flown to a US air base in Spain.

He thought of Jerry Meyerstein back at home in the Chicago suburbs, grieving, his wife, Martha's mother, struggling to cope with the enormity of the loss. He wondered if Jerry had heard anything further. Maybe he should call Jerry later and give him an update. But he didn't have much of an update to give. He didn't know who'd caused the explosion. He had scraps of information. A piece or two of the jigsaw. But nothing more.

Who was behind this? And why? Was it an Islamist plot? Had it all been hushed up?

Reznick needed to clear his head from all the jumbled-up thoughts rushing through his mind. He changed into his workout gear and put on his old sneakers. He headed out of the cool and calm of the hotel and into the broiling Mediterranean sunshine.

He walked over to the beachside bar and got himself another coffee, just enjoying space to think. He realized he'd been sitting in the exact chair and at the same table when he first met Mac. He feared the worst for Mac. But he didn't want to tell Catherine that. She was smart, though, and she knew that her brother had become inadvertently wrapped up in the fallout after Martha's death. Whatever that fallout was going to turn out to be.

A bomb planted on the yacht of an FBI assistant director by a terrorist group would be worldwide news. Her murder would send shock waves around the globe. It would send out the message that no member of the American intelligence services was safe. No one. Not a soul. And that would unnerve and scare many Americans. And rightly so. But it would also invariably enrage America, with some calling for revenge. *Demanding* revenge.

An eye for an eye.

It was the American way. Had been since the Founding Fathers. Retribution. Vengeance. It was in the DNA of America, for better or worse. The very fabric of its being. All the way back. The war against the Native Americans. The settlers being massacred. And settlers avenging in blood. On and on.

His thoughts turned again to what Catherine had said. The crucial fragment that Mac had handed over to the Spanish police and a Fed frogman. The Arabic writing pointed to one thing: an Islamist cell had planted the bomb. How could it be anything else? They had taken out Martha Meyerstein. The fact that she was an American and Jewish would make it all the sweeter for them.

Reznick felt the stirrings of anger. His blood was up. He gulped some coffee. He wondered if Mac had been taken to a secure place to keep him from talking. If it leaked out that a fragment of the bomb contained Arabic writing, there would be a media firestorm the likes of which no one had seen since 9/11. Recriminations. A thirst for blood. The road to war. Nothing would be off the table.

But something was nagging at Reznick, deep within him. Something didn't sit right with him. He couldn't figure it out. He began to game-plan different scenarios.

If Mac had been disappeared to ensure his silence, he could have been taken to a facility controlled by the CIA. A black site. Maybe on Spanish soil. Reznick knew they existed in several European countries. Poland. Romania. But maybe the Americans who'd picked him up from the police station had handed him over to the British. Mac was a British citizen, after all. And the UK and America were part of the Five Eyes intelligence alliance for sharing classified information, along with Canada, New Zealand, and Australia. The Brits might have taken him to nearby Gibraltar in the south of Spain, where they had a significant base.

Reznick gazed off into the distance. The shimmering haze on the water was beguiling. He lingered as if in a trance. He thought again of Martha. Images raced through his head. Haunting images. Her cold dead body. He thought his heart would burst. It was aching with the emptiness. He could only imagine the heartache her family was enduring. The endless nights. The gaping hole in their lives.

Reznick could only do his part. He had made a solemn promise to Jerry. He would find out who killed Martha. Because someone had killed her. Of that, Reznick was certain. But an Islamist cell in the Med? They would have had to know about her trip ahead of time. Or had someone spotted her here and decided to act on the fly?

Probably the first thing on the mind of anyone local would be the 2004 Madrid train bombings, a near-simultaneous coordinated attack on four trains by an Islamist cell. The atrocity had killed 193 and injured nearly two thousand people, the deadliest terrorist attack in Spain.

In light of that, had Martha's assassination been carried out by a similar fundamentalist Islamist cell? Or was this a highly focused attack by a new generation of fundamentalists who wanted to terrorize and force the West into submission?

The more he ran the scenarios around his head, the less he thought it likely. Ordinarily, one-on-one assassinations weren't their modus operandi. Their game was mass terror. Mass casualties. The more the better, as far as they were concerned. Probably the biggest red flag, as far as Reznick could ascertain, was that the Islamists hadn't sent out a message on social media claiming credit. If there'd been anything—a video proclaiming jihad and victory over the infidels—it would be all over the media by now. These terrorists were masters of high-production-value propaganda videos. They saw them as tools to recruit the next generation of Islamists.

Nothing made sense. Except he understood now why the Feds had gone to such lengths to insist, even to Martha's own father, that the explosion had been an accident. If it was known that an assistant director of the FBI had been assassinated on the other side of the Atlantic during a sailing vacation—by anyone, Islamists or not—it would shake the Federal Bureau of Investigation to its very foundations. It would call into question whether the FBI was fit for its purpose. More than anything the credibility of the FBI would be torn to shreds. And it might undermine the confidence of the American people in their domestic security and intelligence service.

He finished his coffee, left a ten-euro bill, and headed across the street. He walked up the dusty sidewalk adjacent to the road that led out of town.

Reznick stopped when he got to the line-of-sight spot on the rocky overlook and surveyed the scene for the umpteenth time. Kids were again jumping off the high cliffs into the water, egged on by their friends.

He spotted the young guy he'd spoken to before.

The kid caught his eye and waved, motioning him down to join them. "Señor!"

Reznick acknowledged the kid and clambered down the rocks, careful not to lose his footing.

"Señor," the kid said, "my friend who was there that night?"

"Sure, is he here?"

The kid turned and pointed to a brawny boy with shoulder-length blond hair. "My friend Loreno, he was there. You said you wanted to talk to him, señor?"

"Sure."

The brawny kid was tapped on the shoulder by his friend and turned around. The two exchanged brief words before Loreno stepped forward.

Loreno shielded his eyes from the sun. "Hey, señor, what do you want? You American?"

Reznick took the kid aside for a moment. "I was told you were here the night the boat exploded."

"Yes, I was."

"Tell me about that night."

"Are you FBI? You an American cop, señor?"

Reznick shook his head. "My friend died on the yacht. I'm just trying to find out if anyone saw anything on the night it happened."

"Well, it was early evening. I had started jumping late afternoon off these cliffs, right here, about an hour, maybe fifty minutes before the explosion. I had finished my job."

"What job is that?"

"Cleaning pools. But I went home before it exploded, thank God."

Reznick looked out at the buoys, wanting to be crystal clear in his head about what had happened. "I need you to think back, Loreno," he said.

The kid looked serious. "I can do that."

"Good." Reznick pointed to the buoys in the distance. "Is that where the yacht was? Really think about what I'm saying."

"Exactly where it was, señor. I know the waters around here. And I remember its position. It didn't move. It was anchored offshore as it was getting dark."

"So the yacht was off there, and what happened after your last jump of the day?"

"After my last jump of the day, I picked up my towel, dried myself, put on my flip-flops, and walked home. I was tired, as I'd been up since six that morning, working, cleaning."

"And that was it?"

Loreno shrugged. "Yeah, I went home."

"And you didn't see anything different?"

"What do you mean different? I don't understand, señor."

Reznick smiled at Loreno. "I'm sorry that I don't speak Spanish."

"Don't worry, I manage."

"What I mean is, you didn't see anyone hanging around, someone you hadn't seen before? Suspicious activity. Anything different."

Loreno scratched his head and frowned as if trying hard to think back. "There was only a guy, I think he was a tourist in the town."

"A tourist? Tell me about this tourist. It was a man?"

Loreno nodded. *"Sí, señor."*

"I'm guessing there are people who stop, like me, and just admire the views from here."

"Yeah, all the time. But this guy was just sitting in a white camper van, VW."

"A camper van, like an RV?"

Loreno shrugged. "I don't know what that is."

"When maybe a family gets in a vehicle and goes on the road, it might have a tiny kitchen, sleeping bunks too. People drive and sleep in the vehicle."

"Yeah, definitely, that was it. A white RV."

"But that wasn't out of the ordinary, I'd guess. There must be many people who travel around in camper vans, RVs, whatever you want to call them."

Loreno shook his head. "I don't think he was traveling around."

"You seem very sure."

"He might've been German. English. I remember his face."

Reznick felt his senses switch on. "Now listen, Loreno, this might be very important. So, you say you remember his face, right?"

Loreno nodded, very serious.

"How do you remember his face?"

"I saw him before that night."

"You saw him before the night of the explosion?"

The kid nodded.

"When? Where?"

"I remember I saw him before. It was him."

"Where? Where did you see him? In town?"

"Just on the outskirts of Cala San Vicente. He was staying in a villa. Well, he was earlier in the summer."

Reznick was struggling to take this in. "Hang on, let's be clear. So, you saw this man at this location, before the explosion, in an RV parked on the roadside. And that's the same man you saw at a villa earlier in the summer?"

Loreno nodded. "That is correct, señor. I help to clean pools in the summer. And I saw him sitting on the rear balcony of the house next door, weeks ago. Maybe a month ago."

"House next door to the one whose pool you cleaned?"

"Exactly."

"And it was him?"

"I swear on the memory of the Virgin Mary herself, it was the same man."

Fourteen

Adam Ford felt his mood stabilize as he clocked laps in the villa's infinity pool, high up in the hills above Cala San Vicente. His gruesome work was complete. The dismembered and decapitated body of the young North African teenager had been safely disposed of in the middle of the night. He had washed down the basement and burned his clothes and the boy's. Not a trace remained. He had used a forensic luminol test and there was no blood, not only to the naked eye, but to a trained investigator. The crime didn't happen. And it certainly couldn't have been attributed to that property.

Besides, what was good and what was evil anyway? It was all about perspective as far as he was concerned. And what did it matter to anyone how he lived his life? Fuck it. Fuck them all. Ford alone knew his own mind. He knew it well. Knew his destiny.

He swam hard, the sun warming his back. His mind felt sharper today. The drugs and the booze had worn off. He was his old self. Smart. Self-assured. Confident. He had allowed his darker nature to take over temporarily. And it had felt good. But he was back to being the rational man. The thinking man.

After a thirty-minute swim, Ford dried off and lay back down on one of the sun loungers by the pool.

His mood began to elevate. He felt glorious. And he was loving it as he contemplated what he had already achieved.

Meyerstein had been taken care of. The North African boy, Abdullah, had served his purpose and was gone. It was all coming together.

Ford felt a smile cross his face. Only Reznick was left. The fact that Ford had been able to act with impunity made the whole thing even more delicious. What was not to like? The years of pent-up frustration and anger were finding an outlet. The hundreds—no, thousands—of hours of planning, surveillance, and attention to detail, covering his tracks. He was on the verge of deleting Reznick. The vengeance would be sweet. And it would be his and his alone.

Ford was never content to think just about the next move, or even the one after that. He thought six or seven steps ahead. Like in chess. His brain operated on that level. He had factored into his plans that a guy like Reznick would start sniffing around. He wanted Reznick distracted.

He felt a frisson of excitement wash over his body. He had counted on Reznick making the trip to the northeast tip of Mallorca after the explosion. The bastard would want answers. From what he knew about Reznick—the tenacity, the ruthlessness—the man would hang around. For days. Weeks. Or even months. He would ask questions. He would build a picture of the chain of events.

Ford knew the FBI would be doing the same. They were predictable like that. And other agencies. But it would take them a long time to figure out what was really happening. And it would mean Reznick had a new reality to contend with. No longer would he have a protector within the FBI covering his back. With Martha gone, Reznick was on his own, thousands of miles from home.

Ford had Reznick in his crosshairs. It was only a matter of time. And the fact of the matter was, Ford had all the time in the world.

He headed inside and took another shower. His body was tingling. Part exhilarated by and part turned on by the whole thing. Then he put on a fresh polo shirt and shorts with sneakers.

He opened a bottle of Chateau Lafite. Then he took out his cell phone and streamed the overture of Wagner's *Rienzi* through the wireless speakers. The purity was like a balm to the soul. He headed upstairs, glass in hand, to the study, pulled up a chair, and sat down at the telescope. He took a sip of the wine, savoring its elegance and nuance.

Ford put down the glass on a marble table. Leaning forward, he lightly held the eyepiece of the telescope, pressing his eye to it. He adjusted the view until it was in pin-sharp focus.

He peered down from the mountainside to the sandy beach at Cala San Vicente. He tracked away from the beach and focused on the bar opposite. A handful of people were enjoying a morning beer in the sun. A couple of tourists sat drinking coffee. A woman who appeared to be alone was drinking a glass of red wine. But there was no sign of Reznick.

Ford maneuvered the telescope and focused on Reznick's balcony at the four-star hotel opposite the beach. It was empty. No T-shirts or trunks drying on the metal clothes rack.

He wondered if this was the time. An opportunity. He ran the scenarios he had in store for Reznick. And one in particular seemed like it might fit the bill at that precise moment. A plan he loved for its beauty, simplicity, and deadliness.

Ford grabbed his backpack, threw it in the back seat of his rented BMW SUV, and drove down the winding dirt road into town.

He was careful not to drive too fast or accelerate down the hill.

Ford knew the town would be watched by the Civil Guard. He drove past the bar where he had obsessively observed Reznick for hours at a time. He negotiated a narrow side street and pulled up at the rear of the hotel, opposite the staff entrance.

From his backpack, he removed the hotel master key card he had stolen from the front seat of a van used by a hotel maintenance guy who had foolishly left his coveralls in his van after work.

Ford felt excited. He knew exactly what he was going to do. He had mapped it all out. He had known Reznick would stay there. It was a nice hotel, right on the beach, many of the rooms with views to where the yacht had been.

Ford was good at planning. He liked details: the time it would take, where the hotel surveillance cameras were placed. He got out of the car with his backpack and walked around to the front of the hotel.

He could've been any other tourist. He went completely unnoticed as he took the stairs to the second floor. He paused to put the latex gloves on, then walked calmly along the carpeted corridor until he got to the third room on the right.

It was Room 206. Reznick's room.

Ford felt a shiver run down his spine.

He stood outside the room for a few moments. How cool was this? How audacious was this? He pressed his ear to the door and listened. No sound, no sign that Reznick was there. Ford swiped the hotel key card, and the door clicked open. He stepped inside and shut the door quietly behind him.

He checked the bathroom first. He saw Reznick's shaving bag. The toothbrush and toothpaste placed neatly in the glass by the sink. He headed back into the bedroom and opened up the wardrobe. Shirts, jeans, all neatly hung up; sneakers and a pair of boat shoes, pristine and clean. He checked a chest of drawers. T-shirts carefully folded, boxer shorts fresh, socks paired.

He ran a latex-clad finger across the top of the drawers, luxuriating in knowing this was the domain of a feared killer. A shadowy assassin. But here Ford was, toying with him. It felt good. Damn good.

He opened the TV cabinet. Inside was what he was looking for. The minibar refrigerator. He took out the three whiskey miniatures and placed them on the carpet. Then he opened up his backpack and took out three identical miniature bottles of Johnnie Walker Red Label scotch. He placed them in the small fridge beside the vodka and gin. The fake whiskey in identical bottles had been ordered from a supplier in Dubai. He checked the seals. Perfect. The label, perfect. The liquor was pristine. Except for the addition of a drop of odorless strychnine, carefully administered by a chemical engineering graduate who had a drug addiction and needed the cash.

Ford lined up the three bottles side by side. He closed the minibar door, put the whiskey miniatures he had taken into a side pocket of his backpack and zipped it up. He unzipped the main pocket of the backpack and took out a clock. It matched the room's existing clock. Except that his clock concealed a miniature spy camera in the middle of the clock face. He carefully hung the surveillance clock on the wall. He smiled. It would mean that when Reznick drank the whiskey, his tipple of choice, Ford would be watching, remotely. Remotely watching Reznick fall asleep. And then die.

The more he thought about it, the crazier he felt. It was beyond brilliant. Its conception and being privy to watching a man like Reznick die would be sweet vengeance.

Ford took one last look around the room. He was tempted to wait for Reznick to return. Sorely tempted. But his work here was done.

He pressed his eye to the peephole. No one around. He put an ear to the door, listening for vibrations of people walking down the corridor. Heard only the thumping of his heart beating.

Ford softly opened the door, looked around, and shut it quietly behind him. He walked down the corridor, headed down a stairwell, and through a door. He dumped his latex gloves in a trash can, then walked past the young concierge and through the hotel lobby into the blazing sunshine.

Fifteen

The sweat was sticking to Reznick's shirt as he headed along a shaded sidewalk, past upscale modern villas, on the southern outskirts of Cala San Vicente. The incessant buzzing of cicadas in eucalyptus trees filled the stifling air. He wondered if the information the long-haired kid had given him might be a breakthrough. The kid seemed sure that the man in the RV was the same man who rented a villa only yards from where he was just now. It could be a long shot. But for Reznick, any lead was worth chasing down.

He checked a street sign, the suffocating heat beating down on him all the while.

Reznick's cell phone vibrated in his pocket, and he removed it. It showed real-time motion-activated footage from the camera hidden in his hotel room smoke detector, five hundred yards away. He thought at first it might be a cleaner. But the guy wearing shades looked like a thief who was robbing his room.

He turned his back to shield the cell phone screen from the sun.

Reznick watched, transfixed, as the guy searched the room, then took off his backpack. *What the fuck?*

The guy reached into his backpack, took out three miniature whiskeys and swapped them with the bottles in the minibar. The average person who viewed the footage might not understand. But Reznick knew exactly what was happening. The guy in his room wanted to poison him. Slowly. Surreptitiously. The guy wanted Reznick dead, no question. And he seemed to know Reznick was partial to single malt scotch. Who the hell was that guy? It couldn't be a coincidence. Who knew he was in town? A handful of people. The Feds. But he had also left a bit of an impression on the Civil Guard.

Could be one of their guys. But how likely was it that the local cops, paramilitary or not, would want him dead? Then again, maybe his antics the previous day had humiliated them enough to want to teach him a lesson.

Reznick wiped the beads of sweat from his brow with the back of his hand and glanced around. He knew he must look weird just standing there on that quiet street checking his cell phone. His gaze was drawn back to the footage. He was intrigued by how the guy quietly and methodically left the room. Then he noticed the latex gloves.

The guy was a pro.

"Hey, señor." A boy's voice. "Wrong street. It's a couple hundred meters farther along. The pink house."

Reznick saw the long-haired kid Loreno running after him. He put his cell phone away. He'd take another look at the footage later. The aviator shades had concealed the guy's identity very well, but not entirely. "The street signs are very confusing," Reznick told Loreno. "I was checking maps."

"Don't worry, they don't make sense to us either and we live here! Anyway, I just wanted to make sure you found it OK. I realized when you left that the street layout is a jumbled-up mess, if you know what I mean. The numbers are running even, then there are odd numbers that head down separate streets, but they have the same street name."

Reznick looked farther down the street. "So how far?"

"Not far."

They walked on in the direction of the villa, Loreno pointing the way. It had to be at least one hundred degrees and climbing. The whirring sound of cicadas seemed to be getting louder.

Reznick's thoughts were racing, knowing there had been an intruder back in his hotel room. He made a mental note to change rooms—and to remove the tainted whiskey bottles without being observed by whoever had installed the camera clock.

A whiff of cigarette smoke caught the breeze, and the smell of flowers from a nearby garden drifted in the stifling Mallorcan air.

Loreno pointed to a beautiful coral-pink villa, up ahead, pretty flower boxes in the window. Lawn watered and green.

"So," Reznick said, turning to the kid, "just so we're clear, the guy you saw in the RV just before the yacht exploded was the same guy who was renting this pink house."

"The pink house, yes. I swear, señor, it was him."

"How can you be so sure?"

"I just know. They had identical mustaches. The same white Lacoste polo shirt. The same sunglasses. But there were two men at the house."

Reznick's interest was slightly piqued after what he'd just seen. "Could you tell what they were? The sunglasses. I mean, were they Ray-Ban Wayfarers, for example?"

"No."

"How can you be so sure?"

"My father has Wayfarers. I want a pair."

"So what did the guy have?"

"Aviators. Mirror aviators."

Reznick handed the kid a twenty-euro bill. "You've been incredibly helpful." He wondered briefly if he should show the kid the picture of the guy in his hotel room. But he decided against it, at least for now.

He turned to look at the pink house. "So the guy was living in the pink house, and you were cleaning the pool next door, and you saw him once on the balcony of the pink house?"

"The other side of the house, away from the street. I could see from the poolside. There was a younger guy with him. He was about my age."

"Did you see the guy on the balcony for long—the one who was in the RV?"

"A few moments, and then he went back inside." Loreno shielded his eyes from the sun. "You want to speak to the lady whose pool I cleaned? The woman next door?"

"She won't mind?"

"No, she won't mind. She is a good friend of my mother."

Reznick followed the kid down a path to the front door of the house next door.

Loreno knocked and stepped forward. A little while later, the door opened. A stick-thin gray-haired woman smiled beatifically. She held flowers in her hands as if she had just cut them in her garden.

The kid spoke in Spanish, turning to point at Reznick.

The old woman looked quizzically at Reznick and signaled him inside.

"Do you speak English?" he asked.

The woman smiled. "Not fluent, señor, but enough to get by." She invited him into the kitchen. The woman put the flowers in a vase with water and washed her hands before they sat down, and she made them both a strong coffee.

Reznick took a sip. "The way I like it," he said.

"My late husband, he was the same. Loved strong, black coffee."

"I'm sorry to bother you. I'm here in your beautiful town because a friend of mine from America was on vacation recently. She died in an explosion on a yacht, about a week ago."

The woman's eyes grew wide. "I heard about that. Terrible. I'm so sorry. An accident, wasn't it?"

"I thought so in the beginning. But I don't know for sure."

"Do you think someone murdered her, señor?" She let out a string of Spanish, and Reznick thought he caught the gist—that this was a safe town, good people.

"I don't want to speculate. Look, I've got a few questions. I hope you don't mind."

"I don't mind at all. How can I help, señor?"

"Tell me, the young man who brought me here, he said he saw a man in a camper van, an RV, at an overlook where he was cliff jumping on the night of the explosion."

The woman shook her head. "I don't like it when the children do that. A child many years ago, way back in the 1970s, he died doing that. I tell them not to."

Reznick nodded empathetically as the old woman went off on a tangent, remembering terrible memories from decades earlier. "The man in the camper van. The boy said he was living in the villa next door a few weeks back. The pink villa. Do you know if he's still there?"

The woman went quiet for a few moments. "The pink villa? Next door?"

Reznick nodded.

"I own that house."

"You own the pink house."

The woman nodded. Her hand had risen to cover her heart. "You think this man might be involved?"

"I don't know. Maybe he knows something."

"I'm surprised. That doesn't sound like the man I knew. He was very kind. He was very quiet. Studious. Highly, highly educated."

"Is he still living there?" When she shook her head, he added, "He rented for how long?"

"Three months, approximately. He said he was a doctor who retired to Spain. He had a friend staying with him, a young man I never met, but they both had Spanish passports."

Reznick took a few moments to process the information. "Tell me about the doctor's friend. Do you know anything about him?"

The woman shook her head. She walked over to a small, highly polished sideboard. She took out a folder, and inside were photocopies of Spanish passports. It showed two men. "This is what they looked like."

Reznick studied the face of the American man, the older man. He saw instantly the similarity to the handsome, clean-cut guy who had entered his hotel room. He then considered the other, younger man. North African, maybe. He turned over the paper. They both had the same stamps on their passports. He scanned the information and slowly digested it. Then the realization crashed through his head like a concrete block.

The stamp on the passports was from Melilla, a Spanish enclave in North Africa. His mind flashed to what Mac's sister had said about finding the fragment in the water with Arabic writing.

"What else can you tell me about the older man? The American."

"He paid me in advance. I had expected them to stay for six months, as that's what they paid. But they were in my villa in total for three months. March to around June. Three months, early summer. He swam a lot. I saw him swimming. Very quiet, wholesome. Lean. He swam hundreds of lengths of the pool. Hours each day. Very, very fit. Strong."

"And you're sure he was American?"

The old woman smiled. "Unmistakable. He was an American."

Sixteen

When Reznick got back to his hotel room, the first thing he did was pour all the booze from the minibar fridge down the sink. He paid the bill and asked to be moved to a new room, citing noise from his neighbors. The manager was most obliging. A couple of bellhops picked up his possessions and carried them to the new room.

Reznick tipped the guys and shut the blinds, then settled into the suite on the floor above his old room, where he had rooftop views of the town and the sea in the distance. He switched out the smoke detector for the one with the hidden camera. Then he sent a photo of the intruder, along with a picture he'd taken of the passport photocopy, to an encrypted email address at the FBI. Then he called up the direct line number for SIOC, the same one he had called before. A short while later he was connected to the same woman. He identified himself after a series of security questions.

"Jon, I've been instructed to tell you, for the last time, that you are no longer operating under the auspices of the FBI. And we certainly have no jurisdiction in Europe. Do you copy?"

"Yeah, but I hear your guys are out here doing more than just advising. Look, I've just sent a photo captured from footage of a guy who was roaming around my hotel room. I believe that this might be the same guy who was seen shortly before Martha

Meyerstein died. He's an American. I want the FBI to try and run him through facial recognition. He claims to be a doctor. I've also sent over a copy of a passport I believe belongs to the same man."

Silence.

"Do you copy that?"

"Jon, I've been informed that you have no jurisdictional or operational capacity."

"I'm giving you a goddamn lead. Use it. Find out who this guy is. Pass it on to O'Donoghue. I believe this American had a Moroccan kid staying at a villa here with him. They both had Spanish passports. There was a Melilla stamp on the passport. The kid might also have something to do with this."

Reznick ended the call. He headed across the street to the bar overlooking the cove and ordered a beer. He sat and drank, trying to process everything he had learned that day. A picture was emerging. The American guy was pulling the strings of the whole operation. Maybe the Moroccan kid was a patsy. Perhaps the Islamist link had been carefully planned to throw investigators off as to the true mastermind of the atrocity, the mysterious American man with a Spanish passport. Misdirection. Misinformation. Did it point to the mastermind having a military background?

As he stared out over the water, his thoughts invariably returned to Martha. Her body might have been washed out to sea. Or maybe she had been blown to bits, nothing discernible left. That wasn't unusual with explosions. His years deployed in Afghanistan and Iraq had seemed to provide a never-ending catalogue of such grotesque murders. Explosions often resulted in bodies being ripped to shreds, torn limb from limb. The thought of Martha's life being ended that way enraged him.

Reznick was no stranger to death. He had tasted it. The loss of his wife had alienated him from the world. And during his work in Delta in Iraq, he saw humankind at its worst. Depravity on all sides. He saw so much it was overwhelming. Bad, bad things. He could compartmentalize the horrors. Others hadn't been so lucky. Some of his American colleagues had gone mad at what they were seeing. What they endured. And the descent into hell that they contributed to. Endless night. That's what it seemed like. Endless goddamn night.

Ankle-deep in raw sewage, dragging Baathists out of ditches. Seeing the fear in a man's eyes as he was about to die. It got to a point where he didn't feel anymore. Not a thing. It wasn't long before he was plagued by nightmares. Waking in the dead of night, soaked in cold sweat. It was almost inevitable that he had found his way into the arms of the CIA. And on it went. He killed undesirables. Whoever the American military wanted neutralized. He, and guys like him, operated in the shadows. No questions asked. It was pure chance that he eventually ran up against the FBI. In particular, Martha Meyerstein. She'd wanted to use his tradecraft and skills and know-how in highly specialized and classified investigations. She'd convinced him he could be one of the good guys.

Now she was gone. The terrible emptiness he'd felt after Elisabeth's death was filling his soul again. He was going to that dark place again. And he had nowhere to turn. Martha wasn't coming back. And he couldn't bear to contemplate not seeing her again. Maybe he should see a clinical psychologist. A few months earlier, Lauren had suggested as much. She thought he needed help. His head was full of images of bodies. Bad stuff. Bad thoughts.

An SUV pulled up opposite the bar, snapping Reznick from his morbid thoughts. A small, stocky white guy wearing chinos, a pale blue linen shirt, and boat shoes walked toward him.

The guy strode through the bar and pulled up a chair beside Reznick. He sat down slowly as if for effect. "Long way from home, Jon." The accent was American. West Coast, perhaps.

Reznick said nothing as the man fixed his steely gaze on him.

The guy wiped the sweat from his brow. "I work for the State Department."

"Is that supposed to mean something to me?"

"You're asking a lot of questions around here, Jon. You don't work for the FBI. And even if you did, this isn't their jurisdiction, is it? Do you understand what I'm saying?"

"Always interesting to get an update on such legal niceties. Thanks for that."

"Pointing a gun at a friend of mine from the Civil Guard was a dumb move. A really dumb move. You don't strike me as a stupid person, Jon."

"Neither do you. So, if you don't mind, I'm enjoying some peace and quiet. Before I forget, any leads on what happened?"

The State Department character stared at him.

"I'm sorry, I missed what you said. Say that again?"

"Jon, don't be a smartass."

"Who the hell do you think you are? I don't answer to you."

"I'm letting you know that you crossed the line. You don't understand the big picture."

"Don't I?"

"So, if this continues, this little investigation of yours into a terrible accident, then there will be consequences for you. You're so out of line it's ridiculous. You're acting as if this was a murder. It was an accident, pure and simple."

"It was no fucking accident. I know. You know. The question is, what are you withholding? What is the American government withholding? What are you concealing? Because from where I'm sitting and from what I know, this is starting to sound like a twenty-four-karat-gold cover-up."

"Take my advice, Jon. Go home."

"And if I don't?"

"You either leave or we will make you leave."

"Go right ahead. What's stopping you?"

The guy stared at him for what seemed like an eternity. "Get the fuck off this island. You've been warned."

"Love the outfit, by the way. It's back in, that look."

"Heed the advice, Jon. Before it's too late."

Reznick reached across the table and grabbed the guy by the throat. The man's face went red. "Don't ever try the tough guy routine. It doesn't work with me. Do you understand?"

The State Department stiff closed his eyes and nodded.

Reznick loosened his grip.

The guy took a few moments to compose himself. "You haven't heard the last of this." He got up and calmly walked across the street, climbed back into the passenger seat of the vehicle, and the SUV pulled away.

Seventeen

Ford watched Reznick grab the guy in the bar. He peered through the telescope and scanned the rest of the patrons. No one seemed to bat an eye. He had quickly checked the plates on a database on his laptop. The SUV was a diplomatic vehicle, licensed to the American consulate in Palma.

It meant Reznick was ruffling feathers. The way he usually did.

Ford contemplated the importance of the situation. Reznick's presence on the island had clearly been noted by the intelligence agencies. The State Department, at least, who'd probably passed on what they knew to the CIA and the FBI.

He wondered if Reznick was going to be arrested and deported. Had the thickset guy Reznick grabbed warned him to back off? To leave the island?

Ford didn't want to get sidetracked. His sole purpose was to kill Reznick. And for that, he needed Reznick here. He wondered why exactly Reznick had changed rooms at the hotel. That was something of a mystery, since the camera clock he'd installed had malfunctioned. Perhaps he didn't like the view. Or he had a noisy neighbor.

Whoever took over the room and drank the poisoned whiskey would be an innocent. But that wasn't what irked Ford. What irked him was that Reznick would have been dead by now if his first plan had worked. But that was only a minor irritant in the grand scheme of things.

There was more than one way to skin a cat.

Still, it was a coincidence, Reznick switching rooms like that, and coincidences never sat well with Ford. He liked order. Everything and everyone in their place. He was used to planning every move, anticipating every eventuality, to the point where people's actions, no matter how idiosyncratic, became predictable.

Was it just a bit of luck on Reznick's part that he had decided to move? Or was it something far more problematic?

The questions raged like a storm in his head. Taunting him. Was it possible that Reznick realized the identical miniature booze bottles had been tampered with? Now, that would be worrying.

Ford was wired. He hadn't considered the possibility that Reznick would find out about the switch. The chances were a million to one.

He kicked over a nest of glass tables, smashing them to the floor. "Think you're so fucking cute, Reznick?"

Ford peered again through the telescope, focusing on Reznick's impassive features. "Well, from where I'm standing, you're not so smart. Dumb fuck. I see fuckwits like you every day. And I know how to deal with them. Think you'll get the better of me? I don't fucking think so."

Ford looked away from the telescope, down the hills shrouded by foliage. It was the most perfect line of sight. He should be feeling euphoric. He had been euphoric for the last day or so. But he felt his mood darkening.

The realization that the bait hadn't been taken, whether inadvertently or by design, needled him.

Ford sensed he could be facing a formidable adversary. He tried not to compare himself to mere mortals. But something about Reznick switching rooms bothered him. Worried him. Obsessed him.

He had Reznick where he wanted him. The bastard had been drawn into the aftermath of Martha's demise. That was the plan from the outset. But part of that plan was taking out Reznick at a time and place of his choosing. That was plan A.

When he realized Reznick was in the hotel, the opportunity was too good to pass up. But somehow, fate had intervened to save Reznick. Why on God's earth was the man not dead? His research had shown that Reznick was a single malt guy. Not a boozer. But a guy who enjoyed a glass or two of the amber nectar.

Ford could understand him skimping on the temptations of the minibar. But it was quite another thing to change rooms. He couldn't risk a second attempt. Damn, why had Reznick changed rooms? Had Reznick gotten spooked? And by what? He tried to put himself in Reznick's shoes. If Reznick did suspect someone had been in his room, it would make perfect sense to get out of that room. But by not leaving the hotel, was Reznick trying to send a message that he wasn't fazed? Perhaps Reznick was hoping the unseen foe would try again. And if he did try again, would Reznick be lying in wait? It felt as if Reznick was getting in his head.

These circular arguments went around and around in his mind. Then again, another way to look at it was that Reznick was just enjoying a stay of execution.

Yeah, that was a good way of looking at it.

Ford's gaze returned to the telescope and lingered on Reznick. He wondered what exactly the bastard was up to. He wondered if it had anything to do with Reznick visiting the kindly old Spanish lady. The same woman Ford had rented the first villa from. His base camp in the small town before his final move into the secluded mountainside retreat. Ford had used a trick the dark web hacker had shown him to remotely access the grainy security camera footage the old lady had rigged up to cover her property. But he couldn't hear a word of what was said. That was frustrating. Reznick was getting closer. Quicker than Ford had expected.

Ford wasn't worried. He'd left enough misdirection behind that it would be a while before Reznick uncovered his true identity. But Reznick was inching closer. He needed to know what Reznick knew.

He began to pace the room before turning and kicking over the telescope and the tripod. The equipment crashed across the marble floor, the lens smashing into the wall. He felt himself getting more and more worked up.

It was then, in a cold, blind fury, that an idea came to him. A germ of an idea. A moment of clarity. The idea was forming. *Oh yeah, that would work.*

Ford made a mental note of what he was going to do. He needed to compose himself. He did what he always did when he was stressed. He went to the bedroom and began to meditate. He closed his eyes and felt himself drifting away to another realm. A realm of peace. A realm of tranquility. He felt himself being blanketed in a cocoon of warmth.

He sensed he was drifting above the wisps of white cloud, toward the rays of sunshine. Basking in the light. It was as if he were floating through space, unhindered by worries. He was lighter. More relaxed.

When he finished with his exercises, he went into the bathroom and stared at his reflection in the mirror. The lean, handsome face. The golden tan. But his eyes were bloodshot. He sometimes got like that. Yet he also saw a coldness in his blue eyes. And then he thought about what he was about to do and smiled. "Let's go and have some fun, Adam, huh?"

Ford picked up the keys to the SUV, headed outside, and got in the vehicle. As he sped off, he caught his reflection in the rearview mirror. His pupils were like pinpricks, and he hadn't even done any coke. This was pure adrenaline. He grinned as he headed straight for the old lady's house on the edge of Cala San Vicente.

Eighteen

A crimson sunset bathed the waters off Cala San Vicente as Reznick watched Catherine McCafferty walk into the beachside bar. She wore sunglasses and a white summer dress, arms pink with sun.

She pulled up a chair beside him. "You mind if I join you?"

"Not at all."

Catherine sat down, surveying the sunset. "This is nice. But it would've been nicer with David."

"Any news?"

Catherine stared at him as if in a daze before she nodded.

"You look like you need a drink," Reznick said.

"Glass of dry white wine."

Reznick signaled the waiter. He ordered another beer and a glass of wine. "You OK?"

Catherine was scrolling through messages on her cell phone. "I've felt better."

The waiter served the drinks at the table.

Reznick waited until the guy was out of earshot. "What happened? Have you heard something?"

"I got a call about thirty minutes ago."

"From who?"

"Military attaché in Madrid. British diplomat."

Reznick recognized immediately the significance of a military expert attached to a diplomatic mission taking the lead. It showed the importance of the matter to the UK government. "Did they tell you what happened to him?"

"They—the Brits—have taken him to a secure location."

"That's what he said? I mean, was that the exact language he used?"

"Exact language. *Secure location*, that's verbatim what he said."

Reznick sighed and sipped his beer.

"What?"

"Your brother knows too much."

Catherine nodded. "I know. It's that fragment he found. It has them spooked."

"So, did they say whether he's still in Mallorca?"

"The military attaché said he couldn't say."

"Couldn't or wouldn't say?"

"Wouldn't say, would be my guess."

Reznick nodded. "I think you're right."

"All he said was my brother was safe."

"I don't want to get you worried, but that sounds ominous."

"In what way?"

"Well, I'm operating under the assumption that the Brits and Americans are working closely on this. And I believe that the Brits are doing whatever they're being told to do. Maybe they've handed your brother over to the Americans. Maybe they're trying to find out what your brother really knows and pass it on. That's what happens."

Catherine picked up her glass and sipped some wine. "I reminded the attaché that under the European Convention of Human Rights, to which Spain and the United Kingdom are signatories, Article 5 guarantees the right to liberty and security."

"Interesting."

"In particular, I pointed out that I would be referring my brother's case to the European Court of Human Rights in Strasbourg."

"How did he respond to that?"

"He said the Foreign Office was doing all they could to *resolve*, as he called it, a fiendishly complex situation."

"He didn't say anything about what country your brother was in?"

"Said he was being held legally within an EU country. Maybe Spain, I don't know."

"And that's that? So, he's just disappeared?"

"The military attaché assured me he was safe."

"How does he know that?"

Catherine shrugged. "I don't know."

"What's the attaché's name?"

"Gerald Essenden."

Reznick made a mental note. "You believe him?"

"Essenden?"

Reznick nodded.

"Maybe. The only problem is, I have to take him at his word."

"They're jumpy, knowing your brother knows something about what happened."

"The problem is, so do we. Which means we might also get the same treatment."

Reznick sighed, only too aware that they already knew too much. "There's more to this than meets the eye. Way more."

"More than an Islamist link?"

Reznick nodded. He hadn't told her about the man who had broken into his hotel room or the mysterious American doctor who bore a striking resemblance. "The whole thing just feels off, you know what I mean?"

"You have no idea how off," she said.

"I'm sorry, what do you mean? Do you mean what's happened so far?"

Catherine shook her head. "I'm referring to what happened in the middle of the night."

"What was that?"

"I got a call from a number I didn't recognize. Which freaks me out, now that I think about it. Anyway, a man told me I needed to take great care. And that I really needed to go home and keep it all quiet."

"Shit."

"My thoughts exactly."

"So . . . what was it? A veiled threat?"

"More or less. But I don't scare easily."

Reznick grimaced. "Catherine, listen to me. I admire your spirit. But this isn't a game."

"I'm well aware of that."

"My friend has been blown up. Your brother has been taken into custody, and we don't know where he's being held. Do I need to spell it out for you? You need to pay attention."

"Whose side are you on?"

"This isn't going to end well. I might be wrong, but we're in the middle of a cover-up. This is a murky game. A game of mirrors, where nothing is what it seems. What is real, what is unreal? You might want to think about that."

"Are you seriously telling me to get out of here?"

"That's precisely what I'm saying."

"What about my brother?"

"Your brother can look after himself. Besides, I doubt this is the end of it. Not by a long shot."

Catherine gulped down her wine. "Do you think I should take the threat seriously?"

"You absolutely should. How did someone get your number? Who was it? Also, what kind of accent did he have?"

"American, I believe."

Reznick wondered if it was the State Department guy who had threatened him in the bar and warned him to leave the island. "Heed the advice. Get out of here. Go home. Whatever is happening here will not end well. You don't want to be around for that."

Catherine was quiet for a few moments, as if contemplating her situation and that of her brother.

"Tell me, the British guy you spoke to, the diplomat who seemed to know about your brother?"

"Essenden. Gerald Essenden."

"Yeah. Are you sure he is who he says he is?"

Catherine nodded. "I checked."

Reznick made a mental note. "Do you know what a military attaché is?"

"He advises on military matters, I'm guessing, or security issues?"

"Exactly. They're invariably senior military officers, sometimes with an intelligence background. So they're aware of espionage, counterespionage, surveillance, terrorism, all those things that their government is involved in."

"And he'll be my link between Spain and the UK?"

"Spanish military intelligence and UK security services. He might be MI6. That wouldn't be disclosed. But he's clearly here to gather up whatever intelligence he can, liaise with the Spanish and also, crucially, with the Americans."

"You believe this attaché knows more?"

"Way, way more than he's letting on."

"With regards to my brother?"

"With regards to your brother and the people on the yacht. With regards to everything. He'll know the big picture. He might even know who threatened you."

Catherine sighed. "Look, for what it's worth, I've got a meeting with the attaché tomorrow morning in Palma. He's hoping to have an update for me. And once I get that, maybe I'll heed your advice and return to Scotland."

Reznick nodded. "Let me know how it goes before you leave Mallorca. Maybe call me when you're at the airport. The attaché knows far more than he's letting on. And I want to know what."

Nineteen

Reznick was floating in a sea of darkness. He felt the water on his skin, endless black sky above. Not a star in the sky. Not one. The sound of whispered voices carried on the wind. He detected an ominous tone. He sensed someone was speaking to him. Talking to him. Maybe they were close. Maybe he was alone. Like in a fevered dream. Dark whispers. Foreboding. He thought he could discern Martha's voice. In the distance, carrying on the breeze.

He awoke, bolt upright, bathed in a cold sweat.

Reznick was breathing hard, heart pounding fast. He took a few moments to get his bearings. It was only a nightmare. The kind he had experienced a thousand times before. Malarial dreams. Torment. The sense he was suffocating.

He reached over and checked his watch on his bedside table. The luminous dial showed it was only four thirty. Still dark. But not long till dawn.

Reznick sat up on the edge of the bed, head in hands. A waking nightmare. No end in sight. His mind was still coming to as he sat in silence. The loss was unbearable. He thought of his father on the day his mother passed away. His blue eyes, haunted at the best of times by ghosts of Vietnam, booze, and having seen too much suffering, seemed frozen, as if knowing things would never be the same. And the thing was, things never were the same. His father, a man he revered, seemed to have an air of resignation about him from that day on. A little bit of his father had died, too, that day. As the doctor arrived to tell him the time of death, as they took her body from the house, a terrifying sadness crossed his face, as if her passing was worse than anything he had witnessed. Reznick saw it. But to a casual observer, his father merely looked stoic.

And he was. Even the day after his wife was buried, Reznick's father got himself dressed, still stinking of booze, and went to work at a place he loathed, the sardine packing plant in Rockland. He didn't moan. He just endured. He was a workingman till the day he died.

Reznick snapped out of his morbid introspection and got up from the bed. He went to the bathroom, took a piss. Then washed his hands before splashing cold water on his face to wake himself up.

He went back to the bedroom and pulled out his running gear: a Dri-FIT running top, shorts, and socks. He laced up his old sneakers, took a bottle of chilled spring water from the minibar, checking the seal carefully. Then he drank it in one gulp.

It was still dark when he walked out of the hotel. He crossed the street and stood on the sidewalk overlooking the small sandy beach, Cala Molins. Waves crashed off the cliffs, and the moon bathed the water in a ghostly white glow.

Reznick breathed in the salty air as he gathered his thoughts. He thought of Martha and all she meant to him. He thought also of what Catherine had said about the threatening phone call she had received, warning her to leave. He pondered that as he began some stretching exercises for a few minutes. He felt as if he was getting drawn deeper into a murky shadow world. A world he knew all too well. A world he had long inhabited. But a world that was conspiring to conceal what had really happened.

He felt a strong temptation to head back home. Get back to Rockland. Stare out over Penobscot Bay, lost in his thoughts. But he knew that deep down he wasn't going to back off, even if he wanted to. It wasn't in his nature. *Semper fidelis.* The motto of the US Marines he always carried in his soul. Engrained in his very being. It meant always faithful, always loyal. He was loyal. He was dutiful. He would see this through.

Reznick sighed long and hard. He needed to clear his head. He ran down the sidewalk, which snaked its way around a road that fringed the beachside town. Higher and higher, sweat already sticking to his shirt. On and on he ran, the humidity eased slightly by a gentle offshore breeze.

Reznick's arms were pumping hard as he ran faster. Harder. Past hotels, an early-morning bakery with its lights on, a Civil Guard cruiser, two cops watching his every move while drinking bottles of water. He jogged on, feeling himself getting stronger. He felt his head beginning to clear. He was thinking clearer. The endorphins were kicking in.

He pressed on until he hit the edge of the town, along a dusty road that led to Puerto Pollensa. Then he turned left and headed down an even narrower road as he doubled back through a sleepy part of town. Past isolated villas with imposing old wooden doors with state-of-the-art video entry phones. Past more modest houses. And then past an occasional bar and restaurant until he was back to the seafront.

It had taken him nearly an hour.

Reznick jumped down onto the sandy beach and walked to the water's edge. He sat down in the soft, warm sand and gazed out over the dark waters lapping at the shore. He felt better now. More centered.

He listened to the waves. Their hypnotic quality. He closed his eyes, listening to his breathing, his beating heart. He sat for what seemed like an eternity, cloaked in the predawn darkness, wondering what lay ahead that day.

The sun was peeking over the horizon as Reznick sat on his room's terrace, enjoying an early breakfast of scrambled eggs, buttered toast, orange juice, and a cup of black coffee with a couple of Dexedrine, when his cell phone began to vibrate on the table.

Reznick answered. "Yeah, Jon speaking."

"Hope you don't mind me calling you so early," Catherine McCafferty said.

Reznick detected a note of tension in her voice. "You OK?"

"I'm on the road to Palma. I think—I think someone is following me."

Reznick's blood ran cold. "Listen to me," he said. "Don't panic."

"He's still there."

"Who?"

"I don't know. It's a Nissan pickup; I can't make out the driver. But I'm scared."

"Can you slow down?"

"That's just the thing." Her voice cracked, a sign of acute stress. "Every time I tap the brakes to slow down to get off the road, the RPMs rise. It's like I'm not in control."

Reznick's heart sank. He understood exactly what was happening. "Can you pull on the hand brake?"

"Tried. And it failed. It's like I can't control it. It's like the car's got a mind of its own."

"Can you carefully veer into a ditch?"

"I've tried that. I don't think I'm controlling the vehicle. Jon, I'm really freaking out. It's like it's been hijacked by someone else remotely."

Reznick's mind was racing. He left the terrace, locked up his room, and strode out of the hotel. "What speed are you doing?"

"Sixty-five. I can't slow down. I can't jump out or I'm dead."

"Catherine, I am on my way. I've got a GPS fix on your location. Stay on the line."

"Jon, please, I don't know what to do."

Reznick headed across the street to the bar by the beach.

"Jon, are you still there?"

Reznick spotted the owner clearing a table and quickly explained the situation. He gave the guy one hundred euros and borrowed his Ducati. "I'm on my way. Do you copy that?"

"Yes, I do, Jon. I'm very scared. I don't like this."

Reznick put on the helmet. "I will get there as soon as I can. I promise you."

"Don't be long. I'm scared, Jon. It seems to be getting faster. I'm doing seventy-five now, but I haven't touched the accelerator."

Reznick ended the call and burned rubber on the way out of town. He negotiated a few winding roads before he hit the highway that led to Palma. He thought about calling the police, warning them about a runaway car. But whoever had rigged Catherine's vehicle—probably whoever was following her in the pickup—might choose to do something drastic in response.

He opened up the throttle to the max and hurtled down the freeway, a terrible sense of foreboding washing over him.

The minutes seemed like hours as Reznick sped down the highway, hoping and praying he would get there in time to help. But only a few minutes later, he spotted the flashing lights of fire trucks and police cars visible on the horizon. A sense of dread enveloped him as he snaked through the gridlocked traffic until he reached the crash scene.

Reznick flipped up his visor. Ahead of him was the mangled, smoking wreckage of the car Catherine McCafferty had been driving.

He got off the bike and ran to the scene. "Señor," he said to a fireman, "she was a friend of mine."

The guy shook his head. "It's too late. She was badly burned by the time we got here."

Reznick stared at the smoking, twisted metal. "Where is her body?"

"She is in an ambulance. Taken to the hospital morgue. I'm sorry. She's dead."

Reznick's mind was racing, a rage building up within him, ready to explode. "Did she have ID on her?"

The firefighter nodded. "British. She had her passport on her." He patted Reznick on the back. "I'm so sorry, señor."

Twenty

Reznick stood by the side of the road, head bowed, as he contemplated the terrible chain of events. "Motherfucker!"

The firefighter nodded as if he understood Reznick's grief.

Reznick turned and stared at the blackened, mangled car, the smell of gasoline and burnt metal filling the air. He thought back to Catherine McCafferty's call only a short while earlier. A Nissan pickup had been following her. At least she thought it was following her. And she was struggling to control the steering. He knew what that pointed to. He knew exactly what had happened. It was a Boston Brakes job. An assassination technique believed to have been pioneered by the CIA. It involved planting an electronic device in the target car, which could then be remotely controlled by a following car. It was known to be used by governments. But it was also a technique that Special Forces operatives could master, given training.

"Señor?"

Reznick looked at the backed-up traffic as dawn broke across the Palma expressway. The Nissan pickup was long gone. He was tempted to ride into Palma to speak to the diplomat Catherine McCafferty was set to meet. But after a few short moments, he let that slide. Instead, another idea had already begun to form in his head.

He knew that a knee-jerk reaction wasn't the smart move. The smart move was to take the time to get the response right. A gut reaction might compound the problem. He needed to slow down and try and figure out his next steps.

"Señor, do you need medical treatment?"

Reznick shook his head. He walked over to the motorcycle, turned it around, and turned the key in the ignition. He accelerated fast past the gridlocked traffic on the freeway as he headed back to Cala San Vicente.

Think, goddamn it, think.

Reznick's mind was swirling with ideas. Overloaded with a thirst for revenge. But he knew from his training and experience that a measured response was needed. He needed space to fully process what had happened. The easiest thing in the world would have been to lash out. But the smart thing to do was to strategize. To figure out what he should do next.

What a fucking mess.

Reznick dropped the Ducati off at the bar, thanked the owner, and walked up to the overlook, staring out at the buoy bobbing in the water. The marker for where Martha and her friend had died. He closed his eyes and thought first of Martha. Then of Catherine McCafferty. She was the one who had told him about the Arabic inscription her brother had found. And someone wanted to silence her. Someone had gotten to her. Was it the guy who'd called her? The American? The car crash had all the hallmarks of a special ops hit, but it could just as easily be a Spanish operation. Maybe military intelligence. Was this their response to Reznick humiliating one of their guys? Or else it was the American government. Taking out a person who could have leaked the information to the press.

On and on the questions bounced around his head. And he was no closer to knowing who'd been responsible for the explosion— Islamist terrorists or someone else.

Reznick looked out across the water. A police boat came into view, once again circling the area. His thoughts turned again to Catherine McCafferty. She'd been en route to a meeting in Palma with a British diplomat. A military attaché.

He took out his cell phone and pulled up a number. The number of a trusted friend.

It rang five times before it was answered.

"This better be fucking good at three in the morning," said the voice of Trevelle Williams, a reclusive computer genius and former NSA contractor.

"How you enjoying your new abode?"

"Hey, Mr. R., long time no hear."

"So how are the cornfields and all that stuff?"

"Gimme a break. Actually I love it. How are things where you are?"

"Not good, my friend. Trevelle, I need to lay my cards on the table. After what happened previously, you might not want to help out." Not long ago, Trevelle had asked for Reznick's help alerting a government whistleblower who had been targeted for assassination. The hacker's fortresslike base in Miami had been breached, and he had subsequently set up from scratch in rural Iowa. Reznick hesitated. He didn't think it was the right time to tell Trevelle about what had happened to Martha.

"I'll always help you out, Jon, not a problem. Don't ever think it is."

"Appreciate that."

"So I can see from your phone's GPS signal that you're not in America. Spain? What the hell is going on there?"

"Long story. I hope you can come through for me on this. I need help. Real bad."

"What do you need?"

Reznick sighed, relieved to be getting some technical assistance. "I want you to find out everything you can about Gerald Essenden. I believe he's British, a diplomat based in Madrid. I want to know more about him. A lot more."

"Why?"

Reznick smiled. "You ask a lot of questions, Trevelle."

"Old habits die hard."

"He's a person of interest. That's all I can say."

"Leave it to me. When do you need info on this guy?"

"Yesterday would be good."

"No pressure. Back at you soon."

Reznick ended the call. The hacker was a specialist at fast turn-arounds. He could get his hands on classified information and have it to you within the hour. He wouldn't take long. Reznick needed to find Essenden, but he wasn't ready to speak to him face-to-face. He wanted to track his movements first. The man knew something. Of that Reznick was sure.

His gaze turned to the turquoise waters off Cala Molins beach. A picture-postcard scene. His mind was racing again. Part exhaustion, part amphetamines still in his blood. He needed to pull all the strands of what he knew or had so far uncovered and try to spot the less obvious links.

Reznick was standing on the spot that tied so many threads together. Where it all began. Where the RV had been seen. Driven by the guy who had rented a villa on the outskirts of town. An American. Who looked like the guy who had broken into his hotel room. Had to be the same guy.

Reznick turned and squinted against the glare of the midmorning sun, edging higher up into the sunbaked hills.

He took a few moments as he focused on the skyline. Far away in the distance, he could just make out little white dots on the mountainside. Like small whitewashed cottages. Holiday homes, perhaps. He had always looked down on the bay. But not up at the mountain.

He wondered why he hadn't turned around and looked up high into the mountain range.

Who lived there? Maybe locals in low-rent old cottages, tending the dusty land. Maybe tending goats. He'd seen a few scrawny animals wandering wild through the town.

Reznick felt his curiosity get the better of him as he contemplated his next move. He could just sit tight and do nothing until he heard back from Trevelle. But that wasn't in his nature. He needed to do something. Anything to keep his mind from going around and around.

A sixth sense, a gut reaction, began to kick in. He was curious about those sun-bleached hills.

Reznick considered what he needed to head up there. He needed some basic provisions. The first thing he did was return to his hotel room. He picked up his backpack, popped in half a dozen bottles of water, and headed to the overlook.

He had a feeling the guy who was behind this, the guy in the RV, wasn't far. Maybe the guy was closer than he thought. Living in plain sight. He had no proof of it. He just sensed it. He felt it in his guts. The bastard was still around. Maybe watching and waiting at this moment. Waiting to make his next move.

Reznick poured some water over his head, cooling him down. Then he gulped down the rest of the bottle and took a few steps onto a dusty trail. He began to climb. A steep climb. The trail meandered as it crisscrossed the barren mountainside. He strode on under a blazing sun along the winding, dusty path. A few hundred yards later it led to a dirt path, goats aimlessly heading up to even higher, rockier ground.

Reznick kept climbing, scrabbling through the bone-hard dirt and scree, clouds of dust getting kicked up in his midst. His throat felt badly parched, sweat sticking his shirt to his skin. He took out another bottle of water from his backpack and gulped it down. He had endured the hell that was Delta training. This was nothing in comparison. It was like a walk in the park. After sleep deprivation, physical and mental exhaustion, eating rancid food, being blindfolded, taking pain and piling on more pain, and then piling on stressful situations. In particular, SERE—survival, evasion, resistance, and escape—taught Delta warriors what it would take to have the guile, guts, and sheer stubbornness to come out on top. But the endgame was being able to make the right decisions when tired, hungry, and in need of sleep. Critical thinking at times of acute stress was tough. Measured thinking. Being able to detach from the emotional situation unfolding amid death. Killings. He needed to stay remote to win.

Reznick could do that. He had done that. Time and time again. A little hike up a steep mountainside in blazing heat was nothing to him. He would find the person responsible for Martha's death, the same person responsible for Catherine McCafferty's, even if indirectly. Somehow.

He turned and shielded his eyes from the glare of the sun. Reznick looked down at the town. The whitewashed villas, the turquoise waters. The line of sight was still good. Very good indeed.

Reznick could see the attraction of the area on multiple levels. He turned around and continued on with the climb, not really knowing what it was he was hoping to achieve. His curiosity was getting the better of him. Perhaps he was being pulled by unknown forces. It was as if he sensed that something in his surroundings might provide a clue to what had happened. But then again, maybe he was just clutching at straws, determined to explore every avenue, every line of sight. Maybe that was it. He just couldn't give up hope that the clues to who had killed Martha were hidden, far higher, up above the town and out of sight from sea level.

He traipsed upward, calves tightening as the broiling heat beat down.

The temperature reminded him a little of his time in Fallujah. Unrelenting, brutal heat. He didn't care. He felt in a perverse way as if he deserved to be punished. Punished for not being able to protect Martha. Punished for not finding the clues to her killer.

More than once, he wondered what the hell he had become involved in. But he also knew that, come what may, he would get to the bottom of the killing. Maybe die trying.

Twenty minutes later, almost blinded by heat and the sun, Reznick stopped and screwed up his eyes toward something on the horizon. He squinted and saw, through the haze, what looked like an abandoned hut. It appeared to be an old shepherd's hut. A broken-down place of rest for shepherds tending their goats. Cracked windows in the side, a dilapidated broken-down look.

The incessant sound of cicadas in olive trees buzzed the air. Getting louder. More shrill.

Reznick wiped the sweat from his brow with the back of his hand. He approached the hut. The bone-dry front door had been blasted for decades by the sun. It was slightly ajar. Flies were buzzing around. He pushed open the door.

The smell of decay hit him. Overpowering, cloying in his throat.

Reznick felt the urge to retch and had to wait until it passed. He stepped into the hut, and his foot went through the rotten floorboards, exposing dry earth. He extricated his foot and looked down at the splintered and broken floor. Slowly he knelt. The floorboards were loose, not nailed down.

A putrid smell permeated the airless hut. A vile, rotten aroma. A dead animal?

He took a pocketknife from his back pocket, flipped open the blade, and pried up a few more of the floorboards. Dust particles hung in the still air. He brushed away the dry earth beneath. Despite the heat, his blood turned to ice. He could see hair, black hair, sticking out through the earth. He brushed away more of the dirt.

It was then he saw waxy human flesh.

Twenty-One

Reznick called it in from his cell phone and sat and waited outside the hut in the blazing sun, knees up to his chin. It seemed like hours before he saw anyone. Eventually, he spotted police and forensic technicians climbing up the scorched dirt of the hillside to join him. A chopper dropped off more police, whipping up the dusty earth as it took off.

Reznick answered questions from one Spanish cop and then another before he was allowed off the mountainside. He was escorted by four Spanish cops until they reached the road. A car was waiting, and Reznick was driven to a small police station on the other side of the island. Forensic samples were taken from his fingernails and sneakers before he was allowed a shower at the station. Then he was shown to a windowless room, where he was given water, coffee, and sandwiches and told to wait.

The hours dragged. Now would be a good time for Trevelle to call, but he still hadn't heard from him.

Reznick sat alone with his thoughts. He felt ill. Drained. He knew the cops were keeping him there while they tried to build up a picture of what had happened. They would also be trying to find out more about him. But the basic point was to let him stew alone. They wanted to get inside his head. Make him scared. Uncertainty bred fear. Reznick knew the psychology behind it. It gave the police interviewers the psychological advantage. The upper hand.

Eventually, two cops arrived.

"You need to move, señor," one of them said.

Reznick was escorted to a stark interview room, metal grilles on the window, air-conditioning unit growling low. Two men were already there, sitting on one side of the desk.

He was shown to the chair on the other side and slumped down.

The two men stared at him for what seemed like a lifetime but might have only been a few seconds.

"Jon Reznick?" drawled the older of the two. To Reznick's surprise, he had an American accent. The guy wore a white shirt, navy tie, and dark pants.

"Who are you?" Reznick said.

"Lionel Finsburg, FBI legal attaché."

Reznick nodded. "Yes, I'm Jon Reznick."

The second guy cleared his throat. "Why are you in Mallorca, Jon? You're a long, long way from home."

"You FBI too?"

The man shook his head. "State Department. Todd Mavor."

"I bumped into one of your guys yesterday, I think. Not very friendly."

"Jon, let's cut the bull. We know why you're here."

"You do? And why is that what I'm being questioned about when I've just uncovered some human remains up a goddamn mountainside?"

Mavor shifted in his seat as Finsburg scribbled some notes on a legal pad.

"Is the State Department leading on this investigation?" Reznick asked. "At least that's what I was told. Are you liaising with Spanish military intelligence? Are they helping you out on this?"

"Let's leave those questions till later. You're here, on this island, because of an explosion, right?"

"You're being rather coy, Todd. What do you think?"

"What do you mean?"

"I mean this isn't about an accidental explosion. It's about an FBI assistant director being assassinated. That's why we're all here."

Mavor stared back at Reznick. "I'm not at liberty to talk about such matters."

"So you're over here in beautiful Mallorca for what purpose, Todd? Working on your tan? I knew Washington spending was out of control, but that's ridiculous."

Mavor pointed a finger at him. "Listen to me, Reznick, I don't give a shit about your reputation. You need to know that you are an American citizen, and you have no jurisdiction out here. You no longer work for the FBI."

Reznick shook his head. "Whatever."

"On whose behalf are you operating?"

Reznick said nothing.

"You seem to have made friends quickly. The Scottish gentleman, McCafferty. He's an interesting character. I'm not surprised you gravitated toward him."

"Where is he? Is he even still alive?"

"He's a British citizen. They're dealing with that."

Reznick made a mental note. He now had confirmation that backed up what Catherine McCafferty had been told. "Tell me about the body I found up in the hills. You want to talk about that? You identified that person?"

Finsburg intervened. "Jon, what Todd was getting at is that your presence here isn't helping matters."

127

"I asked about the body I found up in the hills."

"That's a matter for the local police."

"Is that right, Lionel? So why am I not being interviewed by them?"

Finsburg flushed. "Jon, we all know what this is about."

Reznick stared at him.

"I knew Martha very well. And I know she spoke highly of you. But we're concerned that there are aspects of this one-man investigation of yours that could impinge on national security."

Reznick nodded. "I appreciate your candor. Now tell me about the body."

"I'm getting to that. We believe it was a young man."

"Who is he? And is this linked to Martha's death?"

"You're asking a lot of questions."

"I just want answers. Is the body up there linked in some way to Martha Meyerstein's death?"

"I'm not at liberty to say, sorry. But we're grateful that you have somehow managed to find this person."

Mavor pinched the bridge of his nose. "I'm curious, Reznick. How did you find this site where the body was? Was it just a wild, crazy guess?"

"You tell me."

"You didn't kill this person and cover it all up by claiming to have found him?"

"What an imagination. Do all you State Department guys have such vivid imaginations?"

Mavor fixed his gaze on Reznick. "If it wasn't you, tell me straight. How did you find the body?"

Reznick shrugged. "Just walking around, looking at the lines of sight to where the yacht was blown to pieces."

Mavor made a few notes, as did Finsburg. "Line of sight. Just walking around, huh? Do you really expect me to believe that?"

"Believe whatever you want, Mavor. It began with me trying to find a line of sight. Curiosity. That's where it led me. And yeah, I did stumble upon the body, somewhat."

"You really expect me to believe that, Reznick?"

"Like I said, believe what you want. Since I've arrived, I've discovered a few interesting things. This whole thing doesn't add up. You're spinning a line. It's bullshit."

Mavor scribbled some more notes. "OK, let's just back up for a moment. Let's imagine, just for a moment, that I believe you, Jon."

Reznick nodded.

"So when you say *line of sight*, do you want to explain what you mean? Line of sight from where to where? Give me context. Your thought processes."

"I mean where I believe someone might have been observing the yacht and remotely detonated an explosion. Perhaps via cell phone. And I took it from there, working my way up the mountainside. It was an aspect I hadn't considered. I had been thinking line of sight from land to sea. But then I started thinking that higher elevations might have views of the town. And certainly the sea. The place where the explosion happened."

Finsburg flushed and stared at Reznick. "Jon, there has been no chatter detected that this tragic accident was anything but. There is no intelligence pointing to an explosive device."

"I don't believe you."

Finsburg's face flushed a deeper scarlet. "Let's get back to talking about your finding this body. I want to retrace your steps on this, if you don't mind."

Reznick felt himself getting exasperated. He wondered if he was being deliberately tied up speaking to these two while . . . while what? "I found out where the yacht's last position was and looked for suitable locations to observe. The weather vane."

"Which overlooks the bay?" Mavor said.

Reznick nodded. "Correct. A little rocky outcrop with the weather vane beside it. But then I looked around and climbed higher and higher and higher, and I somehow stumbled on the hut, and the remains of that person. It was a fluke. A coincidence."

Mavor said, "I don't believe in coincidences, Reznick."

"Neither do I. I don't believe it's a coincidence that the FBI and the State Department are out here on a Spanish island if you believe Martha Meyerstein's death was an accident. This was murder."

Finsburg showed his hands, as if trying to calm down the tense exchange. "Jon, there is no evidence of murder."

"Bullshit. Do you really expect me to believe that her death here was an accident?"

Mavor shook his head. "It happens, Jon. Life is hard. And bad stuff happens."

Reznick looked hard at Mavor. "'Life is hard'? Is that your line? Let's talk for a minute about why we're all here. It's not about that body I found. The State Department is getting twitchy. I can see it in your eyes, Mavor."

Mavor stared at him.

"You know something. You've been given information, haven't you? Let's talk for a minute about McCafferty. Did you know his sister is dead? Did you arrange for her death because she knew about the circuit board Mac found with Arabic writing on it? Are you going to scribble *that* information down?"

Finsburg averted his gaze.

"Mac was being questioned after he handed over the pieces, and now his sister dies in a car crash. All within a week after an FBI assistant director and her friend are blown up on a yacht. Do you really expect me to believe this is all just a tragic series of accidents? Seriously?"

Mavor glared at Reznick.

"And now, there's some unidentified body up in the hills? Guys, now *that's* stretching credibility. I don't believe for a minute that these are all accidents. So, please, do me a favor, and start talking some fucking sense and cut the lies and obfuscation."

Finsburg said nothing.

"What do you say, Mavor?" Reznick said.

The State Department lackey tapped his hand against the table. "Who mentioned Arabic writing?"

"Catherine McCafferty. Her brother told her."

Mavor checked his notes for a fleeting moment. "Are there any others she told?"

"I wouldn't bet against it," Reznick said. "She was smart. A lawyer."

Mavor sighed. "You can't talk about such things, do you understand me?"

"Why not?"

"Don't talk about it, do you hear me? National security is involved."

"You said I wasn't working for the government. I can talk about whatever I like. I don't report to you. I don't report to anyone."

Mavor stared at him. "This was a terrible accident, Jon. We're all upset about this."

"A lot of terrible accidents on such a small island. What do you think the odds are? So, have you got any more questions for me, Todd?"

Mavor leaned forward, face inches from Reznick's. "You need to go home, Jon. I don't want the Spanish police to think you're hindering their investigation in any way."

"No one is hindering anything."

"Go home."

"Am I free to leave?"

Mavor looked at Finsburg, who nodded, gaze once again averted to the floor. "Pack your bags, Jon. And get back to the States on the next flight."

"And if I don't?"

"Just get on the goddamn flight. Enough is enough."

Twenty-Two

High up in the hills, nearly two miles as the crow flies from the bar in Cala San Vicente, Adam Ford was in his villa listening to the Spanish police on the scanner. He smiled as he heard the heads-up that the Americans had released Reznick. He was enjoying the game he was playing. A game that had become more complex. But that didn't dim its fun. Quite the contrary. It only added to the growing excitement. The frisson of the chase. Fucking with Reznick was fun. Especially killing the Scottish lawyer. He enjoyed that immensely. She had told Reznick about the Arabic writing on the fragment her brother had found. He was surprised how easy it was to bug her cell phone. He could track her movements. Listen in to calls. Ford didn't have to kill her. But having the power to kill at will was a high like no other. It made him feel good. He decided who would live or die. Omnipotent. It was her bad luck that Ford could see the value in killing the smart and beautiful Catherine McCafferty. It was also a great way to fuck with Reznick's head. Classic psyops.

He had simply followed her in his pickup. And then he had remotely accessed her car, allowing him to control it with a simple Wi-Fi–enabled joystick. Slowly he had moved her car from side to side, watching her losing control. He let the fun continue for miles. Then when he was bored, he casually flicked a switch on the device, crashing her car into oncoming traffic. Now that was cold, even by his standards.

Ford picked up military-grade binoculars from the coffee table and went over to the floor-to-ceiling windows. He scanned the beachside bar. Tourists and a few locals eating lobster and fresh fish and drinking beer at the tables beside the road. He was tempted to head straight to the bar and wait for Reznick's return. He knew Reznick was a creature of habit. Wired to enjoy repetition. The comfort of the familiar. Ford was a bit like that himself in some ways.

He wondered what it would be like to be so close to Reznick. Physically close. Close enough to touch him. Smell him. And eventually kill him.

He thought about what it would feel like to be in Reznick's presence again. The growing excitement as Reznick sat close by. In a way, he was glad Reznick hadn't drunk the poisoned scotch. It increased the challenge. He had to be careful now. Reznick was especially dangerous when wounded.

He allowed himself a minute to fantasize about the final moments of Reznick's life. He imagined the agony. The slow, slow death. That would be the ideal scenario. But he wasn't picky about how it happened. If anything, Ford was a pragmatist.

Maybe it would be a jab in the neck with a quick-acting anesthetic. Maybe a bullet in the head. Sniper rifle. Why not? He could do that. He'd been trained to do that. He might be a brilliant doctor. But he also had skills. Serious military skills. A bullet was a crude, unsophisticated response to Reznick, but it was important to be wide open to all possible endgame scenarios.

Reznick was a strong adversary, but the shadowy operative from Maine was in the dark on this one. Reznick didn't know that Ford had been waiting all these years for just this opportunity. He had been watching Reznick for a long, long time.

When Reznick was drinking in the Rockland Tavern, Ford had been watching. Sometimes from a distance, maybe in a rental car, sometimes up close.

A pair of shades and a beard concealed most people. Baseball hat. Glasses. He could hide in plain sight. Sometimes he was mere yards from Reznick. He often had to calm himself down, knowing Reznick was within striking distance. He'd sometimes fantasized in such moments what it would be like to kill Reznick in cold blood. But ultimately, Ford had bided his time. He had waited.

Ford peered through the binoculars and scanned the bar area one more time. Still no sign of his prey. Not long, though. He knew Reznick would return to the familiar.

Meyerstein had become one of the familiar things in Reznick's life.

Ford had fantasized about killing Reznick for years. He had nursed his grievance to the point of mania. But it was only in the last couple of years that he had realized the power of killing Meyerstein first. That's when his plan took root. He saw how it would work. Not only the gut-wrenching emotional pain it would inflict, but also how Reznick would respond. He would have to. It was in his nature.

Reznick would investigate. He would pursue her killer. He wouldn't believe it was an accident. Ford figured Reznick would see the explosion for what it was: a cold-blooded assassination. Maybe by a terrorist group.

Ford had been counting on all that. He had set the trap. And Reznick had taken the bait. A well-laid plan was a joy to behold.

He felt his mood peaking. Spiraling. It was as if he could not get any higher. Euphoric. His heightened mood always turned his thoughts to retribution. He felt strong and invincible. And he would strike.

Ford was like Reznick in many ways. He could compartmentalize. He would keep his feelings to himself. He worked hard to stay fit. Keep sharp. Keep vital. Maintain muscle definition. Strength. Exercise was a way of dealing with the mental stress that came with his line of work.

Reznick was the same.

But whereas Reznick lived a relatively spartan existence, Ford enjoyed the finer things in life. The little luxuries. Music. Travel. Reznick could sustain himself, if required, with the bare minimum. Reznick was trained to survive in any terrain. Trained to survive on scraps. Reznick could kill rats and mice and cook them and eat them if required. Ford was fascinated by that. A shadowy American assassin who could have been the guy next door. A nobody.

Ford was different. He had taste. Refinement. He was a man of discernment. He liked nice clothes. Bespoke suits. He liked visiting art galleries. He spent hours perusing the grand masters at the Met when he was in New York. And the Museum of Modern Art. The Jackson Pollocks. And of course Roy Lichtenstein, one of the godfathers of Pop Art. Ford was fascinated by creativity. Creating something, art, out of nothing was, in many respects, genius. But like everything, there was a sliding scale. Ford loved beauty in art. Monet. Renoir. He abhorred the banality of *unmade bed as modern art* bullshit masquerading as groundbreaking. Ford was discerning. He had a keen eye for the brilliant. He was sure Reznick liked none of that. In fact, Reznick would probably sneer at the very thought of modern art.

Ford snapped out of his thoughts, back to the glorious present. He felt the need to get back in the zone. He wanted to feel pin sharp. He headed to his bedroom and took off his clothes. Standing naked in front of the mirror, admiring his physique. He changed into swimming shorts—his initials, AF, stitched in fine gold thread beside the pocket. He headed out into the blazing sunshine and dove into the pool. He swam fifty lengths, showered, and changed into Valentino cargo shorts, Tom Ford sneakers, and a pale blue Valentino T-shirt. He poured himself a glass of Chateau Lafite and savored the fine Bordeaux.

He walked over to the floor-to-ceiling windows and stared once again through the superpowerful binoculars, perched on a tripod, which had replaced the telescope he'd smashed.

Ford scanned the bar and saw Reznick was finally there. And he was chatting with a beautiful young woman. "Well, well, well," he said, "what have we here?"

It took him a few moments to recognize exactly who it was.

Well, this was interesting. Very interesting. Reznick's daughter, Lauren, was sitting beside her father.

Twenty-Three

Reznick took a few moments to wrap his head around the fact that Lauren was stepping out of a cab. He got up from his seat in the bar and hugged his daughter, kissing her on the cheek. He looked at her with a mixture of shock and wonder. "What on earth are you doing here? Actually, first, how did you know I was here?"

Lauren pulled up a seat beside him.

Reznick slumped back down in his chair. He felt a wave of anxiety wash over him knowing Lauren was putting herself, inadvertently, in the line of fire. "This is not what I was expecting. I'm serious, I'm working. This is not a vacation."

"Well, that's a nice way to greet your daughter. So, are you going to buy me a drink or not?"

Reznick worked alone. He *could* work as part of a team. But his daughter, despite being eager to help him out, was not in his plans on this particular investigation. He signaled the waiter and ordered a couple of bottles of Heineken, then leaned closer. "What the heck do you think you're doing, Lauren? This is not a goddamn game."

"I want to help you."

"Help me? What are you taking about?"

"You're not the only one with contacts. I heard about the accident."

"People within the Hoover Building?"

"I work for the FBI, in case you forgot. Assistant Director Meyerstein mentored me. I was bound to hear something, don't you think?"

Reznick stared at her as she met his gaze, unflinching. Much as he loved his headstrong daughter, so like her mother in that regard, he didn't want her involved in his investigation. Especially *this* investigation. The dangers were only too apparent. "What really happened is not widely known, even within the FBI."

Lauren shrugged, unconcerned or unaware of the danger she was in.

"What do you know?" he said. "And how do you know?"

"Someone said she'd been involved in an accident. That's what they called it. Very vague."

"An accident?"

Lauren nodded.

"I tried reaching the Assistant Director." She frowned. "I called the cell phone number she gave me when she told me to reach out to her if I needed anything. But there was no answer. Then I made another call."

"A call to who?"

"Her father."

"Jerry Meyerstein?"

"Yes, Jerry Meyerstein. I got his number. And then he told me, in confidence, the news. That's why I'm here."

"Jerry told you?"

Lauren nodded.

Reznick sighed. The waiter put down the two bottles of chilled beer and gave a respectful nod to Lauren. When he was out of earshot, Reznick said, "Why didn't you call me?"

"I knew what your response would be."

"I want you out of here. You have no idea what's happened. It's not a fucking game."

"Don't swear at me."

"I want you home."

"Dad, I understand you're hurting. I am too. But don't shut me out."

Reznick gulped some of his beer. "You're killing me, Lauren. Absolutely killing me."

"Dad, the FBI's working assumption is it was just an accident. At least that's what they're saying."

Reznick closed his eyes.

"I don't believe them. Neither do you."

"What in the world were you thinking, Lauren? I mean, you flew all the way here to do what?"

"I want answers. I want to help. I want to do something. That's what you always taught me: don't be afraid to do the right thing. Didn't you?"

"You're a goddamn child."

"Don't patronize me, Dad."

"Well, you are!"

"No, I am not. What is wrong with you? I'm a college graduate working for the FBI."

"You're a goddamn rookie. You don't know the first thing about what's going on here."

"Have any other objections?"

"Yes, I goddamn do. Have you thought about how this could affect your career?"

"I have." Lauren had the same defiant look in her eyes that her mother had often had. A combination of high intelligence and bullheaded stubbornness.

"And do you think the FBI will look kindly on this?"

"I don't try to second-guess what my employer thinks. Besides, I'm taking vacation time."

"You think that's how they're going to see it? They're not completely stupid, Lauren. When they know that you're in Mallorca, that you joined me here, trust me, that won't look good for you. Not good at all."

Lauren took a small sip of her beer. "Why don't you trust me, Dad? Why is that?"

"It's not about trust, Lauren."

"Isn't it? Then what is it about?"

"It's about knowing when and when not to get involved. This isn't your domain."

"I disagree. I'm FBI. You want to see my ID?"

"You don't have any jurisdiction here."

"Neither do you."

"That's where you're wrong. This is personal."

"It's personal for me too."

"Do you have the first goddamn idea of what exactly is going on?"

Lauren sighed and said nothing, waiting for him to enlighten her.

"Martha is dead. An accidental explosion. That's what Jerry Meyerstein was told. That's all we know."

"You know more than that, Dad. A lot more. I know you. I know you keep your cards close to your chest."

"Why do you think that is?"

Lauren shrugged.

"It's because I don't want you involved in this. You've got a bright future in front of you. Don't screw it up."

"I know how to shoot. I know how to fight. I know how to think."

"And that's all great. But there's a lot you don't know."

"About what?"

"About my world. It's not pretty, let me tell you. And the law doesn't apply."

"You forget, I've seen your world. And I still want to help."

Reznick stared at his daughter.

"You know what I see when I look into your eyes?" she asked.

Reznick said nothing.

"I see a father who loves his daughter. A father who wants to protect his daughter. I love that about you. But please don't push me away. I'm not your little girl anymore. And I sure as hell haven't come all this way just to be lied to."

"I don't lie to you. My job is to protect you."

"Dad, I'm a goddamn full-grown woman. An adult."

Reznick closed his eyes and sighed. "I swear, the last thing I need is you getting hurt."

"Why would I get hurt? Wasn't this just an accident, after all?"

Reznick gave a rueful smile. She was smart. Very smart. And her analytical brain had just picked apart his argument that Martha's death had been an accident. "I really want you to focus on your work in the FBI."

"So do I. But this is a vacation."

"This might jeopardize your career before it even starts. You would be clearly intruding on an investigation in a foreign country, accident or otherwise, which has nothing to do with you. Even if the FBI were inclined to give you a pass, the State Department is involved. They have a lot of pull."

"Martha was my friend. She mentored me. I could talk to her. Do you understand? Mom isn't around anymore. And I miss her. Every day. But when I wanted to talk about things, what's on my mind, I could talk to Martha about stuff."

"What kind of stuff?"

"Boyfriend problems, career paths, about being without a mom for all these years, about wanting to connect with you."

"Connect with me? You talked to Martha about me? About us?"

"Yes, Dad. That's what people do. They want to connect. To help each other. To guide them. I haven't had that from a woman before. A confidante. That's what she was for me. A woman, a confidante, and a freakin' tough assistant director who insisted I ace all my tests or I would have her to answer to."

Reznick took a sip of the cold beer. "She helped you with all that?"

"She advised me how hard I needed to work to not only pass the goddamn FBI tests and exams, but pass with flying colors. She looked out for me. And she wasn't interested in excuses." Lauren's eyes were welling with tears. "I cared about her like she cared for me. I miss her. Do you understand now?"

Reznick felt guilty at having been so hard on his daughter. The way his father had been hard on him. The unyielding tough love. His father had instilled a steeliness, a resilience, and independent spirit that had served Reznick well through the ups and downs of his life. He wasn't one for emoting.

He wondered, with his daughter sitting right there in front of him, what the hell he should do now. She had come all this way.

The reality was Reznick couldn't force his daughter away from his world even if he wanted to. She was here. And now he would have to deal with it.

It was true he'd tried to protect her and inoculate her for all these years from his shadowy world. He had done what any father would do. She knew vaguely that he occasionally worked for the government on classified work and sometimes he'd go overseas. But as she'd grown older, she'd begun to figure it out more. A lot more. She learned he was ex–Delta Force. She knew that he had operated behind enemy lines in Afghanistan, Iraq, Somalia, and other such places. She probably didn't know about the assassinations he had been involved in. The cold-blooded killings. She didn't need to know that. At least not now.

Lauren sipped some beer and dabbed her eyes. "I miss her."

"I miss her too."

"What do you know?"

Reznick said nothing.

"Talk to me, Dad. Don't shut me out."

Reznick finished his beer and ordered another round. "There are forces at work here, Lauren, which I can't easily explain. Things that don't make sense. Goes without saying that what I tell you is not to be repeated for public consumption or for the FBI's files. Am I clear?"

Lauren nodded, face solemn. "That's a given."

"Now that we're set with the rules—and make no mistake, I operate according to strict rules—here's the situation we have. Let's put aside what happened to Martha for one moment."

"I'm listening."

"Yesterday, a guy gained access to my hotel room. He swapped some of the miniature whiskeys in the minibar with an identical selection of bottles."

"Are you kidding me?"

Reznick shook his head.

"Why?"

"I don't know for sure, but I'd wager that he wanted to poison me."

"And you were definitely the target?"

"Welcome to my world."

"Do you know who did this?"

Reznick waited until the waiter, who was attending another table, was out of earshot. He showed her the photo on his cell phone. "This guy in the shades, I need to know who this is."

144

Lauren studied it for a few moments.

Reznick put his cell phone back in his pocket. "That was the first thing that was troubling. The second was a woman named Catherine McCafferty. She's Scottish. But now she's dead. I met her brother my first night here. Sat right in this bar, two tables away from where we are now. He used to be British SAS."

"What's this SAS guy got to do with Martha?"

"Good question. The Scottish guy, Mac, he was scuba diving. He found a fragment of what he thought was an electronic motherboard, with Arabic writing scrawled on it."

"I've never heard this before."

"Well, now you have."

"Which would point to her being killed by Islamists, right?"

"You would think so. But Mac, the SAS guy, was taken to a 'secure location,' according to Catherine, shortly before she was killed in a car crash. And she was the one who told me about the Arabic writing."

"That's crazy. Sounds like a cover-up."

"Tell me about it."

"Who knows about this?"

"Outside of the State Department and FBI guys who are here in Spain? Just us. So far." Reznick took a gulp of his beer and leaned closer, his voice a whisper. "Now do you understand why I'm reluctant for you to get involved?"

"I do. But I'm glad you're not shoving me away."

"The guy who broke into my hotel room, who is he? Listen to this. A kid who was tombstoning off the cliffs the day of the explosion told me about an American guy who rented a property on the outskirts of town a few months back. He was traveling on a Spanish passport with a young man from North Africa."

"Red flag there. Islamist connection?"

"Correct. A big, big red flag."

"I'm intrigued about this American guy."

"I've sent what I know about him to the FBI through SIOC."

"What did they say?"

"You don't work for us, but thanks anyway."

Lauren shook her head. "I'm assuming they'll pass it on."

"I hope so. That guy is important. His identity. Who he is? I have no idea. But I'm going to keep digging. There's one other thing. Catherine McCafferty. She was en route to Palma to get an update on her brother from a British diplomat when she died."

"Do we know anything about this diplomat? Did anyone else know about Catherine's movements?"

Reznick smiled. "Nice questions. Was someone monitoring her movements via the GPS on her cell phone? Was the diplomat aware of her precise movements?"

"There is the possibility that it was just *another* tragic accident," Lauren said.

"Your emphasis answers that point of yours. How can it be *another*? The reality is it could be. Accidents do happen. Bad luck and all. But . . ."

"I'm not buying it."

Reznick nodded. "Neither am I. Which brings me back to my original point. My concern for you. I don't want to play games with my daughter's life or career."

"I hear what you're saying. But I'm going to take my chances. Besides, who's to say that operating in New York for the FBI is any safer?"

"Fair point. There's another thing."

"Another thing? What other thing?"

Reznick finished up his beer and got to his feet. "Want to show you something."

Lauren followed him out of the bar. They crossed the street and headed up along the winding sidewalk above the beach. A few minutes later they were standing at the rocky overlook.

Reznick pointed over the water to the buoy bobbing in the swell. "See that? That's where the yacht was anchored before the explosion."

"That's terrible to think about."

Reznick turned and pointed up the hillside. "The other thing I wanted to show you. About half a mile up the mountainside, maybe three quarters of a mile, is a shepherd's hut, an old dilapidated thing. A body was found underneath the floorboards."

"You discovered it?"

Reznick nodded, shielding his eyes from the setting sun.

"This is just getting crazy, Dad."

"That's what I've been trying to tell you."

"Do we know who it is?"

"I don't know. I did report it to the Spanish police and was interviewed by a State Department guy and the FBI legal attaché on the island."

"Someone burying the evidence? Killing a witness?"

"Perhaps. Then again, maybe someone laying a trail. A false trail."

"This was absolutely, definitely, not an accident."

"Right."

Lauren turned and faced out to the sea. "It's a lot to take in."

Reznick nodded. "I know."

"I can't believe Martha's gone. I really can't, Dad. I'm going to miss her."

Reznick wrapped his arm around her and held her tight. "You're not the only one."

Twenty-Four

Ford spotted Reznick standing with his arms around his pretty daughter, close to the point where he had detonated the bomb. It was all very touching and fascinating. He scanned the sadness etched on her face. He felt his mood elevating. A euphoric sense that he was ready to explode. To devastate. Ford closed his eyes for a moment. He wanted to burst down the mountainside like a lava flow and engulf everything in his path. Incinerate. Extinguish. Turn to ash. "Oh yeah."

His fevered thoughts were seeping into his cerebral mind.

Today could be the day.

Ford gazed long and hard at the fine features of Lauren Reznick. She was smart. He had seen her grades. She was bright. Bright future. All ahead of her. But not for long.

He allowed his depraved thoughts to fill his head as he headed through the villa, down the stairs to the basement garage, and got into the pickup truck. He started the ignition, and the electronic garage doors opened. He adjusted his shades on the drive down the winding mountainside road. He drove hard and fast, accelerating into bends and corners. He felt like he always did before he tuned in to the mission at hand. Primed.

Now was the time to hunt down Reznick and his daughter. There was no time to lose. If not now, when? They both had to die. He couldn't allow the daughter to live.

He might never get the chance again. What if Reznick headed home? His best opportunity to take him down would be gone. Perhaps forever. He couldn't bear the thought.

Ford slowed down as he approached the outskirts of the town, the Cala Molins beach in sight. His heart began to skip a beat. His pulse was quickening. The blood was flowing. He drove past the bar and then slowly headed up the winding road to the spot where he had last seen Reznick. The spot where he had triggered the explosion.

Time seemed to slow. Then for a split second, time stopped.

Ford looked up ahead. He saw Reznick sitting on a bench on the sidewalk with his daughter. He veered slightly off course as he accelerated around the bend. He weighed the idea of mounting the sidewalk. But in that split second, for whatever reason, Reznick turned around, as if sensing danger.

A blink of an eye. The bastard glared at him.

Ford blanked him and kept on driving up the winding road. He checked the satnav as he negotiated the tight roads near the beach, wedged between villas and a luxury hotel. He drove on until he headed down a one-way street at the opposite side of town.

He pulled over for a few moments, breathing hard. Ford felt he was being consumed by a mounting fury. Angry with himself for not plowing straight into Reznick and his daughter. What the fuck was wrong with him? Was he a coward? Had he been spooked when Reznick turned around?

He felt something snap within him. A putrid anger beginning to build within him. Reznick was on guard. Sensing danger. Sensing menace. Like some sentinel.

That was the thing about Reznick. He was wired. All the time. Always watchful. Ford had to be patient. He had to show the same fortitude.

Ford pulled away and drove through a quiet residential area. Huge trees shaded the sidewalk. His head was swimming. He felt his mood plummet. He felt humiliated. He pulled up outside a restaurant off the beaten path. Wood-beamed dining room and ceramic tile floors. He ate alone, enjoying roast suckling pig, washed down with a half bottle of a full-bodied Rioja. He savored the wine as he ruminated on the missed opportunity.

As he thought about it—the fleeting encounter, a split second almost—he realized it hadn't been the right moment. He hadn't passed up a chance to kill Reznick in cold blood. The speed he had been traveling at wasn't fast enough. He needed to be doing at least fifty miles per hour to feel confident that Reznick would either die or be permanently maimed.

So, in hindsight, Ford had made the right call. He had ensured the mission was still on. And he hadn't blown his chance with an impulsive act. No, Ford needed to just wait. He would get his chance. He had time. The opportunity would arise. And when it did, this time he would take it, no matter the consequences or outcome.

Ford paid his bill and returned to his pickup. He felt better. Slightly more calm than before. The fine wine had soothed his nerves. Calmed him down. He had rationalized his actions. Ford would get Reznick another time.

He started up the pickup and pulled slowly away from the curb.

Ford decided to head home. But as he got closer to the center of Cala San Vicente, he spotted them. Again.

Up ahead, walking on the sidewalk beside a low wall, with their backs to him, were Reznick and his daughter. Ford's heartbeat quickened. He felt a rush of blood to the head. He put his foot on the gas. He accelerated hard and drove straight. And slammed into them.

Ford screeched to a halt as Reznick and his daughter were propelled through the air and over the low wall. He reversed and quickly sped away, burning rubber, the sound of screeching metal echoing as he disappeared from the scene.

Clouds of dust in his wake.

Twenty-Five

The moment of impact was sudden and hard and disorienting. Reznick gasped for breath. He saw it all as if in slow motion, out of order. The lights of the vehicle reversing away, the sounds of scraping metal. The bone-crushing impact. The feeling of losing control as he and Lauren were catapulted into the air and flung headlong into a fast-moving drainage channel. Swallowing filthy water, fighting to stay afloat. Dragged under time and time again. He looked around, frantic. But he couldn't see his daughter.

"Lauren! Lauren!" he spluttered.

Reznick spun around, spitting out water. He began to panic. "Lauren!" He turned around. Still nothing. Suddenly out of the corner of his eye he saw movement in the water to his left. Twenty yards from him. He turned again and saw a hand grabbing for an overhanging tree.

Reznick swam furiously in the dirty water. It was chest deep. He reached out and seized her hand. "Hang on!"

Lauren grabbed ahold.

Reznick clawed his way through the channel, dragging his daughter up the concrete bank. A surge of adrenaline coursed through his veins. He managed to get her on his shoulder as the water threatened to topple him over. But he stood up, his daughter motionless on his back, and climbed over the small concrete wall.

He laid her down on the sidewalk. Lauren was like a drowned rat, eyes rolling around in her head. Blood spilling from a cut on her forehead where she'd probably hit the drainage canal wall. He turned her onto her side; water spilled out of her mouth.

Then he flipped her facedown and compressed her back. More water poured out.

"Lauren! Can you hear me?"

No response.

Reznick pressed her back, expelling more water from her lungs. He turned her on her side again and kneeled down beside her, water oozing from her mouth. A group of British tourists rushed to her aid, also kneeling down. A woman held her hand, others frantically calling emergency services.

"Lauren!" Reznick said. "Can you hear me?"

Lauren coughed up some more water and gasped as if trying to speak.

Reznick held her hand and stroked her soaking-wet hair. "You're OK, honey, Dad's here."

Lauren spluttered some words he couldn't comprehend.

Reznick looked up as some tourists began filming on their cell phones. "What the hell is wrong with you people? Get help, you morons!"

It was the dead of night when Lauren awoke in her hospital bed in Palma. She sat up looking dazed, pale, eyes bloodshot.

Reznick squeezed her hand, gazing down at her.

"Hey, Dad," she said.

Reznick stroked her hair. He was wearing a hospital gown; his own clothes were still soaking wet. "Hey, honey."

"What happened?"

Reznick told her about how he had traveled in the back of an ambulance with her until they got her to the hospital, as she lapsed in and out of consciousness. "The prognosis is good. They've checked you over, and you don't have a concussion. You'll live."

"I'm sore."

"You've got bruising on your back and a cut on your forehead."

Lauren scrunched up her face as if trying to remember what had happened. "It's all coming back now. We were hit. By a car?"

"A pickup truck, I think."

Lauren blinked away tears.

"Some vacation, huh?"

She started to cry. "I'm an idiot."

"You're not an idiot. You're just a major league pain in the ass."

Lauren touched the bandage on her forehead. "What's this?"

"I told you. Cut to your forehead. You had seven stitches."

"Am I going to be scarred?"

"The doctors say it will heal nicely, as long as you don't do any tombstoning or diving into concrete pools."

"Nice."

"It's a reminder of what happened. Look at it like that." Reznick bowed his head and put his hand on her brow.

"Who was it?" she said.

"We'll find out. I'm just glad you're going to be OK."

Lauren grimaced. "My head hurts."

"I love you, Lauren. I thought I'd lost you."

"Not a chance, Dad."

Twenty-Six

It was late morning when two American guys in suits arrived at the hospital.

"You need to come with us," one of them said. "We've brought a fresh change of clothes for you both. We need to talk."

Reznick had a feeling it was the State Department wanting to lay down the law. He was tempted to tell them to go to hell. But he was just relieved his daughter was OK, a few scrapes, bumps, and scratches aside.

Besides, she was employed by the FBI, and Reznick needed to take that into account and perhaps be less confrontational. At least until he figured out who'd tried to kill them.

Reznick and Lauren were shown into an SUV with diplomatic plates and whisked to a suite of offices in Palma Old Town overlooking a Gothic cathedral. The two guys in suits escorted them to a room at the back of the building.

The door opened.

Reznick looked around. Sitting at a table were FBI legal attaché Lionel Finsburg, who was cleaning his glasses with a cloth, and Todd Mavor from the State Department. A third man, a black guy, was sitting in the corner, eyeballing him. The guy wore dark jeans, a navy polo shirt, sneakers. He stared long and hard at Reznick, as if trying to unnerve him.

Reznick had seen it all before. He and his daughter pulled up chairs beside each other, opposite Finsburg and Mavor. "So, you guys like my company so much you want to go on a double date or something? I mean, what is it with you guys?"

The door slammed shut behind them.

Mavor looked at Reznick and then Lauren. "I'm sorry about what happened to you, Miss Reznick. Really I am."

"It's Ms. Reznick, thanks."

Mavor shifted uneasily in his seat. "Of course. How's the head?"

"Sore. But I'll live."

Finsburg gave a weak smile. "Lauren, we know why you're here. And legally speaking, you're putting us in a very awkward position with the Spanish government."

Lauren said nothing, face impassive.

"We believe you're here on your vacation with your dad, which is fine, but your father's investigation is not something we believe is in America's national interests. He doesn't work for the FBI in any capacity. We don't want your position with the FBI to be jeopardized."

Lauren said, "That's not too subtle, if you don't mind me saying so."

"You need to consider where your priorities lie, Lauren."

Reznick's protective instincts kicked in then. He was going to say something, but then Lauren spoke.

"My priorities are very clear, sir. I have to be frank—I don't appreciate the insinuations and veiled threats."

"I'm merely stating that it is important that you not intrude on matters that don't concern you."

"Mr. Finsburg, with all due respect, you used the word *jeopardized*, implying a threat."

156

"I assure you, there was no threat intended. I just want you to be aware that your boss in New York might not look very kindly on this."

"I hear what you're saying. And I'll take that under advisement. But I'm on vacation with my dad."

Mavor cleared his throat. "You tell your daughter about the body you found, Jon, up in the hills?"

"Yes, I did."

"That wasn't smart."

Reznick leaned forward. "Don't ever tell me what I can or cannot say to my daughter. I don't have secrets from her."

"Let's cut the bull. Since you've been so openly talking about what you know or have unearthed, I'm going to get straight to the point. You are investigating the death of an American citizen—you know who I'm talking about."

"You know I do," Reznick said.

"You are becoming embroiled in matters that don't concern you. National security matters."

Reznick shook his head. "Unbelievable."

"In addition, since you have arrived, you've found a body, made contact with an ex-British Special Forces soldier and his sister—a lawyer—and you seem to be convinced that the lawyer's death wasn't a tragic accident."

"Catherine McCafferty called me—check the records from the NSA—saying she couldn't control her car."

"That happens, Jon."

"All the time. I know. But she was murdered. By a highly sophisticated operative who knew exactly what they were doing."

"Jon, you're making connections that don't exist."

Reznick shook his head. "You'll have to do better than that, Todd."

"Not content with dredging up all these spurious connections and conspiracies, you have also passed on photographic details to the FBI about a Spanish citizen who may be an American, who you are claiming might be involved in this whole affair."

"Have you guys identified him yet? If not, why not? Christ, you're making it seem like I'm the bad guy here. I'm helping the FBI out."

Mavor shook his head. "No, you're not. You're following a personal agenda. A vendetta of sorts. Jon, look at it from our point of view. It's like you've gone batshit crazy."

"Are you finished?"

Mavor leaned back in his seat. "I'm just getting started."

"Well, how about you start by telling me why we were both nearly killed last night?"

Mavor said nothing as Finsburg scribbled notes on a legal pad.

"Some nutcase," Reznick said, "deliberately rammed us off the sidewalk. We nearly drowned in a goddamn drainage channel. Lauren had to spend the night in the hospital. You want to talk about that? Is that me just making shit up again? Was that just a bad fucking dream? Well, was it?"

Mavor averted his gaze for a moment.

"Your silence speaks volumes."

Mavor pointed his finger at Reznick. "Who the hell do you think you are? You're an American citizen on Spanish soil. We are helping the Spanish authorities with various sensitive national security issues. Your presence is only complicating matters. Do you know what they're saying?"

"What?"

"You're unstable. You're a crazy person."

"You guys need to wake the fuck up. I'm not going to have the wool pulled over my eyes. Your bullshit does not wash with me. Got it?"

Finsburg cleared his throat. "Jon, no one's trying to pull the wool over your eyes."

"Lionel, let's just forget about the explosion on the yacht for just a moment. Are you seriously saying the death of Catherine McCafferty, the body up on the hillside, and my daughter and me getting rammed into a drainage canal is just a sequence of bad luck?"

"It is very, very troubling. I'll give you that, Jon."

"Very troubling? Is that what you call it?"

"But we can't take the law into our own hands."

"You've got a problem. The reality is—and let's cut this bullshit once and for all—something stinks. You know it. I know it. There's a cover-up in place."

Finsburg put his finger to his lips. "Let's try and keep this civil. Jon, I think what Todd is saying is that there are aspects of the yacht explosion we can't discuss. I'm sure you'll understand, with your background."

"I understand there may be an Islamist link. I understand why you wouldn't want that to come out. I get that. But I'm wondering if that's just a red herring. The Islamist kid a perfect cover to get the blame. A false flag. It's brilliant. It's elaborate. And it was lethal."

Finsburg scribbled more notes on the legal pad.

Reznick looked over at the guy in the corner, who was staring back. "What's your name, pal? What's your position?"

Finsburg leaned closer. "He works for the government. Our government."

The man got slowly to his feet and pulled up his chair beside Finsburg and sat down. He leaned over and shook Reznick's hand. "Jeremiah Johnston. Nice to meet you, Jon. I work for the CIA."

Reznick leaned back in his seat. "This just got a bit more interesting. So we've got the Agency involved too."

Finsburg smiled as he looked across at Lauren. "The FBI, as you will no doubt be aware, requires uncompromising personal integrity. But they also expect you to accept responsibility for your actions and your decisions."

Lauren nodded. "Yes, sir, I understand."

"I'm quite prepared to give you the benefit of the doubt in the circumstances, knowing you were mentored by the Assistant Director," Finsburg said. "But what happened last night has changed matters, so you're going to have a choice to make. Either you head back home and continue your recuperation in the States, or there may, at a future date, be disciplinary actions against you. I'm just laying it all on the line."

Reznick shook his head. "You turning the squeeze on a young FBI rookie? My daughter? Really?"

Finsburg looked at Johnston before fixing his gaze on Lauren. "No one is turning the squeeze on any rookie. We are simply reminding Lauren that she has responsibilities. So we're giving you forty-eight hours before you head home. A day to recover. And the day after to get to the airport and arrange a flight home."

Reznick said, "This is bullshit."

"Jon, the individual who entered your hotel room, whose passport you passed on to the FBI . . . We're concerned that you're becoming involved in things you don't understand," Johnston said. "We believe you might be confusing and conflating different strands of our investigation."

"Are you protecting a CIA asset? Is that what's happening?"

Johnston stared at him. "Don't fuck with me, Jon."

"You didn't like that, did you? Why is that? Did I hit a little close to the mark? Why has this guy been able to operate with impunity? No one seems to be able to lay a glove on him."

"Go home, Jon. And your daughter too."

160

"Or what? We're gonna be disappeared? Like David McCafferty?"

"I've heard just about enough."

"Likewise. I'm not going anywhere. And my daughter will be with me."

Johnston said, "Jon, I have no beef with you or your daughter. But you need to heed this warning."

"Why?"

"Just get the fuck off the island. That's your final warning."

Twenty-Seven

The first thing Reznick did when he returned to Cala San Vicente was check into a new hotel with his daughter. It was only a hundred yards along the coast, overlooking a rocky promontory by the sea. The guests seemed mostly to be young Europeans, predominantly German, Dutch, and Scandinavian tourists. Laid-back, tanned, largely blond. Most were Lauren's age. But there were also a few young Englishmen, heavily inked and noticeable in their polyester mesh soccer shirts.

Reznick requested an adjoining room to his daughter's and took her to a pizza restaurant across the street. He had a mineral water, as did Lauren, still feeling woozy after the hit-and-run the previous day.

When she had finished her meal, she wiped her mouth with the napkin. "I haven't thanked you, Dad," she said.

"You have nothing to thank me for. A father looks after his children. Those are the rules."

"You're always saving people. But what about you?"

"What about me?" Reznick said.

"No one's looking out for you."

"Don't worry about me."

"You need saving too."

"From who? Myself?"

Lauren smiled. "I'm serious."

"Martha, in her own way, always looked out for me."

"I know you're hurting. I can tell."

She'd touched a raw nerve. It was true. He didn't like to show it. But he missed Martha so much it hurt. He felt like he had fallen into a swamp or quicksand and was slowly being sucked under, unable to escape or call for help. Maybe that's why he was so stubbornly refusing to leave the investigation to the Feds. Except, as he reminded himself, he had his last remaining reason to live sitting right in front of him. "I'm OK if you're OK."

"Dad, you mentioned the guy who broke into your hotel room. The guy wearing sunglasses?"

Reznick nodded. "Sure, what about him?"

"I'm trying to figure it out."

"Join the club."

"The thing I don't get is, what's the connection between that guy, who we believe is an American, and the fragment of the bomb with Arabic writing? Could he be an Islamist convert? Radicalized?"

Reznick nodded. "His travel companion was a younger guy from Morocco. They both had passport stamps for Melilla. It's a Spanish port city on the northwest coast of Africa. Near Morocco. A country with a large Islamic population."

"Tell you what, I'm interested in that angle. I read, quite recently, a report—not classified—that said that while Islamic converts are a tiny proportion of the Muslim faith, extremists and terrorists are disproportionately represented."

"Hmm. We can't discount that with this guy. Then again, there's an angle we might be overlooking as we try and connect the dots."

"What's that?"

"A false trail."

"You're saying this American guy is laying a false trail? Why? Why so elaborate?"

"To conceal the real threat."

"Dad, seriously?"

"The only reason I got the image of him is because I installed a fake smoke detector in my hotel room. I got lucky. And I saw him stocking the minibar with substitute booze bottles. This guy is very smart. He knows me, I think."

"You think this is about you?"

Reznick shrugged.

"So you think *you* are the target?"

Reznick nodded. "I do. It's crazy, I know."

"And you think he was also the guy behind killing Martha?"

"Maybe. Maybe the same guy that was in my hotel room was also the same guy who mowed us down last night."

"The same person?"

"I don't know. But what I do know is finding that man is the key."

"So who is he? A guy from your past, perhaps?"

Reznick nodded. He had been wondering the same thing. "It's a possibility."

Lauren sipped her drink. "The State Department guy was really interested in getting us both out of the way."

"It's understandable."

She tilted her head. "So the killing of Martha Meyerstein? How does that fit into this guy being after you?"

"That's what I'm trying to establish."

Lauren's cell phone rang. She rifled in her handbag and took it out. "Yeah?"

Reznick watched his daughter grimace as she listened. She looked confused.

Lauren screwed up her face. "I'm sorry, who are you? You want to speak to him? Who are you?" She put her hand over the microphone. "That's weird. A guy who wants to talk to you. Said he's from the State Department. But didn't give his name."

Reznick took the cell phone. "Yeah, who's this?"

There was a brief silence. "Jon, what a pleasure it is to hear your voice after all these years."

Reznick sensed it was *him*. His blood ran cold. Like ice in his veins. He looked at his daughter before his gaze wandered around, scanning the street and down the road. No one but a smattering of tourists. "Who am I talking to?"

The man laughed. "You're a long, long way from home, Jon."

"You must have the wrong number."

"Lovely voice Lauren has."

Reznick felt his stomach tighten, blood surging. "Who is this?"

"I'll get to that in a minute, Jon. You don't mind me calling you Jon, do you? I feel like I know you so well. Intimately, almost."

Reznick knew this was him, the guy they had just been talking about. He reached into her bag, took out a pen, and scribbled on a napkin, *It's him.*

Lauren nodded.

"You've gone so very quiet on me, Mr. Reznick. You don't strike me as the shy type. Quite the opposite. Your psychological profile shows you as outgoing, assertive, confident, and cold-blooded. Not exactly a wallflower, are you?"

"You finished?"

"Not even getting started. I know so much about you, Jon, it hurts. And your daughter. A credit to you and that late, lamented wife of yours. Elisabeth, isn't it?"

"You listen to me . . ."

"Temper, temper, Jon. I'm in the driver's seat. You just don't realize it. Speaking of, a most unfortunate incident last night. How very careless of that driver."

Reznick said, "Give me a time and place, and I'll meet up with you and we'll sort this out."

The man laughed. "You'd like that, wouldn't you? All in good time, Jon. Always quick on the draw, weren't you?"

Reznick leaned over and whispered the gist of the conversation to Lauren.

"Don't whisper too loudly now. I hope her head isn't too sore, Jon."

Reznick sat back. "I want to know who you are. Let's talk about it."

"The time for talking is over. You and Lauren had a close call, but sadly, it wasn't a close call for the lovely Martha Meyerstein, previously of the FBI, or so I heard. Bang! Bang! That's how it went. How does that make you feel? Do you want me to describe how it made me feel? So alive! What a night that was."

"You sick fuck! When I find you, I will finish you. And I will bury you."

"Talking of finding, you've been a very busy boy since you landed in Mallorca. Finding bodies up in the hills."

Reznick sensed he'd been watched since the moment he landed. The caller seemed to know just about everything he'd done since he had arrived.

"And spending time with that very attractive Scottish lady, a lawyer, I believe, who had a nasty accident."

Reznick closed his eyes, nursing a silent fury.

"She had excellent bone structure, Jon. Quite a looker. A bit younger than Martha, if you catch my meaning."

Reznick felt himself wanting to lash out at the needling. He had to steady his breathing.

"Or maybe older women are your type. A little birdie told me you met up with a kindly old Spanish lady. Rented the house next door to an American, she said."

Reznick felt sick to the pit of his stomach.

"Do you want to know where she is now, Jon?"

Dread washed over him. "You better not have touched that woman or I swear to God, you're going to pay."

The caller laughed. "Touched a raw nerve, Jon? A man of honor, a patriotic American . . . That's you, isn't it? But for what? You think your country loves you? What's in it for you, all this sacrifice, and the killings? What's it all been for?"

"Where is she?"

"Do you have a pen and paper, Jon?"

Reznick picked up a fresh napkin.

"Are you listening carefully?" The guy gave GPS coordinates.

Reznick scribbled them down, the foreboding that had washed over him deepening.

"You've found one body, Jon. It'll be really helpful if you could find this one too. I'll be in touch."

Twenty-Eight

The mutilated body of eighty-nine-year-old widow Luciana Lopez was found at the bottom of a well, high up in the rocky Serra de Tramuntana mountains.

Reznick could only watch as her body was retrieved in a painstaking operation by mountain guides using safety ropes and harnesses. A police screen was erected around the top of the well, concealing the body. Reznick wrapped his arm around Lauren as a forensics team arrived. A police photographer took pictures of the corpse. A local priest arrived and said prayers for the dead woman, making the sign of the cross, looking up at the flawless blue sky as if beseeching God to explain why he had allowed this to happen.

Reznick felt like he was unraveling in slow motion. A gradual descent into hell. First Martha. The death of Catherine. The body found up in the hills. Now this abomination.

A series of events, seemingly unrelated, unfolding day by day, hour by hour. And he was at the center of all of them. It was like there was nothing he could do to stop it. But one thing was apparent. The man who called him was behind this. The American. He was orchestrating it all.

Reznick held his daughter tightly, riven by doubts. Running scenarios around his head again and again. He looked at the bleak sun-scorched mountainside, tinder dry. There was nothing for miles around. In the distance, the far distance, on the horizon, on the tip of the mountainside, he saw the military radar tower that had been installed by Americans way back in the 1950s. He was a military history buff. He knew about all that sort of stuff. The tower was located on Puig Major, a mountain pass thousands of feet above sea level. The system had been put in place to detect planes or missiles violating Spanish airspace during the Cold War. An early-warning system for America's Eastern Seaboard. But it would not have detected the person who had dumped the body in such a location.

This burial spot had been carefully chosen. No cameras for miles. Maybe tens of miles.

An ambulance arrived, and the corpse was zipped up into a body bag before being lifted onto a gurney. A short while later, a couple of SUVs arrived.

Two men in suits stepped out of the front vehicle as Lionel Finsburg emerged from the back seat.

The FBI legal attaché walked over to Reznick and his daughter. "The Director wants to speak to you, Jon." He cocked his head, indicating the SUV. "He's on the line right now."

Reznick looked at Lauren and smiled. "I'll just be a minute, honey."

She wrapped her arms around herself as if for comfort and nodded.

Reznick slid into the back seat beside a guy in a suit he assumed was also a Fed.

Finsburg got in the front and handed Reznick the cell phone. "He's waiting. Line's secure, obviously."

"Director, how can I help?"

Bill O'Donoghue's voice was brusque and no-nonsense. He'd never been a fan of Reznick's, but Reznick knew he'd respected Martha Meyerstein, and that she'd respected him. "I want to talk frankly, Jon. I don't want to get into the blame game or pointing fingers. Never does any good. You told the police that you were alerted to the presence of the body by an unidentified call that came in on Lauren's cell phone. I want to be clear—are you absolutely positive it was her cell phone?"

"It was her cell phone issued by the FBI, sir."

"Jon, do you understand what I'm saying?"

"I know exactly what you're saying."

"Someone managed to get a number that's not listed in any public database, only in the FBI computers, and make an untraceable call."

"Then you've got a problem."

The Director sighed long and hard. "You don't have to tell me that. We have cybersecurity professionals doing tests to find out how the intrusion occurred, whether it was through our system or whether the number was obtained by other means."

"Listen, I appreciate the heads-up on that. And just so you know, my daughter hasn't broken any FBI rules or regulations."

"She is employed by us, Jon."

"I know. But she's scrupulous about her security. And she was nearly killed last night. Did you hear about that?"

A sigh. "Yes, I did. I'm sorry about that."

Reznick looked at Finsburg, who was staring through the front windshield toward the screen shielding the top of the well. "I sent over photographs of a guy, a white male. Have you made any progress identifying him?"

"Jon, you know as well as I do how we work. We appreciate your help on this, and what you've uncovered we believe could be significant, but I'm not at liberty to say any more than that. I hope you understand."

"I keep being told to leave Mallorca. The State Department and the Agency are hanging around."

"I can't comment on that."

"I don't actually want you to comment. I want you to *do* something."

"Not in this case, Jon. I'm sure you can appreciate what I'm saying."

What O'Donoghue was saying was that he had limited ability to encroach on the State Department's territory.

"One final thing," Reznick said. "And this is something that's been bugging me. Why is there no body? There was an explosion on a yacht. Two people were on that yacht. But there's no body. Nothing. No clothes. Nothing."

"Jon, let's not go there."

"It's a simple question. Does that sound plausible to you? Divers have been out there for what, a week now? And nothing. Unless you know something."

The line was silent.

"I'll get to the bottom of this. I'm not going anywhere. Just so you know."

"This is not your concern, Jon."

"It most certainly is. Besides, I don't work for the FBI, right?"

Reznick was about to disconnect the call when he sensed the guy next to him in the seat turn slightly. He felt a sharp jab in his thigh.

And everything went black.

Twenty-Nine

Adam Ford discreetly followed the two American consulate SUVs containing Jon Reznick and his daughter back down from Puig Major. He had them in his sights. But he didn't want to get too close.

Driving down the winding mountain road, he felt invincible, wildly happy. He had watched the whole operation, a sordid and prolonged effort to retrieve the old woman's body, with his high-powered binoculars.

Reznick had stood alone most of the time, cell phone in hand. Occasionally his daughter hugged him tight. It was fascinating to see him through the pin-sharp binocular lenses. Like he was right there in front of him. But Ford wanted to be closer. A lot closer. Maybe close enough to smell him.

Ford had concealed himself about a mile back from the well. The distance was probably for the best.

He'd studied Reznick's hooded eyes. The grief etched on his face. The type of grief he had only dreamed of seeing there. The type he wanted Reznick to endure. Ford understood the pain only too well. He'd felt it five years ago, knowing he would be denied the chance to be revered for killing the delinquent President. He had been chosen to kill the fucker. And his chance had been snatched from him. Immortality had been snatched from him. They would have spoken his name in the same breath as Lee Harvey Oswald. But the name of Adam Ford would not enjoy or revel in such infamy.

Reznick was going to pay. It was going to take time. But there was something about watching Reznick, a cold-blooded assassin, show his humanity that fascinated Ford. Something almost touching. Reznick wasn't a machine, after all. He had a soul. A heart. But that heart was breaking.

The thought that Reznick was hurting gave him a fleeting moment of pleasure. But he had to keep his eye on the real prize. The endgame.

Reznick had gotten lucky twice so far—he'd avoided the poisoned booze and he'd survived the fall into the water. But his luck was about to run out for good.

Thirty

Reznick was in blackness. A faint whisper spoke in Spanish. Then an American voice. He felt himself drifting and floating. He sensed he was being carried. A warm wind on his skin. The roar of what sounded like a business jet engine. He wondered if it was a Cessna. Maybe a Gulfstream.

He felt himself being strapped in. Then takeoff. The drone of the engines. Quiet chatter. More American voices. This time a harder edge.

He needs to go now. He needs to be dropped in minus one minute.

Reznick was gripped by panic. He realized they were going to drop him from the plane. He tried to struggle but he couldn't. He was paralyzed. He had a sense of being slightly conscious. But unable to do or say a thing.

He willed himself to move. But nothing. He could hear the sound of his breathing under the gag. It was getting faster. His mind was racing. But his pulse was virtually dead. Or so it seemed.

A feeling of weightlessness. A fierce blast of cold air.

"Time for a long sleep, Jon," a voice said.

Reznick awoke in a cold sweat and sat straight up. He was blindfolded. He struggled, but he was handcuffed to what seemed like a metal bed. His ankles too. He tried to move again, and heard the clanking of heavy steel chains on the floor. The bed seemed to be bolted down. His mind flashed back to the seconds before they'd taken him. He had been on the phone with O'Donoghue. He'd felt a prick. Then darkness.

Suddenly, Reznick sensed he wasn't alone. A moment later his blindfold was carefully taken off. The ankle restraints and handcuffs were briefly unlocked, detaching him from the metal bed, before both ankles were cuffed together and wrists were tightly secured. He squinted against the harsh artificial strip lights overhead. He looked around. He was sitting on a bed in a windowless room. Staring down at him was the CIA guy, Jeremiah Johnston.

"How you feeling, Jon?"

"How do you think?"

"We had to do what we had to do; I'm sure you understand. We needed to get your attention."

"Was that your friend in the back seat who jabbed me? What did he give me?"

Johnston pointed to a chair behind a desk. "Sit down there."

Reznick struggled to get to his feet. "Where's my daughter?"

"She's safe."

"What does that mean?"

"It means, Jon, she is with the legal attaché of the FBI at this moment. And some State Department people, I believe."

Reznick shuffled to the chair and slumped down, handcuffs chafing against his wrists. "Are they interrogating her?"

"You ask a lot of questions." Johnston pulled up a chair opposite and sat down. He leaned across and undid the right-hand cuff, opened it up, and clicked it onto a steel ring on the bolted table, allowing Reznick one free arm. "Just so you don't get any ideas."

"You want to take off the ankle cuffs?"

Johnston sighed. "Don't fucking try anything, you hear me?"

Reznick jangled his wrist. "I'm bolted in. Gimme a break."

"I know who you are. Don't try any cute stuff." Johnston unlocked the ankle cuffs. "Better?"

"A lot, thanks. Appreciate that."

"Spanish military intelligence insisted on it. They do stuff differently in Spain, trust me."

"So under what pretext am I being held? Spanish law? If so, where are the Spanish? Also, I wanna see a lawyer."

Johnston leaned back in his seat and shook his head. "I've already cut you a break."

"I want to see a lawyer."

"All in good time."

"So, what do you want to know? And why the fuck are you drugging me?"

"I never drugged you. Listen, I've read all about you, Jon. I know a guy who worked with you in the Middle East. Said you're the best. But he also told me to be careful. So, you can appreciate why I'm being a bit cautious with you."

"You got the name of this person?"

"Can't say."

Reznick felt the chafing on his wrist. "Goddamn, you want to loosen this cuff?"

"Not just now. Maybe later."

"I want to see my daughter."

"You will. Right now she's talking to Finsburg. Nothing to be alarmed about. She's working with the FBI, they're trying to ascertain what she knows."

"Is she being held here?"

"Nope."

Reznick stared at him.

"You, my friend, are in deep shit."

Reznick shook his head. "Oh boy, here we go."

"How many fucking times do you have to be told?"

"I don't work for the government. I'm here on vacation. You're infringing on my freedom."

"Bullshit. We know what you're up to."

"Is this all classified?"

"I can't disclose that, Jon, you know how it works."

"Answer me this: Have you identified the American who called Lauren's cell phone? I'm telling you, this American, who's traveling on a Spanish passport, is involved in the explosion. He's fucking with me. Who the hell is this guy?"

Johnston stared at him as if not wanting to get involved.

"I feel like I'm repeating myself, over and over again. There is an Islamist link. But there's also a guy who might be running this thing. The American. Maybe it's a parallel operation. Who knows, maybe . . . a false flag."

"A false flag?" Johnston rubbed his eyes and shook his head as if he'd heard enough. "Here's what's going to happen. I've been given instructions, and the Spanish government is aware of what we're going to do."

"And what's that?"

"We're going to drive you to Palma airport, you will board a flight operated under the auspices of the State Department, and you will have several Agency and State Department officials to accompany you on your journey back to the United States. It's the end of the line for you, my friend."

"What about my daughter?"

"She's not my problem. You are. And we're shipping you out of here within the hour."

Thirty-One

A sharp knock at the door snapped Reznick out of his morose contemplation. A guy in a gray suit popped his head around the corner.

Jeremiah Johnston spun around. "Yeah, what is it, Bob? Can't you see I'm busy?"

"Station chief on the line from Madrid."

"Tell him I'll talk to him in fifteen minutes. I'm not finished here."

"It needs to be now. Right now. His words."

"Tell him I'll be there in a minute."

Bob nodded and shut the door again.

Johnston got to his feet, hitching up his pants, adjusting his suspenders. "You need coffee, food?"

Reznick shook his head.

"I won't be long. Sit tight." Johnston grinned. "I'll be right back. And just to make doubly sure, I'm going to lock the door behind me. Don't try anything dumb."

"Like what?"

"I don't know. Just don't try and test my patience. Sit tight, got it?"

"Yeah, like I'm going somewhere," Reznick said.

Johnston smiled. "It's nothing personal, man. It's just the way it is."

Reznick nodded as the CIA guy slammed the door hard behind him, key turning in the lock. Reznick waited for a few moments, knowing Johnston would be watching him through the peephole into the room. He sat still until he heard heavy footsteps heading down the tiled corridor outside. He waited until he didn't hear a sound.

He had bided his time patiently. This could be his opportunity.

Reznick knew he didn't have long. He began to twist the handcuffs, using the torque to put pressure on the steel chain linking the two cuffs. He clenched his teeth as he twisted farther and farther. Tighter and tighter against his skin. He wrenched the steel handcuffs another half inch. He felt his skin twist, virtually cutting off the circulation. The pain was like a pinched nerve.

Reznick grimaced, absorbing the agony as he had been trained to. The seconds were flying by. He was trying with all his might to burst it open. But nothing. "Come on, you fucker."

He twisted harder and tighter until he felt he was going to pass out. The pain was overwhelming, biting into the skin, cutting off the circulation. Suddenly, the chain holding the two cuffs snapped. He was breathing hard. His senses switched on. He got up and moved the chair a couple of yards away, deliberately positioning it out of line of sight from the peephole.

He stood up on the chair, reached up, and pushed back one of the ceiling tiles. He could see attic space beyond. He reached up to a metal beam and dragged himself up. Then he carefully slid the ceiling tile back into place.

Reznick crawled along a wooden joist, past a huge duct, then past some air-conditioning vents. Staring down through a ceiling vent, he saw a corridor. He crawled farther along and looked down again. He could see a shaft of light below. A door opening.

Reznick watched as a Spanish guy in a suit, maybe a cop, maybe intelligence, spoke into a cell phone. He held his breath for a few moments, waiting until the conversation was over and the guy began to walk away. The guy headed down the corridor, past a bathroom, and out of sight around the corner. Reznick crawled a few yards more until he was looking down into an empty office.

A few moments later, a FedEx delivery guy wearing sunglasses, carrying three large padded envelopes, pushed through the door.

Reznick slid back a tile. He jumped down and seized the guy by the neck. With one hand over the delivery guy's mouth, he hustled him down the corridor. Then through a bathroom door. He pressed his thumb hard against the guy's carotid artery. "You speak English?" he whispered.

The guy nodded, eyes frightened.

"What is this place? Where are we?"

"This is a police station. We are in the middle of Palma."

Reznick pointed to the bathroom window. "Can I get to your van through there?"

"Yes, it is outside. That's where I park it every time."

"Keys?"

The man rifled in the pockets of his pants and pulled out his keys.

Reznick took the keys and the guy's cell phone.

"Please don't hurt me, señor."

Reznick pointed to the man. "Lie facedown, eyes closed, and count back from three hundred very slowly. When you reach zero, you can go. But not a second before. Yeah?"

"Yes, señor," he said, lying facedown on the linoleum floor, eyes shut tight.

"Start counting."

"*Trescientos, doscientos noventa y nueve, doscientos noventa y ocho . . .*"

Reznick leaned over and took off the guy's sunglasses and base-ball cap. He put them on and shoved the cell phone in his back pocket. Then he reached up for the open window and pulled himself up.

Reznick spotted the van no more than fifteen yards away. He had to risk it now. He clambered through the narrow window, quietly dropping down onto the other side. He waited as he heard voices, Spanish voices. He spotted them in the distance, maybe one hundred yards or more away.

He adjusted the sunglasses and strode to the van. He started up the engine and pulled away, driving down a narrow road and onto the baking streets of Palma.

Thirty-Two

Reznick drove for a couple of miles along narrow, winding streets until he got to Palma's historic Old Town. He pulled into an underground parking garage and called the beachside bar in Cala San Vicente.

The bar owner answered.

"Hi, it's Jon Reznick, the American."

"Hey, Jon, you OK? I haven't seen you for a little while."

"I've been working on some stuff. Look, I need a ride. I'm willing to pay a thousand dollars for your help."

"Why not catch a cab?"

"Long story. A little run-in with law enforcement. I need someone to pick me up and get a cuff off me."

The bar owner laughed. "You been fighting?"

"No. Just a slight misunderstanding with the Civil Guard."

"Not a fan of them myself. Neither was my grandfather. Locked up by Franco."

"So, can you help me? I need someone to pick me up in Palma."

"Palma? Now?"

Reznick gave him the location. "I need to know that I can trust you."

"You can trust me. I'll call my son. I trust him with my life. He can drive up, he isn't working until later."

"Tell him to bring bolt cutters. Goddamn cuff."

"Man, are you crazy?"

"Can you do it?"

"Sure, why not? For a thousand dollars, hey, what's it to me?"

Reznick smiled. "Appreciate that. Tell your son to look out for a FedEx van. I'll be in the back. And remember, don't tell a soul."

Just over an hour later, a small red Seat, a Spanish brand of car, drew up alongside the FedEx vehicle. Reznick was watching from the rear window. A rap on the side of the van and Reznick opened up the back door.

The kid carefully aligned the bolt cutters and snipped off the handcuff in a matter of seconds without breaking the skin.

Reznick shut the back door of the van and got into the front passenger side of the Seat. He put on the sunglasses. Forty minutes later, he was dropped off at his hotel. He was reluctant to hang around in case he was tracked down by the Civil Guard or in case the hotel staff tipped them off. He picked up his backpack and belongings and paid his hotel bill. Then Reznick handed the kid his thousand dollars.

"I want another favor," he said to the kid.

The kid shrugged.

"I need to freshen up nearby. And I want your dad's motorcycle again. Thousand extra dollars work for you?"

The kid grinned. "You got a deal."

Reznick was whisked away to the bar owner's house on the outskirts of town, where he had a shower and put on a fresh T-shirt. Just as he was about to ride back up the freeway to Palma, his cell phone rang.

"Mr. R., it's Trevelle."

"Trevelle, what the hell? I can't believe you tracked down this number. I'd given up on you."

"You should know better than that, Jon."

"I know."

"Listen, sorry this took so damn long. Gerald Essenden was a tough, tough one to crack."

"How come?"

"Long story."

"So, what did you find out about the British diplomat?"

"A lot. You want to talk about it?"

"Do I want to talk about it? Are you kidding me? Of course I want to talk about it."

"You want to do it face-to-face?"

"What do you mean, through Skype or FaceTime?"

"No, I mean, me and you, in person."

Reznick wondered what Trevelle was saying. "I think you've lost me."

"Jon, I'm here."

"What?"

"In Mallorca. I just landed. In Palma. What do you want to know?"

Thirty-Three

Just over an hour later, Reznick was back again in Palma's Old Town after locking up the bar owner's Ducati against a streetlamp on a quiet side street and checking in at a new hotel. He met Trevelle in his hotel room overlooking the city's historic cathedral. The ex-NSA contractor wore loose-fitting cargo pants, a gray Metallica T-shirt, and black Adidas sneakers. Reznick hugged the lanky black twentysomething cybersecurity expert tight.

"This is a long, long way to come."

"Tell me about it. I'm jet-lagged out of my brain. By the way, I'm sorry about Martha. I know you were close to her. And she was a good person. She cut me a break."

Reznick sat down in an easy chair. "Word is getting around, huh?"

Trevelle paced the room like a caged tiger. "What the hell is going on, Jon? I've been trying to figure it out on my way across the Atlantic."

Reznick told him what he knew. From the explosion on the yacht to having to escape from the clutches of the CIA. "It's all gone to shit."

"This is just crazy, I mean, an FBI assistant director? You think she was assassinated?"

"Yes, I do." Reznick had filled him in on the fragment of the electronic motherboard with Arabic writing. Mac's disappearance. His sister's death in a car crash. The body up in the hills. The old lady who'd rented a house to a mysterious American gentleman with a Spanish passport, and ended up dead down a well. And the car ramming him and Lauren into the drainage channel.

Trevelle nodded. "A pattern of cover-ups. Some person or organization is trying to cover their tracks."

"Precisely. But I think there's more to it than that. That's why I needed your help."

Trevelle grinned. "Well, you're in luck. I'm here. And I'm going to help you any way I can. I want to be your eyes and ears where you want to be but can't."

Reznick was intrigued. "Why are you doing this for me, man? You don't owe me."

"Don't I? You know, it's funny, I was thinking about this after you called. Thinking long and hard about the lengths you went to, to save Rosalind Dyer in DC. Remember, the whistleblower woman?"

Reznick nodded.

"We all need help. Even you. I have IT skills, cybersecurity insights, computer skills, knowledge that's only found in high-level government agencies, notably the NSA. My former employer, God forgive them."

Reznick smiled. "First things first. The British diplomat. I believe he may hold the key. After all, Catherine McCafferty was en route to see him when she was killed. He knows what's going on."

"Essenden, yeah. I found out quite a lot about him. I also have a photograph of him, so we know what he looks like." Trevelle looked at him curiously. "But how do you know he's not just a nobody diplomat? A bureaucrat."

Reznick shook his head. "I don't think so. First, the facts. Essenden is a military attaché. He's a senior diplomat for the British consulate. And he has immunity. But I'd guess that with the highly sensitive nature of what Mac found on his dive, he's also the point man liaising between Spanish military intelligence and the State Department, not to mention the CIA, on this issue."

"He's a cutout?"

"That's what I think. He's the intermediary."

"So, the American connection is in the background."

"Correct. The fragment of the device that Mac found is highly classified, highly sensitive. The consequences of this getting out would be huge. Just imagine the media firestorm."

"It would be crazy."

Reznick sighed. "Yeah. But getting back to Essenden, if I had to guess, I think he's not just an ordinary diplomat. He's MI6."

Trevelle whistled. "That's interesting."

"Britain's foreign intelligence service. Our equivalent of the CIA."

"I get the picture."

"I've known people who work for them. They're smart. Resourceful. And they have amazing connections to the American intelligence community, at all levels. Do you see where I'm going with this?"

"So how would it work? The British diplomat passes on information to the State Department on the ground in Mallorca?"

"That makes sense. An individual, in this case a Brit, someone who is trusted and who can ferry information between the Spanish intelligence agencies and, crucially, the Americans. Like I said, the Americans, the FBI, the CIA, and the State Department, they're all in town. They've interviewed me."

Trevelle nodded.

"Think about it. Both MI6 and the CIA are adept at gathering vital intelligence using interpersonal contacts. Especially when it comes to national security. The traditional area of tradecraft. Spying. We're talking old school, human intelligence gathered by real people, not through analysis or electronic surveillance. And trust me, if an FBI assistant director is killed on a boat in the Med, and there's Arabic writing discovered, this is the stuff they deal with."

"Shit, can you imagine what would happen if the press got their hands on this story?"

"It would be a kerosene wildfire," Reznick said.

"What about the mysterious American?"

"We'll find him. But first things first, we need to see what Essenden knows."

"And that's my cue." Trevelle got up from the sofa and pulled out a suitcase from underneath his bed. He unzipped it and took out a MacBook Pro and placed it on the coffee table in front of Reznick. The hacker flipped it open and logged on to a virtual private network in Switzerland that would conceal both his location and his electronic traffic from any interlopers.

Trevelle adjusted the computer screen for Reznick to see better, then tapped a key, and a Google map appeared, a street view of the center of Palma. He clicked another key, and a red arrow appeared.

"What's this?"

"The GPS location of Gerald Essenden. British consulate in Palma. Real time."

Reznick stared at the screen. "Are we sure?" He glanced at Trevelle. "You're tracking a British diplomat's cell phone?"

"Here's the thing, Jon. He has two cell phones, I've discovered. His Foreign Office–issued iPhone, with state-of-the-art encryption."

"I thought you could hack anything?"

"I can. But I know that if I attempt to hack Essenden's MI6-encrypted cell phone, it would ping all sorts of alerts notifying them that there was a remote entry attempt. And I'm guessing you wouldn't want him to be aware of that."

Reznick nodded. "True. So what am I looking at?"

"This is his personal cell phone, which he bought here in Palma a few days after being transferred here from Madrid, around the time your friend Mac went missing."

"Interesting. So we have his exact location?"

Trevelle nodded.

"Good work."

"You want me to keep an eye on him?"

"The guy, if he is a military attaché, will use countersurveillance techniques, so getting a visual on him would be incredibly dangerous. So, electronic surveillance is good. Very good."

"What are you hoping for?"

"I want to know who he visits. I want to know his whereabouts at all times. This guy knows a lot."

Thirty-Four

Three hours later, the GPS signal of Essenden's cell phone began to move.

Trevelle handed Reznick a brand-new, specially encrypted cell phone and earbuds. "So we can communicate," the hacker said.

"You really need to get out more."

Trevelle stared at the screen. "I've got the app running on your phone and mine, in the background."

Reznick watched as the GPS arrow moved slowly through Palma's narrow streets. He got to his feet and put in the earbuds. "I got this."

"I want to help."

"You are helping."

"No, I mean I want to get out there on the street and help. Keep track of him."

Reznick wondered if that was a smart move. He didn't want to put Trevelle at risk. But he also knew that an extra pair of eyes and ears on the ground would be helpful in addition to the electronic surveillance.

His mind flashed to images of Lauren being interrogated by Finsburg. He'd trusted Johnston that she was safe, and he knew she was smart and tough. But as a father, he couldn't help but worry.

Reznick's thoughts snapped back to the present. "Keep at least fifty yards from me."

"The app will be like a GPS, telling you to turn left or turn right as you lock on to the target."

Reznick took a deep breath. "Let's do this."

The surveillance began.

Reznick got a visual on a middle-aged man meandering through the streets. The man wore a pale blue shirt and chinos, and he had a backpack on. The target was about a hundred yards down the street from Reznick, who held back for a few moments. He turned around and saw Trevelle cross the street, keeping sight of the target. "Not too close," he said into the phone. "Back off."

"Copy that. I want to get a bit closer."

"I'll shadow you," Reznick said.

Trevelle continued down the street toward Essenden. "He's stopped to check out an art gallery."

"Head in a different direction, countersurveillance move."

Reznick watched as Trevelle headed down a side street away from the target. "Keep walking, due southwest like you're doing."

"Copy that."

Reznick waited until the target moved on and turned a corner. He counted to ten before he resumed walking. The voice from the app said, *Turn right, and then continue for twenty yards.* Reznick bought a Coke from a street vendor. He waited for another minute before he walked on. *Head along this route, then due east.* A few moments later, Reznick turned into an affluent street with a huge imposing building opposite. *The target is at this location.* It was a hospital. Clinica Rotger.

"You there yet?" he heard Trevelle say through his earbuds.

Reznick walked on for another twenty yards before he stopped. "Copy that. Hospital."

"Stand by, I'm approaching from a southeast direction. Location is an exclusive private hospital, one of the best in the Balearics."

"Maybe he's getting treatment."

Trevelle said, "Website I'm checking says it's used by VIPs, wealthy individuals, etc. Very exclusive."

"I'm going in."

"Hang on, Jon. I'm going to try and get a more specific location." There was silence for a few moments. "He's on the first floor. Can I make a suggestion?"

"What's that?"

"I'm going to activate the microphone on his cell phone."

Reznick smiled. "The old roving bug, huh?"

"Copy that."

Reznick spotted a coffee shop opposite and headed inside, glad to feel the cool air on his skin. He ordered a latte and sat down.

"The conversation, it's only coming to me," Trevelle said.

"What's he saying?"

"He's inquiring how his friend is."

"Who's his friend?"

"Jill Buchanan."

"Who's she?"

"I'm checking online . . . stand by. Negative. Nothing on any relevant databases. But Jill Buchanan is the name of the patient in the hospital's system."

Reznick touched the earpiece to make sure it was still in place.

"The doctor he's speaking to is in charge of the intensive care unit," Trevelle said. "So, it sounds like he's just checking on a friend or relative of his, maybe a British expat, I don't know."

"I'm wondering if we're wasting our time with this guy."

Trevelle was quiet for a minute. "Yeah, he's talking about her condition. The doctor is saying she's critical. And Essenden told the doctor to only speak to him about Jill Buchanan. Essenden has given the doctor his card."

Reznick finished his coffee. "Stay out of sight."

"Got it."

Reznick only had to wait for a couple of minutes. The diplomat emerged, sunglasses on, talking into a cell phone. He wondered if it was the personal phone or his Foreign Office cell phone. "Got a visual on him," he said.

"Copy that. We've got his position tracked."

Reznick weighed whether they should head back out onto the streets of Palma. "We're definitely tracking his position?"

"Every step of the way."

"And you'll be able to determine where he goes?"

"Copy that."

Reznick sat in the coffee shop for a few moments longer, wondering who Jill Buchanan was. His curiosity got the better of him. If nothing else, it would be useful to rule her out as being pertinent to the investigation. "I'm going in," he said.

"Into the hospital? You want me to keep track of Essenden?"

"Electronically. Get some coffee or water. I'll see you outside in ten minutes."

Reznick needed a bit of cover, so he headed to a nearby shop and bought a bouquet of flowers. He walked into the hospital and headed up a flight of stairs. He followed a long corridor whose signs pointed to the intensive care unit.

A nurse approached him. "Señor, can I help?"

"Jill Buchanan. I'm a friend."

The nurse gave a sympathetic smile. "Are those for her?"

"Well, her room. I'm guessing she's too poorly to receive visitors."

The nurse nodded. "That's right, señor. If you want, you can look at her through the window to her room. She can't receive any visitors."

Reznick followed the nurse down the corridor until she turned around, pointing through the window to Jill Buchanan's room. Reznick looked inside—and his legs nearly gave way. Lying on the bed on starched white sheets, neck, arms, and legs swathed in bandages, pale face, bluish lips, cheeks red as if scorched, hands bone white, eyes closed, ventilator beeping away, was Martha Meyerstein. Still alive. Just. But it was unmistakably her.

Reznick's throat tightened. He put down the flowers. He wanted to go into her room and kiss her. To tell her he was elated that she was alive. To tell her so many things. His mind was racing. He'd been sent on a mission to find out how Martha had died and who'd killed her. But he'd found her. Alive. Though barely.

He felt a mixture of shock and overwhelming joy. And so many questions.

Reznick took out his cell phone and snapped a few pictures.

The nurse swung by again and said, "Are you family?"

"I'm a friend of the family. Very close friend."

"There are usually no visitors for patients at the ICU, señor. We are under strict instructions."

"I understand." Reznick walked down the hallway away from the ICU, then took out his cell phone and called Finsburg.

The number rang three times before it was answered. "Lionel Finsburg." His voice was tentative. "Who's this?"

"Jon Reznick, that's who it is. Lionel, you got a problem."

"Jon? Do you know that they're looking for you?" he hissed. "What the hell is going on?"

"I was about to ask the same question. Listen, I want to talk about a lady in the hospital. You know exactly who I'm talking about?"

Finsburg was quiet for several long moments. "I have no idea what you're talking about," he said finally.

"I think you do, Lionel. You're using a British diplomat as a cutout on this. Gerald Essenden. I'm assuming it's to pass medical updates on to the Americans without hospital staff being made aware of the true identity of this woman. Maybe find out when the woman will be fit to be flown back home. A woman who is definitely not Jill Buchanan."

"Oh my God, Jon, have you lost your mind?"

"I don't know what the fuck you guys think you're doing, but it stops now. I want the patient transferred back home to an American hospital, immediately."

"Jon, I swear to God, I have no idea what you're talking about."

"Find someone who does. I want this woman transferred back to American soil, and I want it done right fucking now or I'm going to explode. So help me God. I'm going to wait here until I'm satisfied that plans are being put in place. Don't disappoint me, Lionel."

Reznick ended the call. He texted a photo to Trevelle, then dialed his phone and relayed the news.

"Are you serious, Jon?"

Reznick was still reeling from the discovery. "That's one hundred percent her."

"What do you want me to do now? This is freaking me out."

"I've got a feeling the State Department is going to be crawling all over this place soon. You need to let me deal with this now."

"What do you want me to do?"

"You've done your bit. I don't want you getting dragged into this."

"It's not a problem, Jon."

"Trust me, it will become a problem. The Agency and the State Department don't fuck around. I don't want you facing charges. I don't want them to close down your new operation in Iowa."

Trevelle went quiet.

"My advice? Get on the next plane home. I'll catch up with you when this is over. I owe you one, buddy. You found her. Amazing work."

"I want to help."

"I know you do. But you don't want to get embroiled any further. We'll speak soon."

"Anytime, Mr. R."

Reznick ended the call and headed back toward the ICU. The same nurse watched him approach, arms folded.

"It's time to go, señor. We don't allow visitors here."

"Miss, I need two minutes with her. She's a very dear friend."

The nurse grabbed a passing doctor and they engaged in a heated discussion in Spanish.

The doctor stepped forward and sighed. "Two minutes, señor. And then you must go."

"Thank you, Doctor."

Reznick followed the nurse into the room after washing his hands with quick-drying antibacterial gel. He pulled up a chair beside Martha's bed and reached out to hold her pale white hand. She was surprisingly warm to the touch. He leaned close, listening to the machines humming and clicking in the background. "Thank God you're alive," he said. "I thought we had lost you. We all did. I don't know if you can hear me or not. But I just want you to know that I'm here. Right beside you. Martha, your family is missing you so, so much. You'll be back home before you know it."

The machines hummed.

"That's all I wanted to say. Except . . . I've missed you. And I need you to fight your way back. I know you can do it, Martha. You're not going to give up. That's not you. You're going to get better. And when you do, I want to take you up to Rockland for a long vacation. How does that sound? Clam chowder and beers, what do you say?"

The nurse, standing at the window, pointed to her watch.

"I love you." Reznick kissed Martha's forehead. "Till the next time."

Reznick watched over Martha like a sentinel from outside the ICU until a group of guys in suits arrived with Finsburg. He took Reznick aside.

"What exactly do you know, Jon?"

"I know what you told me was a fucking lie. How long have you been keeping this a secret?"

"I don't want to get into a discussion. Frankly, you don't have clearance."

"I have all the clearance I need. But anyway, fuck your clearance. I want her protected and taken home to get the best care in the world."

Finsburg nodded. "If you'd let me finish. We couldn't risk moving her in this condition since it might leak to the press. So that's why we kept her here. It was a national security issue. I didn't want her true identity known to the doctors and nurses at this hospital. The explosion and the intended target, if the media got hold of the story, would have resulted in the biggest media coup for Islamists since 9/11. And that's why we had to come up with this plan. The false identity. The British acting as go-betweens."

Reznick sighed. "I want her moved. To an American hospital."

"We had planned to move her in a week or so. But under the circumstances, you're probably right."

"Is she strong enough?"

"Her medical prognosis is better than it was twenty-four hours ago. She is now stable. I have authorization to put plans in place to transport her. American medical crews are waiting to fly her back. They're at the airport. I've spoken to her doctor. He says there is a risk in moving her, but he also said there are always risks. He said as long as we had a full medical team on board, he'd sign off on it."

"OK."

"I want you to know that this is top secret. Highly, highly classified. We both know you don't have the highest security clearance anymore. But I trust that you will treat this information as highly confidential, classified. You get the gist. I'm talking national security. Do you understand?"

"Get her home. Get her well. I want your word that what you're saying is true."

"You have my word. She's flying home."

"One last thing. Who knows about this?"

"A handful of people. And I mean a handful. The President is being informed as we speak."

"We'll save the discussions about how this whole thing happened for another day. Can I assume your men are going to back off of me? And where's my daughter?"

"She's fine. She's back in Cala San Vicente." He smiled. "I think she's a chip off the old block, Jon."

Reznick turned and looked through the window at Martha before he fixed his gaze on Finsburg. "Are you traveling back on the plane?"

"Yes, I am."

"I'm holding you personally responsible for her until she's in an American hospital."

"I can't make any promises, Jon."

"Make an exception for me, what do you say?"

Finsburg nodded. "OK. One final thing, Jon." He handed him a business card embossed with the CIA seal. "Jeremiah Johnston is waiting for you."

Thirty-Five

It was a short drive up the coast to a swanky townhouse in Puerto Pollensa, two blocks from the main drag.

Reznick followed an Agency guy called Ray into the townhouse and walked up a flight of stairs to a first-floor drawing room.

Jeremiah Johnston was sitting in an easy chair. He looked almost annoyed to see Reznick. He pointed to the sofa opposite.

Reznick sat down.

"You're quite something, Jon," he said. "Out of sight, actually."

"What do you want?"

"I've just finished a rather heated video conference call with the State Department people and Spanish intelligence."

"That must've been fun."

"Far from it. You know what they want to do with you?"

"I've got a good idea."

"They want to grab you and get you on the next flight home. Physically remove you. You're a problem. An irritant for them." Johnston smirked. "I told them we tried that once already."

Reznick said nothing.

"I've also spoken to my boss. He says to stick with you. Says you're a means-to-an-end guy. That you're a pain in the ass, but you're also very creative about solving problems. Also said you're a cold bastard."

"Sounds like a bio from a dating website."

Johnston gave a rueful smile.

"What's your point, Jeremiah?"

"My point is we don't want this turning into a war, Jon."

"This is already a war. Except you guys at the Agency don't realize it yet."

"You have shared valuable, truly valuable, information with SIOC. I know you didn't have to. But they in turn passed that on to us. So thank you for that."

"You're welcome. You want to get to the point?"

"I'm going to be honest. We're still trying to get a handle on it. But we think we know who we're facing."

"Who?"

"Someone with a personal vendetta. Someone who wants blood. Your blood."

Reznick stared at Johnston, wondering who the hell they were talking about.

"He wants you to suffer."

Reznick realized Johnston was talking about the guy who'd broken into his hotel room. "The guy with the shades? You identified him?"

"We believe so. We believe he's behind this whole goddamn thing."

"Why are you telling me all this now?"

"We need you. You're the ultimate target. And this guy wants you." Johnston went over to the window and shut the blinds. He picked up a remote control on a table and switched on a huge TV on the wall. A surveillance photo appeared. It showed a good-looking, clean-cut white guy.

"Is this him?"

Johnston stared at the TV. "Just over five years ago, this guy, Adam Ford, a former Special Forces medic, and one of DC's finest surgeons, hatched a plan to kill the President. You stopped him. Remember now?"

The memories came flooding back like a torrent. Flashing through his head like strobe lighting. The race to track down Ford, a long-range sniper who'd been chosen by a cabal to kill the previous president. But despite being under arrest and the plot having been foiled, Ford had managed to escape by the skin of his teeth.

Reznick had pursued him through the streets of New York on a motorcycle until Ford escaped into the waters off Jamaica, Queens, close to JFK.

"Yeah, I remember," Reznick said.

"He's still alive. And he wants to kill you. He wants to hurt you."

"I thought he might've drowned."

"No drowning. This is him."

Reznick struggled to wrap his head around the whole thing. A ghost from the past. *His* past. "Why?"

"The Feds and a special team at Quantico, alongside our guys at Langley, are trying to figure it out. We believe Ford blames you for stopping him from achieving what he craved. Immortality. He wanted to be remembered for killing the President."

"Bullshit."

Johnston shook his head. "But first, he wanted to get to you by getting to someone you care about. Martha Meyerstein."

Reznick sat in silence, numb, maybe even in shock.

"NSA has unearthed messages between Ford and a kid in Morocco. He groomed him."

"Groomed in the sexual sense?"

"Perhaps. But mostly grooming him to help pull off his plan. Two years ago Ford made contact with this kid. Persuaded him that he was an Islamist too. Duped the kid into believing he wanted to kill infidels."

"Seriously?"

Johnston nodded. "The guy is very charismatic, apparently."

"So what was the kid's involvement?"

"We think he swam underwater, then planted the bomb underneath the yacht."

Reznick ran his hands through his hair. "In the name of Christ, how did we miss this?"

"False flag operation. Ford's a very, very smart guy. He knew we'd bite on the Islamist link, and he used this kid to carry out the attack to reinforce that and conceal his identity. The body you discovered up in the hills? That was the Moroccan boy. He'd been decapitated."

"Why would the sick fuck do that?"

"It's probably Ford covering his tracks. We have now formally identified the boy and tracked his movements into Spain, possibly linking him with Ford. Ford's a psychopath. A hugely intelligent psychopath. IQ off the scale, apparently."

Reznick nodded. "That figures."

"And he's been outsmarting us all. It's all been too fucking easy for him."

"It fits with what he said on the phone. He knew me, knew Martha. And he bragged about the murders. This guy's something else—"

Lauren. He'd also known Lauren.

"If this guy's still on the island, my daughter—"

Johnston held up a hand. "We've got people watching her. She's safe."

"She'd better stay that way," Reznick growled. "So where the hell is this guy?"

"We're working on that."

"Yeah, well, whatever you're doing, you need to come up with a new plan fast."

Johnston walked across to a framed picture hanging on the wall and lifted it up, revealing a wall safe. He entered a five-digit number, pulled open the safe, and brought out a cell phone. The CIA operative shut the safe, making sure to put the painting back in place. Then he handed Reznick the cell phone.

"Why are you giving me this? I've got a phone."

"You were saying we should get a new plan. Well, this is it. This is a specially modified phone. Calls to your daughter's FBI number will reroute here."

Reznick stared at Johnston.

"You know what I'm talking about?"

"You want to use me as bait to get Ford, right?"

"Nothing personal, Jon. It's business, right?"

Thirty-Six

It was dark when Ford checked into the junior suite. The room was located on the top floor of a small boutique hotel in the upscale town of Port de Sóller, nestled on the north coast of Mallorca. The hotel was one block from the sea. And it was quiet. The whole town was quiet. Perfect.

Ford had sensed it was time to move from the villa. He had been listening in to Civil Guard radio frequencies on his scanner as they scoured the area only a mile or so away. He could see it was a dragnet, and the Spanish cops had begun to throw resources at uncovering where he lived.

He had anticipated all this. His contingency plan was already in place. After his hour-long drive from his hideaway in the mountains, Ford pulled up outside his new hotel and headed inside. He showed a fake American passport at the reception desk. The guy checked the details, entered them in the computer, and welcomed him to the hotel. It was almost too easy. He poured himself a glass of chilled white wine and picked up his laptop from his bag.

Ford stepped out onto the terrace. He sat down on a leather chair and placed the glass of Chablis on the table.

He opened up the laptop and logged on to an encrypted website that allowed him to remotely watch everything in the villa he'd just left, no matter where he was. The motion sensors, with night vision capabilities, would be activated if anyone approached or breached the property. He checked the garage, the bathroom, dozens of cameras. Even the car outside his garage was rigged to sense movement.

Ford picked up the wine and took a long sip. He smiled and put down the glass. His gaze was drawn to the hotel's underwater-lit outdoor pool, where a British family was enjoying some family fun. Laughing. Splashing. Throwing each other around. He thought of his own mother and father. His father was a lawyer. Solid. The sacrifices he had made so Ford could attend medical school at Yale were astronomical. The punishing hours his father had worked so his son could get the very best education, from elite private schools to the Ivy League college. His father had been proud of the accolades Ford had earned working at the Red Cross in war zones across the world. Of his time as a Special Forces medic in Afghanistan and Iraq. And then, the plaudits as he became a renowned surgeon.

To Ford, none of it meant a damn. He didn't want to be respected. He didn't want a family. He hated family life. He enjoyed solitude. Listening to his own breathing. Thinking of his own concerns. Not having to accommodate anyone or anything. He only wanted people to remember him for a long, long time. He wanted immortality. But Reznick had stolen that from him.

At first, Ford had been content just to be alive after his encounter with Reznick. To have survived. But over time, he began to nurse his grievances. He'd suffered, thinking what he could have been. To have a name that would live on for a thousand years. In history books. On the internet. And whatever invention followed. The name Adam Ford would have lived on. But he'd been thwarted by his nemesis. Jon Reznick.

Ford was now ready to avenge that wrong. Reznick had eluded him for too long. That was about to end. He knew Reznick was still on the island. He had followed the SUVs that had taken Reznick and his daughter to the police station. A guy like that wouldn't be going anywhere. Not until he had tracked down who had caused Meyerstein's death. What bothered Ford was that he hadn't seen Reznick in or around Cala San Vicente for a day or so. But he was around. Somewhere.

Ford sipped his wine, savoring the taste—and the game that was in full swing. He enjoyed pressing buttons. Manipulating people. Most of the time they didn't know they were being manipulated.

This was Ford's most elaborate game so far. And he had never felt so crazy. So alive. So emboldened. He was really on the cusp of something huge. It was like fireworks going off in his head, ricocheting around his brain. Exploding his thoughts. Detonating life-changing grief for Reznick.

He laughed softly.

Reznick's major weak spot was that he cared. Deep down, the cold-blooded assassin had not only a soul, but a heart. Which meant if he thought he could help those he cared about, Reznick would go to their aid, no matter the personal cost.

Ford had exploited Reznick's Achilles' heel, first by killing Meyerstein, then by targeting Lauren. Reznick had seemed invincible when he'd been sent to stop Ford all those years ago. But now Ford knew he could be gotten at. And Ford would get him. All in good time.

Not long now, he thought, scanning the villa's surveillance footage on the laptop. He reached again for his glass of wine, the laughter from the pool filling his head until he thought it might burst.

Thirty-Seven

The call came just after midnight.

Reznick snapped his fingers as Jeremiah Johnston and another Agency operative put on headphones. A silence fell over the top-floor room of the townhouse in Puerto Pollensa. The plan was underway. Someone had called Lauren's number, and the call was coming through on the specially encrypted cell phone.

"Hey, Lauren." The voice on the line was a whisper.

Reznick knew it was Ford. Had to be.

"How you feeling? Feeling sore? I know I am. Bad luck with that hit-and-run."

Reznick listened but said nothing.

"What's wrong, Lauren? Why aren't you speaking? I was so looking forward to hearing that voice of yours. So cultured. So sweet. I've been looking out for you. Can't see you or your dad anywhere."

Reznick closed his eyes and said nothing.

"I want to speak to your dad, Lauren, the tough guy. Can you put him on?"

Johnston turned a laptop and pointed to a GPS location. They had him.

Reznick nodded, stomach tightening.

"I would've thought Daddy would be close. You like your dad, Lauren? He seems really uptight to me."

Reznick sighed. "I think you have the wrong number, pal."

"Well, well, well, I was beginning to wonder when we would speak again, Jon. I have to be frank. I've missed our talks, haven't you?"

"Not really."

Ford laughed long and hard, clearly enjoying causing discomfort. "You see, I love that sense of humor. Self-deprecating, low-key, downbeat. Am I right?"

"Who are you?"

"Small talk not your thing, huh? I don't blame you. It's a drag, right?"

"If you say so."

"You know, I've been following your career for quite a while. Well, I say *career*, but maybe that's not the right word. Can't really call assassination a career. Or can you? These days, who knows, right? The world we grew up in is so different now. The old certainties have gone. Christianity. Capitalism. Family. It's all in crisis, or so they say. No one believes anymore. I think it was G. K. Chesterton who said it best."

"Never heard of him."

"You should read his stuff."

Reznick sighed. He was at the mercy of a cocky smart-ass who was milking every moment for his own gratification.

"He said, 'The first effect of not believing in God is to believe in anything.'"

Reznick wanted nothing more than to hang up on this fucker, but he looked across at Johnston, who was nodding, wanting the conversation to continue so the teams en route could get to the GPS location before the call ended.

"When Martha was blown to pieces, Jon, did you turn to God? Did you beseech him, wondering how he could have allowed such an abomination to happen?"

"I'll tell you what I turned to. An old biblical quote. 'An eye for an eye.'"

"So, you are a believer, Jon. That surprises me. It's all rather touching and wonderful that a man like yourself could still believe in God."

"Go to hell."

"Not quite yet. Tell me, where is Lauren? I had been so looking forward to speaking to that daughter of yours. Is she still in the hospital? Hopefully she pulled through. Beautiful girl you have there. They don't make them like that anymore, do they?"

Johnston was tapping his keyboard, sending out instructions to the CIA guys who were closing in on Ford's location along with the Civil Guard. His sidekick left the room as Johnston gave the thumbs-up sign. But Reznick knew it was best to keep Ford talking, distracted.

"I'm sorry, who am I speaking to?" Reznick said.

Ford laughed. "Very droll, Jon. I like that. I'm not going to give you my name. At least not now. Maybe in a few moments."

"You want to get to the point?"

"It hurts, doesn't it? The loss of Meyerstein."

Reznick felt as if his guts were being ripped out. Knowing Martha Meyerstein was alive had been the best moment of the last week. But he also knew she wasn't out of the woods yet.

"I know how much you cared for her. I can only imagine the depths of despair you're feeling. But guess what. It's payback time, that's what this is."

"Payback? What the fuck are you talking about?"

"You know—even if you don't realize it yet. I was going to be fucking immortal. But you, you stopped me. I wanted to kill that degenerate president. And my name would've lived forever. But you, faithful American servant Jon Reznick, decided you, along with your friend Martha Meyerstein, would intervene. You have no idea how much that hurt me, Jon. The depths of despair I felt."

"Adam Ford, right? I didn't take you for a narcissist. You learn something new every day, I guess."

"Don't try teasing me, Jon. I don't like being teased."

"I thought you drowned, you sick bastard."

"I almost did. I really almost did. But I managed to disappear only yards from you, underwater, hidden from sight. I eventually swam farther from shore. And by the time I reached the surface, I was hidden by rocks and trees."

"You got lucky. But luck eventually runs out."

"I'm still in the game, Jon. Very much still in the game. And I nurse my grudges for a long, very long time," he said. "Now you're starting to feel the pain I felt and still feel. The pain at what should have been mine—immortality. Snatched from me, but by who? A nobody. A dirt-poor nobody. But I've been watching what you've been up to from afar, Jon. I can't believe you were fucking an FBI assistant director. I mean, that's crazy, Jon. What were you thinking?"

"Listen, you fucking psychopath, I will find you. And I will kill you."

"You'll never find me, Reznick. You're too fucking dumb."

"You want to meet up and discuss this further, man to man?"

Ford laughed hard. "You haven't lost that special way you have. Did they teach you that along with the rest of the Delta clowns?"

"When we meet, and trust me, we will meet, I will destroy you. And I'll enjoy doing it."

A sigh reverberated on the line. "This may be a bit above your head, but are you familiar with the Apollonian and Dionysian philosophical concept?"

Reznick said nothing.

"Apollo and Dionysus were sons of Zeus in Greek mythology. Apollo reminds me of you—rational, believes in order, prudence, and restraint. Whereas Dionysus is just a bit like me, don't you think?"

"What are you talking about?"

"Or is it that I'm a bit like him? Why is that? Dionysus is all about chaos, destruction, irrationality, and, of course, the pleasures of the flesh. Do you see what I'm getting at?"

"Not really."

"The struggle to become who we really are. The two sides, in a fight to the death to see who will triumph. It's all about who we want to be. You want to be, well, just as you are. The heroic deeds. Doing the right thing. You represent that side of the human psyche. I represent the other. You represent the pure. You want order. But me? I want to do whatever the fuck I want. And I don't give a fuck what anyone thinks about that."

"You need to see a shrink, pal."

The guy roared with laughter. "You think so? You don't like me talking about you, do you? Does it make you feel vulnerable? But I'll tell you what you do like. You're not so dissimilar to me. You like killing, Jon, don't you? They trained you well. But I think there's a bit more to you than that."

Reznick looked over at Johnston, who gestured that he should keep Ford talking.

"You know what was great about setting up this operation? Knowing the delayed pleasure I was going to get. Knowing what lay down the tracks for me. The surge of excitement knowing the beautiful, talented Martha Meyerstein was going to be blown to bits. The same hands you had touched: Severed. Gone. Dead. How did that feel to you?"

Reznick got to his feet and began to pace the room.

"I take it from your silence that I'm getting under your skin, Jon. You see, it was you that got under my skin first. And now? Well, this is going to play out like a nice slow-motion car crash. Except I'm the one who's going to decide how and when to strike."

Reznick looked at Johnston, who was moving his hands like he was stretching out some dough. *Keep him talking.* Reznick rolled his eyes. "Know what I don't understand?"

"What's that, tough guy?"

"Why you don't just come after me now. I'm here on the island."

"And so am I. Like I said, *I* will choose the place and the time. Not you, Apollo." A raucous laugh. "I'm sorry, Jon, relax. We're going to have fun. Speaking of which, why aren't you on Instagram? I would've thought that would be a great way to keep in touch with your daughter."

Reznick suppressed a growl. He knew the sick bastard was just trying to get inside his head. But he was succeeding.

"Know what's so great about social media, Jon? I've got to be honest, I'm a bit behind the curve on this. I know young people are very savvy with regards to this new digital world. But you know what's really cool? It's that nothing is real. Fascinating stuff."

Reznick looked across at Johnston, who gave a thumbs-up sign. They had Ford. Finally. They would apprehend him, maybe in a matter of minutes. Reznick's only regret was that he wouldn't be the one to neutralize the twisted fuck.

The cell phone he was speaking on pinged, indicating he had a message.

"You'll want to open that, Jon. It's interesting stuff."

Reznick looked at Johnston, who nodded. He opened the message. It showed screenshots of his daughter's Instagram page.

Lauren was wearing a bikini on a vacation to Miami Beach with her college friends.

"I've got to give you some credit," Ford said. "Compared to those skanky friends of hers, she is beautifully turned out. Nice bit of breeding. I guess your late wife's genes were strong. Very attractive, I would gather. But Jon, seriously, if I had a daughter, I would be very concerned about how skimpy that bikini is. Aren't you? I mean, it leaves nothing to the imagination."

Reznick turned away from Johnston's gaze. "I cannot wait until the moment I have you in my sights. Then we're going to see a very different side of things."

"Idle threats, Jon? That's so unbecoming. You know, maybe you can help me out here. I was thinking about Meyerstein just before I called. And I believe I have some pictures of her in a bathing suit taken poolside, Palm Beach. You wanna see what she looks like?"

"Do you know how tragic you sound?"

"Oh, Jon, you disappoint me. I would've thought a man like you, a man of the world, would enjoy perusing such pictures. She was a real beauty. Pity what happened. Boom!" Ford laughed. He sounded like a jackal on the savanna. Crazed by the sun. By the taste of blood. Feeding on bones.

Reznick took a few moments to compose himself. "What happened to the Hippocratic oath, Adam?"

Ford laughed again, this time louder. "How very touching that some people still attach value to physicians. Medical ethics? Well, it's been revised for the modern age. Nowadays, doctors are supposed to pledge to uphold the humanitarian goals of their profession through the Declaration of Geneva, if you must know. Frankly, it's all bullshit."

"Is it?"

"I know what you're doing, Jon. You're keeping me talking, aren't you?"

Reznick closed his eyes.

"You see, I'm smart. Guys like you will never find me. I'm one step ahead."

"You're going to rot in hell."

"We'll see about that, Jonny boy. Night night."

Thirty-Eight

Ford felt omnipotent, laptop on the table in front of him. He was sitting on his penthouse terrace at the boutique hotel in sleepy Port de Sóller, headphones on. The sound of Bach's monumental Cello Suite no. 1 in G Major filling his head. His mind. His soul. He felt a frenzied excitement building within him.

The conversation with Reznick had gone well.

Ford sensed he was pulling Reznick in. He felt it in his bones. He had him. He was reeling the fucker in. He scanned his laptop. The real-time footage from the surveillance cameras covering his modernist villa high up in the hills was pin sharp. He watched half a dozen vehicles slowly approaching. He panned left and right. He clicked to bring up the cameras at the rear of the property. He scanned the screen. The rear-door camera showed two men with guns approaching, the villa's security lights activated. *Come to Daddy.*

He tapped a couple of keys, panning the camera to the periphery. The night vision image showed an algae-green figure talking into a headset.

Ford smiled. *Don't be afraid, little ones. Uncle Adam doesn't bite. Well, not much.* He laughed. His dark thoughts were congealing again. Like old blood. *Come on. Another yard. See what's in my home, why don't you.*

He clicked on a rear-view camera overlooking the floodlit pool.

Ford saw a smartly dressed white man directing a Spanish cop to move in the direction of the pool changing room. The guy had to be FBI. Maybe CIA. Ford watched, intrigued, as the cop headed down the steps that led to the basement.

The music filled his head and he closed his eyes, feeling the euphoric aural pleasures of Bach course through his black soul. A strange sensation was beginning to stir within him. Was it joy? Well, maybe not much. Just enough to distinguish it from the blind fury he worked hard to conceal so much of the time.

Ford looked at the real-time images and smiled. His head was swimming with new, fresh ideas. He was on the cusp of another major step toward his end goal. A slow march to the vengeance he would wreak. The blood would spill. And he would laugh. The laugh of the damned. The mad. Who cared? It would all soon be over. He would have the last laugh.

He watched the footage from the rear property camera.

The men were using sledgehammers to smash the back door. He clicked on the front-door cameras. A two-man team was drilling into the front door.

And all the time he, Adam Ford, was thirty-seven miles away, having the time of his life. Watching. Waiting.

What a time to be alive.

Thirty-Nine

Reznick stared at the computer screen showing real-time footage from the body camera of a CIA operative. The guy was headed through the basement as part of a classified joint US-Spanish task force to apprehend Ford. They had quickly tracked down his location via the GPS from his cell phone signal. It had shown the signal was coming from a huge villa high up in the hills above Cala San Vicente. But the apparent ease with which they had located Ford sowed seeds of doubt in Reznick's mind.

Had a guy like Ford not foreseen that they would have tracked down the cell phone signal eventually? It didn't make much sense to Reznick. Ford was smart. As it stood, the villa surrounded and the task force closing in, no way in or out, this was just way too easy.

He watched as the front-door lock was drilled and the door pushed open. Then the CIA operative began a sweep through the sleek house. Massive pieces of modern art on the whitewashed walls, minimalist vibe. When the ground floor was secured, the guy headed up the stairs. Three other Spanish police officers were ahead of him. Blank looks and shrugs.

"Someone lives there," Johnston said. "We'll find him. The fucker might be in the closet. Maybe even catch him in bed with his goddamn pants down."

Reznick stared at the screen. "Something doesn't feel right about this."

Johnston looked up from the monitor. "What do you mean? This is the place."

"I don't know."

"The GPS showed *this* was the location."

"What if you're wrong?"

"It's possible. But this has been verified. Trust me, he's there. Somewhere on that property."

Reznick sensed something was wrong. Badly wrong. "Are we absolutely sure this is the location?"

"What do you mean?"

"I mean is he physically there?"

"Jon, I hear you. But we've checked. The coordinates couldn't be clearer. That's where he was calling from."

"Unless he's fucking with us. Unless . . ."

Johnston sighed, annoyed at Reznick's apparent negativity. "Unless what?"

"Unless he's spoofing the location. Have you thought of that? Think about it. How goddamn easy was it to suddenly get a fix on him?"

Johnston cleared his throat and shrugged. "We have considered that. But the goddamn NSA has the same coordinates as us. We're all on the same page."

"I don't like this. He was on the call for a long time. It was as if he wanted us to find him. He seemed very relaxed. Something about this isn't right."

"Maybe he's just gotten complacent. Arrogant."

"What if this is a trap?"

Johnston nodded. "Do you mean he's luring us there and laughing at our expense?"

Reznick gazed at the video. An operative was pointing to surveillance cameras in the kitchen, living room, bedrooms, basement. "I don't mean that."

"So, what do you mean?"

"I mean a goddamn trap."

"What the hell are you getting at?"

"I mean booby-trapped!"

"Jon, you need to calm the hell down."

Reznick shook his head. "There are countless cameras in there," he said. "Maybe dozens. What for?"

"Stopping thieves?"

"He's up a huge isolated mountainside in Mallorca. There's no one for miles around."

"Maybe he's just security conscious."

Johnston tapped a few keys. "The owner is Juan Garcia, a businessman in Madrid. He owns seven properties. He rents his Mallorca villa out throughout the year."

"So Mr. Garcia is security conscious."

"He's renting to Alvin Cameron, an Arizona doctor."

"Alvin Cameron? So that's an alias. It's gotta be Ford. Another fake ID, right?"

Johnston stared at the screen, watching the team continue to spread out across the huge property. "We'll wait till he comes back. We'll find him."

Reznick began to pace the room again. "He's not there. He's simply reeling us in."

"You're overthinking this, Jon. The guy is arrogant and didn't realize we'd find him so quickly."

"You're not listening. Adam Ford is a cunning, manipulative, and highly intelligent predator."

"I said we'll get him. Jeez, what's wrong with you?"

The sense of dread Reznick felt was only getting stronger. "Johnston, you need to get your guys out of there."

"What?"

"Get them out! Right now!"

"What the fuck are you talking about?"

"Don't you get it? He's watching your every move within the house."

"Bullshit."

The specially modified cell phone rang. Reznick looked at Johnston. "You want me to answer?"

Johnston nodded.

Reznick put the phone on speaker mode. "Yeah?"

"I don't see you, Jonny boy." The arrogant tone of Adam Ford. "Why is that? Why haven't you visited me? I was so looking forward to seeing you."

Reznick leaned across the table and whispered in Johnston's ear. "Get your men out of there! He's watching your guys!"

"I've got to say that sending an eight-strong team after one guy seems like overkill."

The danger finally seemed to click with Johnston. He was whispering urgently into his headset, instructing his men to get the hell out of there.

"We're going to find you," Reznick said. "And when we do, you'll wish you'd drowned in Jamaica Bay."

Ford began to laugh. "History repeats itself, first as tragedy, second as farce. It was the only thing Karl Marx got right, Jon."

The line went dead.

Forty

Ford ended the call and smiled. He was reveling in the situation he had manufactured. He sensed Reznick might know what he had in store for those poor saps prowling around the rental property. He watched the real-time footage on his laptop, enjoying the show on this balmy night from the terrace in Port de Sóller. Miles away from the scene at hand.

He watched the Americans, perhaps CIA or State Department officials, and Spanish intelligence officers scouring the house. No one had an inkling of what was about to happen. Which made it all the sweeter.

He waited until he saw them all gathered in the living room. He watched them look bemused as they tried to figure out where he was. One of them put his finger to his earpiece. Then he started gesturing wildly and shouting at the others.

Ford had seen enough. He picked up his cell phone again and called the landline number of the villa. The phone was on a sideboard by the front door.

The men on camera all froze at the sound of the ringing. He watched a Spanish policeman walk across to the phone.

Ford gazed at the real-time image. The somber-looking cop had no idea what was about to happen. "Come on, you know you want to." He smiled as the guy reached out to pick up the ringing phone.

Forty-One

The sheer power of the explosion sent debris and flames erupting out of the mountainside villa into the night sky, visible for miles around.

Reznick thought it sounded like the world was exploding. Even the ground began to shake. He ran out onto the balcony of the townhouse in Puerto Pollensa. Car alarms wailed. People began to scream in a nearby square. In the distance, a few miles away, he saw the night sky had turned a burnt orange.

Twenty minutes later, Reznick arrived at the villa with Johnston. Firefighters were hosing down the smoking ruins. The smell of burnt wood and flesh filled the stifling night air. The firefighters weren't even able to enter the house to retrieve the bodies, concerned about secondary explosions or gas leaks.

"I'm going in," Reznick said, pushing past a still-stunned Johnston.

"Are you crazy?"

Reznick soaked a handkerchief in water and tied it like a mask over his face. He headed into the smoking remains. Slippery marble floors were awash with surface water. He rubbed his eyes and saw three charred bodies lying twisted in the doorway of the living room; they'd died as they tried to escape. He found another three collapsed in a heap in the kitchen.

Reznick picked each one up individually and carried them out. He carefully laid them side by side. He pointed at the paramedics. "Cover them up!"

A paramedic nodded and draped the corpses with gray blankets.

Reznick went back inside and brought the other two out. The paramedic covered them too. Reznick ripped off his blackened mask. Then he washed his hands with some antibacterial hand wash and pulled Johnston aside. "Are you going to call in some help?"

The man looked utterly defeated. "What do you suggest?"

"I suggest you get some serious technical support in place, electronic expertise from the NSA, and a few dozen men and women on the ground."

Johnston scowled. "That isn't your call. Besides, that kind of operation won't go unnoticed."

"Ford is a fucking maniac. And he's not going to stop until either I'm dead or he is. He's killing for pleasure. For kicks."

"Jon, the Agency has lost good men. We'll deal with this our way."

"Yeah? And when is that going to happen?"

Johnston raised a palm. "Don't push me. I'm not going to take any bullshit from you, or anyone else, at this time."

Reznick turned and pointed at the eight corpses covered in blankets. "We need to find this guy. We need to get serious and stop dicking around."

Johnston grabbed Reznick by the throat.

Reznick clamped a hand around Johnston's wrist, wrenching it free of his neck. "Don't fuck with me. And don't ever grab me. Do you understand?"

"You need to learn that we play by the rules."

"The CIA? Don't make me laugh. Do you think the bastard who did this plays by the rules? Fuck no. We need to find him. And kill him."

"We don't work like that anymore, Jon. There's oversight."

"The time for rules and oversight has come and gone. You might not have the stomach for the fight, but I sure as hell do. I'm taking Ford down, no matter what you say."

"You're letting it get personal."

"Damn right it's personal."

"We need to adhere to the law. That's what we're obligated to do."

"Why do you think they sent me after Ford the last time? I wasn't one of you then, and I'm not one of you now." Reznick turned to leave, then looked back at Johnston. "I'll find him. And when I do, just so there's no misunderstanding with you or your State Department pals, I'll kill him myself."

Forty-Two

The hours that followed for Reznick were hours racked with guilt. *He* had been the target. *He* was the one Ford was really trying to get to. *He* was the one who should have been dead. He felt sick. He should have been on the mission.

Day after day, there had been only more bad news. More deaths. And all because of him. Ford wasn't going to stop until one of them had drawn their last breath.

Reznick began to cough hard, a souvenir of the smoke he'd inhaled. He walked across to an olive grove, bathed in the headlights of an SUV, and was violently sick. He blamed himself. He should have seen the play as soon as Ford's fake GPS was detected. He should have known the length of the call indicated that Ford had turned the tables.

Johnston came over and handed him a bottle of chilled water. Reznick gulped it down, trying to wash the smoke residue from his throat. He waited until first light, the ruins of the house still smoldering, the corpses taken to the mortuary in Palma, to accept that there was no point in hanging around the burnt villa much longer.

"Let's get out of here," Reznick said.

Johnston nodded, and they drove one of the SUVs back down the dirt mountain track.

Reznick was quiet throughout the journey back to his hotel. Johnston had been occupied throughout the night, fielding calls from the FBI, the State Department, and the CIA in Langley.

The enormity of the crime and its simple execution had stunned everyone. But still they were chasing shadows trying to find Ford.

Reznick had gotten a sense of the interagency recriminations. Screaming over the phone. Where the hell was Ford? What the hell were the Feds doing? How the hell didn't they see this coming? But he knew whatever device or software Ford had been using to spoof his actual location had almost certainly been ditched and Ford was holed up somewhere else. Wherever Ford was, one thing was certain: Reznick was still in his sights. That hadn't changed.

Johnston dropped him off at his hotel. The staff in the lobby looked appalled at his disheveled appearance, his hands partly burned and red from the smoking ruins.

"Are you OK, sir?" the young receptionist said.

"Just a rough night, that's all," Reznick said.

He was relieved to get back to his room. He took a long, hot shower and put on some fresh clothes. A black T-shirt, jeans, and sneakers. He was physically and mentally drained. So he did what he usually did. He took three Dexedrine. It only took fifteen minutes to rouse him.

He wasn't going to allow the terrible loss of life to stop him from tracking down and killing Adam Ford. He wasn't going to sleep it off. And he sure as hell wasn't going to mope around. Enough was enough.

Reznick headed back out of the hotel and down the road to the beachfront café. He ordered breakfast and a cup of strong black coffee. He spent a few moments thinking about Lauren. He trusted that Johnston had been correct when he said she was safe.

The owner smiled. "You OK, Señor Jon?"

"A lot on my mind. Thanks for asking. And thanks for letting me borrow your bike."

"For one thousand dollars, you can keep it!"

Reznick smiled.

"Did you see the explosion last night? Did it wake you?"

Reznick nodded.

"They said on the radio it was a gas explosion. Another one."

Reznick said nothing.

"No one injured or killed, thank God."

Reznick nodded. Another media blackout. He knew the truth would emerge eventually. Maybe days or weeks later, when the State Department had decided it was in the national interest to reveal the full extent of the carefully planned attack. But it might be too late to stop another attack. It was clear Ford was the mastermind behind the whole operation. A special ops–trained medic. He had to be apprehended and stopped. Ideally killed. Ford understood military tactics but also understood medicine. Psychology. He knew how to press buttons to produce behavior patterns. Everyone else was running around like headless chickens.

Reznick looked up at the bar owner. "Sounded bad."

"If there's anything I can get you, don't hesitate to contact me."

"You've been very kind to me. Thank you, my friend."

Reznick sat alone with his thoughts for a minute before he started his breakfast. He was famished. He wolfed down the toast and omelet, followed by a couple of croissants and a couple of black coffees. He couldn't remember the last time he'd eaten. Afterward, he felt marginally better. But his mood was dark, even with the amphetamines coursing through his bloodstream.

He thought of the villa up in the hills where Adam Ford had stayed. Long-distance line of sight into the town. Now the observation point was gone. So where was he now? Was Ford lying low?

Was he watching in plain sight? Was he planning a final move in his quest to kill Reznick?

Reznick had gotten lucky so far. And others had paid the price.

He stared across the bay. The sparkling blue waters shimmered in the blazing early-morning sun. He thought of the families of the CIA and State Department guys, not to mention the Civil Guard officers, who had perished in the night. He thought about the wives being called in the middle of the night in the States. Maybe a door-step call from the Civil Guard to the family of a fallen officer. Their men wouldn't be coming home. Each family's emptiness and anger would engulf them. He knew those feelings all too well.

The American dead, three of them, two CIA and one State Department, would be flown to an American military base in Europe. Then back to Dover Air Force Base in Delaware. He'd lost count of the times he'd been there as fallen comrades and friends were returned to their loved ones.

The suffering went on for years. The dead were returned. The politicians who sent them off to fight were nowhere to be seen. It was all done in the name of freedom. But whose freedom?

Whenever he thought about it, he wondered what the hell it had all been for. What had any of it been for? The endless wars were just that: endless. America funded people in one conflict, then ended up fighting against them in the next. And on and on it went.

Reznick's cell phone rang—his personal phone—snapping him out of his dark thoughts.

"Jon, it's Lionel Finsburg."

"Lionel . . . what's the latest? How's Martha?"

"She's alive. I'm calling from the plane. But I want you to listen to me. I have a message I've been asked to pass on."

"What kind of message?"

"In the parking lot, fifty yards behind the bar, there's a BMW SUV. It's located at the farthest corner of the parking lot."

"The CIA planning on drugging me again, Lionel? I don't take too kindly to that."

"Your daughter's waiting for you. We have an apartment in town for you both; we thought that would be prudent."

Reznick closed his eyes for a moment. "Sorry, I sound like an ungrateful idiot. I haven't gotten any sleep. My main priority now is to keep my daughter safe."

"Then she should think about going home."

"I agree. But she's stubborn."

"She's tough too, Jon. She's got the Reznick genes, that's for sure."

"Can I see her now?"

"Sure, she's waiting."

Reznick ended the call and left a twenty-euro bill under the ashtray. He walked down the side street and toward the parking lot. He spotted the BMW and strode over. The back door opened.

Lauren was sitting on the other side, smiling. "What took you so long, Dad?"

It was a short drive in the BMW to a secluded part of Cala San Vicente. The apartment had a wraparound glass terrace, shielded from prying eyes by huge cypress trees. State Department officials had dropped off their bags, along with some groceries.

Finally, when they were alone, Reznick hugged his daughter tight. "Thank God you're safe. I've missed you."

"Me too."

"Where did they take you?"

"A place in Palma. They said an operation to catch the person responsible had gone south. I feared the worst."

Reznick helped his daughter by chopping up some mushrooms for risotto. They ate it on the terrace with a bottle of Rioja. While they ate, he took a few minutes to update Lauren on the events of the previous night and finding Martha alive in the hospital.

"Thank God she's alive."

Reznick nodded.

"When does this end, Dad?"

"It ends when either Ford is dead or I am. Not before."

"Don't joke around."

Reznick shook his head. "It's not a joke. It's a fact. He's out there."

"And this is all about him wanting you dead?"

Reznick sighed. "Long story. It's personal with him. He wants to get under my skin. And he's succeeding. And he's been one step ahead the whole time."

"And no one can seem to locate him? That's crazy."

"He's a devious bastard."

"I think we'll find him," Lauren said. "The FBI and NSA are seriously involved now. I just think we need a bit more luck."

"Listen to me, after the Agency gets lured into a trap, which incidentally was meant for me, you realize what kind of guy you're dealing with. This guy is clearly in possession of some high-tech equipment, surveillance, cell phone hacking, you name it. And he's had years of planning to prep for contingencies."

"We have to find him."

"How many times do I have to tell you? This is not your fight. You need to go back home. Do you hear me? It's over for you. You know what I did in the dead of night? You want to know the grim reality?"

Lauren stared at him.

"I had to drag the burned corpses of some of our guys out of a still-smoldering fire. So, Lauren, the time for bravado is long gone, trust me on that."

"Why are you pushing me away? I'm trying to help. Did I or did I not take down that Aryan Brotherhood guy I was trapped in the car in New York with? *He* was highly dangerous."

Reznick shook his head. He wanted his daughter back home in the States. She was at the early stages of learning to be an FBI special agent. But she was still pretty green. Very inexperienced. "You got lucky."

"Lucky? Is that what you call it? What did you once tell me, Dad?"

Reznick turned away, feeling uneasy that she was still in Mallorca after everything that had happened.

"*You make your own luck in this business. You earn it. But you've got to shed blood to get it sometimes.* Did you say that?"

"I did say that. But listen to me. You are my daughter. And I want to protect you. It's in my nature."

"What is it going to take for you to understand that I have the right to decide if I want to help you?"

"OK, answer me this. Let's imagine, just for the sake of argument, that we find this nut. Just imagine that for a moment. So, how are you going to kill him?"

Lauren went quiet for a few moments.

"You don't have a gun with you, do you?"

Lauren shook her head.

"You see my point?"

"It's not a very subtle point, Dad. It doesn't make me feel good when you try and put me down."

"This is not about putting you down. I don't mean to belittle you. This is about stark reality. Cold reality. How the fuck are you going to kill this guy? You going to fight him? Knife fight?"

"I would if I had to."

"Adam Ford, you checked his file?"

Lauren shook her head.

"I know about this guy. While he's a doctor, he's also a trained killer. Hand-to-hand combat. Top-notch sniper. He's a cold-blooded killer. And you know, the guy has already escaped my clutches once before."

"When?"

Reznick sipped some red wine. He took a few minutes to tell Lauren how he'd foiled the attempt on the President's life. "I brought down Ford before the hit was carried out. Ford was in custody. But some backup crew freed him. And I had to chase him down. He escaped into the waters near JFK."

"You never told me about that."

"There's a lot you don't know. This guy is a survival expert. And he's as tough as they come. What makes him even more dangerous is his compulsion to kill. I think he enjoys it. Thank God they got Martha out of the country before he realized she's still alive. But you know what concerns me now? Keeps me awake at night?"

Lauren shook her head.

"You. I worry about *you* all the time. When you're here, my job is to keep you safe."

"Who gave you that job? I didn't give you that job."

"I'm a father. That's my job. That's the rules. If you have children you'll understand. Your number one duty is to protect them until they can protect themselves."

"I can protect myself."

"Which leads me back to my question. How would you kill him?"

Lauren gazed at him, tears in her eyes. "I'll never be good enough to match up to you, will I? I'll never be good enough for you."

"You're completely missing the point. And don't turn this into some sob fest, OK? I don't want to hear it."

Lauren shook her head. "I'm trying to reach out to you."

"And I'm trying to keep you alive. Don't you think he'll try and get to you? As long as you're here, you're at risk. He was calling your cell phone. He accessed your FBI cell phone, goddamn it. Think about that. Do you understand that means that all your contacts may have been compromised?"

"I know that. Finsburg and a couple of the State Department guys debriefed me on this whole thing."

"They don't want you here either."

Lauren stared straight ahead, blinking away the tears. "Too bad, I'm staying."

"You still haven't satisfactorily answered my question. How do you kill that guy if you come face-to-face? Answer me that."

"I need a gun."

"Are you really thinking this through? I mean, you work for the FBI. I'm sure Lionel Finsburg has already quoted every goddamn FBI rule to you."

"Over and over again."

"He's not wrong. If that maniac does come face-to-face with you, and you have a chance to take him out, you have no gun."

Lauren looked at him, eyes fierce, like her mother's. The same defiant, beautiful glare.

"Even guys that had guns, the Agency crew that went up there last night—that didn't save them."

"I want a gun so at least I can defend myself if I do come face-to-face with him."

"If you're caught with a gun in Spain, and it's not authorized or you're not on official business, then you could be prosecuted by the Spanish courts."

"I'm talking to you as your daughter. I would like a gun, to defend myself, at the very least."

"Like I said before, Lauren, you have to realize that your career could go up in smoke if you fire a gun in Europe, if you're not on official business or have TSA authorization to carry. I have still got that authorization. At least they haven't taken that away from me yet."

"Didn't you once say that a gun is a great equalizer for any woman?"

Reznick nodded.

"I don't want to be at a disadvantage."

"You're my daughter, and I love you. And you're right, you're a goddamn adult. And you know the consequences, right? And you're prepared to face those consequences if things go wrong?"

"I'd rather be alive and face the consequences than be dead."

Reznick leaned back in his seat and sipped some wine. He gazed off into the distance, birds in flight, the cypress trees swaying in the hot Mediterranean air. "So would I."

"I know you always pack two guns. I want that second gun."

Reznick said nothing as he contemplated allowing his daughter to jeopardize her career. But the worst option was her being defenseless. The fact was, there were no good options for her.

"What is it, Dad? What are you thinking?"

"Why don't you ever make it easy for me, Lauren?"

"This isn't about making it easy. This is about standing with my father. Shoulder to shoulder, side by side. If need be. That's how I was brought up."

Reznick smiled. "I have two guns. I have one on me. But if I give you that second gun, it will open you up to all sorts of problems in the eyes of the FBI."

"I'll take my chances."

"Alright, then," he said and took a large gulp of wine. "So be it."

"So, what now?" Lauren asked. "What are you thinking?"

"I'm thinking it's time to bring this guy to us."

Forty-Three

Ford could barely suppress the smile on his face as he checked out of the small boutique hotel in Port de Sóller and took a short tram ride up to the picturesque town of Sóller. He sat at a table underneath the shade of a tree in the town square, sipping a glass of wine, listening to an American couple beside him talking loudly, as they invariably did, as if *trying* to attract attention, about the highlights of their vacation. He listened as they emoted over the wonders they had witnessed firsthand. They talked cathedrals. All across Spain. All over Mallorca, including the beautiful church in Sóller. They were simple people from Iowa. A farmer and his wife. Ford listened as the urge to laugh out loud came and went. They talked about their children. And how they were thankful that they were following the path of Christ.

The man sounded like Ford's own father. Stern. Quiet. A man who believed in the Bible. The literal interpretation of the Bible.

Ford never could reconcile how a smart lawyer like his father could have faith in a collection of stories written centuries after Jesus was supposed to have been around. But his father had faith. An undying faith. Ford grudgingly respected that.

His own faith was that of the individual. The primacy of one man. Self-reliance. It was a Darwinian approach to life. Only the strong survive. Kill or be killed. His father, by contrast, showed kindness. True kindness. No matter how much Ford tried, he could never care. He could feign caring. And he often did. He was good at that. But genuine concern for other people, no matter their social standing, was something that simply wasn't within him.

Ford didn't worry. He recognized his lack of empathy for what it was. Classic psychopathy. It was a strength. He wasn't saddled with worrying about doing the right thing. Thinking of his fellow man. He wanted something—he figured out how he was going to get it. When he was working full time as a surgeon in DC, his lack of empathy had been useful. Essential, even. He didn't get drawn into feeling emotional about a patient. So, he could do the job. And he did it better than anyone alive.

"Excuse me, sir, do you speak English?" The voice of the American man at the next table snapped Ford out of his reverie.

Ford looked up and pretended to smile. He took a few moments to answer, weighing up whether to engage with them or not. "Yes . . . yes, I do."

"What luck!" the man said. "You're American?"

"Born and bred, sir."

"That's amazing. Say, would you like to join us?"

Ford felt conflicted. He didn't want to attract attention and questions. He wondered if he should make up some lame excuse. But in the blink of an eye, he realized he didn't want to stick out like a sore thumb by refusing to join them. "That would be lovely, thank you for asking," he said in his most polite voice. He turned his chair around and sat down beside the husband. "Well, this is nice."

The man shook his hand. "Brian Fairfax. This is my wife, Lesley."

Ford took the man's firm grip. "Lovely to meet you guys. James Forgan. I'm from Washington, DC."

"So what brings you here to beautiful Mallorca?" Lesley said.

Ford considered how to answer that. He was very adept at creating imaginary life stories. But he was also smart enough to know not to say anything too outrageous that made it likely he would be caught in a lie. "I'm taking my first vacation in five years. My wife died six months ago. And I'm just trying to reconcile my faith and I guess try and mend my heart."

Lesley was already nearly looking for the tissues, eyes welling with tears. "Oh my Lord. You poor thing, I am so sorry. That's heartbreaking."

Ford put on his best sad face. "She suffered terribly. I did all I could. But you know, I know she's at peace now with the Lord."

Brian now also had tears in his eyes. He put an arm around Ford's shoulder as if they were old friends. "You're a brave man. God bless you."

Ford sighed, enjoying the synthetic drama. He loathed emoting. It betrayed a weakness of character. A softness. "We're put on this earth to suffer, aren't we?"

Lesley nodded. "You need to have faith. To endure."

Ford was tempted to burst out laughing; it was ridiculous. But he kept up the pretense. "So very true. Thank the Lord for my faith, Lesley. And thank you for your kindness. So, tell me, where are you guys headed?"

Brian cleared his throat. "Twenty-fifth wedding anniversary and thought we'd treat ourselves. We love exploring these old churches, and where better than some of the oldest in Spain. Beautiful buildings." He turned around and pointed to the cathedral. "Have you ever seen anything so stunning?"

"I believe the original church dated back to the thirteenth century. Amazing. Have you seen the museum with the works of Miró and Picasso?"

The couple looked at each other. "I'm not sure that's our thing," Brian said.

Ford didn't doubt it. He could tell a country hick a mile off. "Well worth a visit."

"We might check that out if we get a moment, James," Lesley said. "Thanks for the heads-up."

"So, are you staying in Sóller for a few days?"

"Just overnight," said Brian.

"How are you guys getting around?"

"We got a great deal on a beautiful RV."

Ford had earlier overheard Brian telling his wife that he had parked the vehicle nearby, down a side street, around the corner from the Seat garage. "Nice."

"We're going to have an early night, and then head out at first light for Palma."

"Now, Palma has got an amazing cathedral."

Brian nodded. "So I've heard. Never been to Europe. Quite something."

"Southern Europe has a different pace of life than we're used to," Ford said.

For the following hour, they made small talk. Ford bought them a drink and they bought him one. It was all very civilized. Eventually, the couple called it a night, saying they would offer a prayer for him at the cathedral.

Ford finished his drink and thanked them as his mind began to race. He watched them amble across the square to their hotel. He waited a few minutes before he retired for the night as well. But he wasn't interested in sleep. Quite the contrary.

He walked five minutes to the Seat garage and located the Mercedes RV parked underneath a lemon tree.

Ford took out an electronic dongle from his pocket. He pressed a switch, and it deactivated the car's alarm and clicked open the central lock. The wonders of the dark web. He slid into the driver's seat and adjusted the seat position. Then he leaned forward and pressed the start button, and the engine purred to life. "Here I come, Reznick!"

He turned up the air-conditioning to maximum, thankful for the cold blasts on his warm skin.

Ford smiled. By the time the couple discovered their vehicle wasn't there, he'd be long gone.

The GPS showed his location. He carefully entered his destination, Cala San Vicente. It showed he was sixty kilometers away. Thirty-seven miles or so. Maybe an hour's drive.

Ford pulled out from the curb slowly, knowing that Jon Reznick and his daughter wouldn't be far away.

Forty-Four

Reznick watched as two cars pulled up outside the apartment in the dead of night. He held the 9mm Beretta.

The buzzer rang.

Reznick checked the security intercom. He relaxed when he saw it was Todd Mavor, the State Department official.

"Jon, you want to let me in?"

"What the hell do you want at this time of night?"

"A word."

"About what?"

"Adam Ford. He's on the move."

Reznick buzzed Mavor and three of his State Department pals in. He looked across the room as Lauren emerged bleary-eyed from her bedroom. She wore jeans and a wrinkled T-shirt.

"What's going on?" she asked.

"State Department. Relax."

A couple of sharp knocks at the door and Reznick let them in.

Mavor waited until the door slammed shut before he spoke. "Sorry to bother you at this time of night, folks."

Lauren rubbed her eyes as she looked at Mavor. "So what's going on?"

"We've got a break. The first one so far."

Reznick said, "Why are you telling us? I thought I was out of the loop."

"We believe he's coming for you."

"I knew that already," Reznick said.

Mavor handed him a surveillance photo of what looked like Ford. "Taken only six hours ago in Sóller town square. He was chatting with two Americans. Then he stole their RV."

"So he's broken cover. I'm surprised he got so sloppy. How did he register on your system?"

"When he stole the RV, it pinged Civil Guard in Madrid. The voice in the car wasn't a match of those who rented it. We were alerted. The NSA quickly retrieved the image from the town's surveillance network."

Reznick thought it seemed strange.

"You don't look convinced."

"Adam Ford, as you know, is a very, very intelligent man. He's cunning. And he's supersmart. I'm surprised he was just suddenly found. He's eluded detection so far. I'm assuming he's been using a portable jammer to evade detection up to this point. Standard gadgetry, right?"

Mavor sighed. "I think he's assumed he would go unnoticed. But I've been told that the RV he stole is very high end. It doesn't rely on the GPS signal to keep track of the vehicle."

"So, what happened?"

"The vehicle indicated that it was probably stolen, through unfamiliar voice recognition. So, it transmitted, in very short, low-power radio signals on random frequencies."

Reznick felt his heart rate hike up. "Now, that is interesting."

"We checked the GPS remotely—well, the NSA did. The directions. He's headed for Cala San Vicente."

"Why haven't we intercepted the vehicle?"

"We found it thirty minutes ago. At the bottom of a cliff, five miles up the coast."

"Was anyone in it?"

"We don't believe so. No sign of anyone."

Reznick contemplated the move. "He's ditched the vehicle and is heading into town on foot?"

"That's what CIA analysis is showing. Might've stolen another car. But so far, nothing has been reported stolen within twenty miles of here."

Reznick looked across at Lauren. Her arms were folded.

"We want you to know, Jon—you too, Lauren—that there's still time to get out of here. That would be the smart move. That's the advice I would give you both."

Lauren stared at Mavor but didn't speak.

Reznick sighed. "Is that the official State Department advice?"

Mavor nodded. "I just got off the phone with Finsburg. He agrees. It's best for you both to get back to the States while you still can."

Reznick looked at his daughter. "What do you think, honey?"

"I'm not going anywhere. This is not the time to run."

Reznick fixed his gaze on Mavor. "Guess that's settled. We're not going anywhere."

"He's headed this way. And he will find you and your daughter. And he will kill you both."

"Not if I kill him first."

Forty-Five

Ford stood on a bone-dry dirt trail, checking the luminous face of his watch under the pale moonlight. He adjusted the backpack slung over his shoulders. He wasn't far from Puerto Pollensa. He knew the area, having lived in Mallorca for the last six months. He would approach Cala San Vicente on foot. The long way. But it was almost certainly the safest way, knowing the Civil Guard would be all over the area.

He felt the sweat sticking to his T-shirt, running down his back. He took a bottle of water from the backpack and gulped some down. He strode on. He headed northwest and walked for a few hundred yards, then turned onto a goat track.

He hiked for a short while before he came to an iron gate that was open. He continued on. He passed by piles of stones that had been assembled by hikers as waymarks and painted with red dots.

He took the gentle climb on the old fishermen's trail.

Ford stopped for a breather and turned around. In the distance, he could see the shimmering lights of Alcudia Old Town and the boats on Pollensa Bay.

He walked on, hiking hard, until he was atop the Coll de Siller hill.

But from there, it was a gentle descent.

He stayed off the main path and took one on the left, indicated by two cairns.

Ford walked on for twenty more minutes until he came to the end of the narrow path. He saw the lights of Cala Molins Bay sparkling in the distance. He afforded himself a smile. Not long now.

He had imagined it would be easier to kill Jon Reznick. He reflected on that. The first attempt, the poisoning, had failed. The second attempt, crudely smashing into him with his car, catapulting him and his daughter into the drainage channel, hadn't been successful either. And the brilliant third attempt, remotely detonating the modernist home in the hills while he watched from Port de Sóller, only took out eight men. Reznick, he assumed, would have rushed to the location. But the fucker hadn't taken the bait.

The more he thought about it, the more Ford wondered if he was overthinking the operation. The closest he had come to killing Reznick was crashing into him with his car, nearly drowning both him and his daughter. Maybe it needed to be a rough-and-ready strategy.

The cat-and-mouse game he was playing was coming to an end. He would find Reznick in the little seaside hamlet. And he would kill him. He didn't care how. Only that Reznick would take his last breath. And Ford would get to watch. His fantasies and the myriad ways he had conceived of killing Reznick had to be pushed aside. The window of opportunity was slowly closing.

Ford had to strike, even if it meant blowing his cover. It was a high-risk strategy. But that was fine. The time for playing it safe, playing the long game, was over. He sensed the endgame was in sight. He would hunker down for the night. And strike first thing in the morning.

He headed through the trees and down onto a dark, narrow residential street.

Ford quickly headed north out of the town and back onto the rural track. He walked on for a few miles until he reached the caves. The white caves. Punta de Coves Blanques. He pulled a flashlight off his belt and shined it into the main cave. He headed inside for twenty yards.

Ford had found his shelter for the night, away from prying eyes.

Forty-Six

Reznick insisted on a punishing early-morning run. He wore a backpack with his two 9mm Berettas inside, and he ran hard in the predawn light. He turned around and saw Lauren puffing hard, red in the face, sweat beading her forehead.

"Is this really necessary, Dad?" she said.

"You didn't have to join me," he said. "You could've slept in. Would've been safer."

Lauren was breathing fast. "I never want to be a sitting target. And I don't intend to be."

"You prefer being a moving target? Because that's what you are right now. That's what I am."

"I'll take my chances."

Reznick glanced back again and grinned at his daughter. Her face was flushed crimson. "You OK?"

"This gradient and conditions are harder than Quantico's Yellow Brick wooded trail. And that was six point one miles of hell."

"Suck it up, Lauren," he said. "No gain without pain."

"I know. This is what we did at Quantico each and every day. Twice a day."

Reznick grinned, his lungs burning. "Stop bitching. You gotta love the pain."

"Tell me about it."

Reznick ran faster up a steep incline alongside the Cala Molins beach. Waves crashed onto the rocky shore. His daughter was struggling to keep up. But before long she'd gotten a second wind and was matching him stride for stride.

Lauren turned and smiled at him. "I'm still here," she said. "Still hanging in there."

"That's my girl."

Reznick slowed down as they approached the overlook. He stopped, catching his breath, hands on hips as Lauren did some stretching exercises. He looked over the bay, the amber dawn light reflecting off the dark waters. The police launch boat was still there, as was the buoy. It was chilling to see the spot where the yacht had been blown out of the water. "Can't believe what happened in such a peaceful spot," he said.

Lauren wiped her brow with the back of her arm. "She's alive. We've got to be thankful."

"Indeed we do. You're absolutely right."

Lauren climbed up the rocky outcrop as Reznick followed suit. He wrapped an arm around her. "I'm glad you joined me here."

"Could have fooled me."

"It's just the way I am. You do realize that we're sitting ducks?"

"Which does have the advantage that it might lure the target to break cover, one more time."

Reznick grinned. "Smart girl."

"That's not to say I'm not a little scared."

"We all get scared."

"Even you?"

"Even me. It's how you manage the fear that counts. Overcome it."

"I wonder when he'll show up."

"He's been calling the shots from the get-go. I guess we'll know soon enough."

"He must really have it in for you. He set this whole thing up. Just to get you."

"It's crazy, I know."

"You think he'll find us?"

"He'll be back, alright. We just need to be alert."

Lauren's gaze was drawn to the buoy out on the water. "You must have some effect on people, Dad."

"What do you mean?"

"That this guy, Adam Ford, so badly wants to kill you that he lured you here by blowing up the yacht Martha was on."

"True story."

Lauren sighed. "Do we have any news on her condition?"

"No, but I'm sure the hospital is taking good care of her."

Lauren forced a smile. But he could see the tension in her face.

"It's natural to be scared. Shows your senses are working. It's important to be switched on to danger."

"I just don't like being a sitting duck."

"Nobody does. But here's the thing. Sometimes you have to put yourself in the crosshairs."

"You really believe that?"

"There are always risks. If you don't like the odds, you need to get out of the game."

"At Quantico, they stress the importance of managing risk and assessing and managing threats. It's very nuanced."

"It's all good stuff. In my line of work, in the field, on the front line, the reality is different. Kill or be killed. But sure, you need to work the problem. Think of the threat. And sometimes you have to get your hands dirty. Lines get blurred. Good and bad."

"I've got a lot to learn, I guess."

"You're going to do fine."

Lauren went quiet for a few moments.

Reznick thought it was time to change the morbid subject. "So, how are you finding living and working in New York?"

"Long days. But it's great. There's a new opening coming up for me."

"In New York?"

Lauren shook her head. "Not quite. The Special Agent in Charge spoke to Martha before all this happened. He recommended me for a fast-track leadership course at Quantico. And once it's finished in a couple of months, I'll be heading back to the field office in Manhattan."

"That's fantastic. Grab the opportunity."

"I intend to."

"You can go back to the FBI and tell them all about this. Though I'm guessing this might not be on the curriculum at Quantico."

Lauren smiled, tucking some loose hair behind her ear. "I don't think so."

Reznick looked at his beautiful, strong-willed daughter and couldn't help thinking of his late wife, Elisabeth. The same expression on her face. The same way she accentuated some words. And a fierce intellect. He was so, so proud of their daughter.

"This can only end one way, can't it?" Lauren said.

"What?"

"This, here, in Mallorca."

"Pretty much. Either he'll be in a box, or it'll be us. Don't be under any illusions. This is real."

Lauren's gaze flicked back to the endless sea in front of them.

"We're the hunted. He's the hunter. We just need to make sure that we don't become his latest prey."

Forty-Seven

Daylight broke, and light flooded into the cave. Ford had stayed out of sight, the way he wanted. He slowly opened his eyes, got his bearings, and crawled out. He needed to move before the troublesome hikers and tourists turned up. He reached into his backpack, grabbed a bottle of water, and took a few welcome gulps.

Ford put the bottle back in the pack and rifled inside, pulling out a handheld radio scanner and switching it on. Distorted, crackly Spanish voices. The batteries were working well.

Ford's Spanish was proficient. Passable. Not fluent. But good enough to get by.

He adjusted the scanner's position to get better reception.

A few moments of garbled communications from the control tower at Palma International Airport. It randomly jumped frequencies for the next few minutes. Switching between Pollensa police arresting a British tourist for spitting at them and a paramedic trying to revive a Dutch tourist who had overdosed on Ecstasy in his hotel room in Alcudia.

The incessant chatter on police and Civil Guard frequencies filled the still early-morning air.

Ford gulped down some more water as the sun began to bathe the hills and sea in a tangerine glow. Shimmering water in the distance, waves crashing off rocks.

He switched frequencies.

A few short bursts of conversation from the Civil Guard observing two people in Cala San Vicente.

Ford listened closely. *Americano y su hija.* It translated as "American and his daughter." *Bastardo duro.* That meant "tough bastard," if he wasn't mistaken. He began to piece together what was happening. Two Civil Guard officers had cruised past a pair he believed to be Reznick with his daughter. Their job was to pick them up and take them straight to the airport. Immediately.

Ford couldn't allow that to happen. He knew this was the time. The last opportunity to strike. It had to be done now. And to hell with a carefully choreographed assassination. He listened to exactly where Reznick was. And then it became clear that Reznick was sitting on the rocks adjacent to the weather vane on Carrer del Temporal. The location overlooked the sea and sported great views, if viewed from high enough, over Cara Clara Beach.

Ford built up a picture in his head. He knew the location. It was the exact spot where he had observed the yacht and detonated the explosion that killed Meyerstein. Now he knew precisely where Reznick and his daughter were. At least at that moment. The good news was that they were in town. Right now. But he had to act. No further delays. This was his chance. Maybe his only chance.

Ford packed the scanner and his things away in the backpack, then slung it over his shoulder. He headed toward a narrow path that led down to the sea. A small dinghy used by tour guides was tied up there.

He made a mental calculation. The town was only one mile away, across the water.

Ford thought he could be there in a few minutes. Then a short walk across town. In ten minutes, he would be face-to-face with Reznick and his daughter. Catch them unawares.

Ford stepped into the dinghy and set off across the water. He felt the salt water in his face, the sun glinting off the blue sea. Closer and closer to land. He imagined what he would do when he saw Reznick and his daughter. Who would he kill first? The thoughts were running around his head, an endless stream of ideas.

A few minutes later, the dinghy approached the soft, undulating beach. Ford switched off the engine and let the boat's momentum guide it onto the deserted sands.

He jumped down onto the sand, walked up the steps, and looked around. Whitewashed hotels and apartments. His gaze lingered.

A Civil Guard cruiser was parked not far away, opposite the beach. He brushed off the sand from his trousers and put his backpack on.

Ford smiled and walked on. He had to assume they were looking for him. The cop sitting in the passenger seat had his arm out of the window. The driver was drinking a cup of coffee. Neither looked too pleased to see him.

Ford nodded. *"Buenos días, señor."*

The cop had dull eyes. Lifeless. His arm was draped lazily out of the window as if the dumb fuck owned the town. "Señor, papers, please. Passport?"

Ford smiled his best smile. "It's in my bag," he said.

Both cops nodded. Truth be told, he was amazed they understood a word of English.

Ford sighed, trying to appear more bored than he really was. He had to stifle a smile as he rifled in the side pocket.

"Señor!" the cop snapped. "Please hurry up!"

Ford felt something break inside his head. He didn't like being told what to do. And certainly not by some shitkicker Spanish cop. He calmly reached into the side pocket and pulled out a silenced Smith & Wesson M&P22 Compact. Then he pressed the gun tight up against the cop's head. He pulled the trigger twice. Double tap to the temple. Blood spurted everywhere, a dull *phut* sound.

The cop in the driver's seat fumbled for his gun. But it was too late.

Ford fired one shot to the driver's forehead, blood splatter hitting the windshield. The smell of smoke rose from the gunshots. He looked around. Not a soul in sight. What a time to be alive. Killing cops in cold blood.

He laughed at the extremity of it all. Ford casually opened the passenger door and hauled out the first cop. Then he reached over and pulled out the second cop, dropping their bodies onto the dusty roadside.

It was just past dawn, and he was already in the kill zone.

Ford slid into the blood-splattered seat. The smell of gun smoke and human tissue ignited his senses. He put the cop car into gear and pulled away slowly. He began to laugh. "Now do you believe me, you fuckers?"

Next stop: Jon Reznick.

Forty-Eight

The cop car appeared on the crest of the hill.

Reznick watched the car as he sat with Lauren in the beach-front bar. It appeared to approach at a normal speed. Then it slowed and stopped halfway down. Reznick stared at the car. A lone cop. The car eased down the hill and approached. The windshield wipers sluicing fast. Reznick sensed something was wrong.

He instinctively grabbed Lauren's hand and dove for cover among the tables and chairs of the beachfront bar. "Stay down!" He took the 9mm from the backpack and handed his daughter the other Beretta. The car began to accelerate, moving fast toward them. The sound of screeching tires split the dawn air. "Heads down! Lie flat! Now!"

A ripple of panic spread through the bar. Some people started sobbing as they clung to each other under tables. Reznick crawled to the front of the bar and saw it was a Civil Guard vehicle. Speeding fast down the road into the town. On the other side of the road he saw a mother pushing a stroller toward the beach. *"Cuidado, señora,"* he yelled, warning her of the danger.

The woman glanced up and hurriedly pushed the stroller toward the sidewalk, fear on her face.

Reznick turned around and saw Lauren beside him. "Don't be afraid."

Lauren nodded, fear in her eyes.

Reznick turned over a table, and they both took up defensive positions, guns drawn. He wondered why the hell it was a Civil Guard car speeding through the town.

Time seemed to slow.

Reznick spotted the driver. It was Ford, gun drawn, teeth clenched. *Fuck.* The bastard fired off four shots, strafing the bar. The bullets shattered glass behind them. Thudding into the thick wood.

Reznick took two quick shots at the driver's window. A direct hit to the guy's shoulder.

The car screeched around the corner as Lauren stood up and fired off some shots, shattering the cop car's rear window.

Reznick jumped to his feet and ran up to the owner, who was crouched behind the bar.

"What is happening?" the bar owner shouted.

"Where's the bike?"

The owner pointed to the back of the bar and put the keys on the counter.

Reznick grabbed them. "Call the cops! It looks like someone has stolen a Civil Guard vehicle."

"What?"

"Just do it!"

The bar owner pointed to the vehicle accelerating fast up the hill, out of the town. "There he is!"

Reznick ran down the side alley and climbed on the Ducati. He put the key in the ignition and revved up the bike hard. He saw Lauren running toward him. "Climb on!"

She got on the bike, one arm draped around his chest. He skidded away, moving through the gears, as he tore up the hill toward the stolen Civil Guard car.

"Dad! I see him! Two hundred yards due north!"

Reznick crouched down low on the tank, Lauren hanging on for dear life, as they gave chase. He was going to get the fucker. No matter what.

Forty-Nine

Ford screamed at the excruciating pain like burning lava in his right arm. "Motherfucker! God damn you, fucker!"

He saw the blood dripping off his arm.

Reznick had fired at him. Hit him as he drove past. He'd gotten some shots in. But it was a scattergun approach.

Fuck!

Ford was accelerating up the road out of town, wondering whether to turn around at the next opportunity and head back down and finish the job. He cursed himself for not getting out at the bar and taking Reznick out at close range. But something within him had balked at that.

Had Ford blinked first? Did he fear what would happen? Face-to-face?

Fuck!

Had he lost his nerve? Did he not want to go toe-to-toe with Reznick? Was that it?

The mere thought enraged him. His mind flashed back to that split-second decision. Whether to stop and fight or drive on and live to tell the tale? He wondered why on earth he had fired and sped by. He had prayed for that opportunity for so long. But he had blown it.

Fuck!

Suddenly, a flash of light in his rearview mirror.

Ford glanced back. A motorcycle was bearing down on him. And it was Reznick, head down, coming full speed for him. He began to smile. Maybe he was going to get a second bite at the apple. Pain shot up his arm, and he clenched his teeth. "That the way you want it, you fuck? You wanna catch me? Come and get me!"

Fifty

Reznick accelerated hard as he approached the stolen cop car. "Take the rear tire!" he shouted.

Lauren was holding on with one hand around his waist. Two shots rang out.

Reznick was momentarily deafened. The car's right rear tire exploded. He gripped the bike as it jolted when Lauren adjusted her position. The car swerved violently on the narrow winding ascent, revving hard, burning rubber. Sparks flew from the steel rim of the wheel.

"Hang on!"

Reznick edged closer, eyes scrunched up against the sun and the noise of the screeching metal on the asphalt. He saw a sharp bend up ahead. He accelerated fast and got level. He turned. Adam Ford was bleeding, sobbing, and screaming.

The bastard glanced around and raised a gun. It was pointed straight at Reznick. Ford's eyes were wide open, crazy, his mouth contorted as if sneering. It was as if Ford had lost his mind. Completely gone.

Reznick braked hard and came to a stop, Lauren gripping him tight around the waist. He watched as the car careered fast up the mountainside, getting away from them. "Motherfucker!" He turned and looked at his daughter. Fear in her eyes. She was breathing hard, gasping for air. "You OK?"

She closed her eyes for a moment. "I'm fine."

"Are you sure?"

"I'm sure."

Reznick took a moment to catch his own breath. "Let's get him!"

Fifty-One

Ford gripped the steering wheel, struggling to control the car. He was losing control of the vehicle. Losing control of his operation. He felt it all slipping away from him. The stifling air billowing through the shot-up car windows. The police radio crackling into life. The pain erupting in waves. "Motherfucker!"

He glanced in the rearview mirror. Half a mile behind him was the high-powered motorcycle. Reznick and his daughter were still on his tail.

His instincts were telling him this was his last chance. He had one shot. He had to make it count. His hand was trembling, holding his gun, trying to control the car.

Ford wanted to turn the cop car around and ram them off the mountainside cliffs and into the blue waters far below. But the car was screeching and billowing smoke as it powered up the steep incline. His foot was to the floor, the car struggling to hit sixty.

The radio buzzed. "Señor, identify yourself. Do you hear me? Identify yourself!"

Ford grabbed the radio and flicked the switch to speak. "Are you fucking kidding me? Now listen here, you fucks! I just iced two of your laziest officers. You tell their wives and family it was for the best. Fuck them! And fuck you! Survival of the fittest! Do you understand? Do you copy!"

The voice on the radio began to shout. "Who the hell is this?"

Ford laughed as he fought to control the steering with one hand. "I'll tell you who this is. This is me. A free man. Exerting free will. I decide how I live. And I also decide how to die. I don't want to live like a dog."

"Señor!"

"Shut the fuck up! I'm a man who will never live on his knees. My name will live on."

"Identify yourself!"

"I'm an American. I'm a free man. Do you *comprender*?"

The radio went silent.

Ford ripped it out by the wires, exposed and sparking. "Happy now?"

He glanced again at the rearview mirror. The motorcycle was approaching. Fast. The bastard was definitely closing in. Two hundred yards. Maximum. Tearing up the mountain road toward him.

Ford smiled through clenched teeth. The pain was burning deep into his flesh, and tears filled his vision. His mind flashed memories of his childhood. His graduation. His proud parents watching him. The faces of patients he'd treated. The faces of people he had killed. The face of the North African kid before he decapitated him. And he began to laugh. "You next, Reznick? You ready to play? Come and get it, you fucker! Come and fucking get it!"

Fifty-Two

Reznick accelerated hard around the bend, chest on the tank, as he headed toward the cop car. Sparks were flying as the metal rim screeched. Black smoke billowing out of the front. His mind raced as he quickly approached the vehicle. The car was weaving, recklessly, as if Ford was trying to block their approach. "No you fucking don't!"

He opened the throttle to the max. The bike was hitting one hundred on the mountain road.

Reznick pulled up alongside the vehicle. He saw Ford staring, cackling like a jackal, gun shaking in his hand. Reznick aimed the barrel of the Beretta straight at Ford's laughing face. He fired off two head shots. The bullets tore into Ford's head, through the skull, and exploded out of the brain, erupting in a mess of blood against the shattered driver's window. Ford's head was lolling.

The cop car veered sharply across the road, through a metal barrier, and over the mountainside.

Reznick braked hard at the mountain's edge. He watched as the car, with Ford inside, tumbled and tumbled, propelling itself at high speed to the foot of the cliffs. The car exploded. It sounded like a bomb going off. A fireball, flames licking the sky, scorching the tinder-dry hillside. Black smoke filled the air. Choking Reznick and Lauren. He turned and hugged his daughter tight.

The bastard was gone. Good and gone.

Fifty-Three

The hours that followed seemed like a fever dream to Reznick. Events flashed by. The adrenaline, amphetamines, and raw emotions were running through him. Cops arrived, guns drawn.

Reznick and his daughter were handcuffed and whisked away to Palma by the Civil Guard. The Civil Guard cops initially thought they were responsible for the murders of two of their fellow officers.

A few hours later, Lionel Finsburg arrived, having returned from the States. He asked for the handcuffs to be taken off Reznick and Lauren. Then they were led to a windowless room in the basement.

A desk with two chairs on either side.

Reznick and Lauren sat down on one side.

Finsburg sat down on the other. The legal attaché opened his briefcase and took out some papers, laying them carefully on the desk. "This is very, very irregular," he said.

Reznick held his daughter's hand. "It's OK, honey."

Finsburg looked first at Lauren. "How are you holding up?"

"I'm OK."

Finsburg gave a sympathetic smile. "Some vacation, huh?"

"One I won't forget, that's for sure," Lauren said.

Reznick said, "What do you want to know, Lionel?"

"Are you both OK?"

"We'll live," Reznick said.

"So, quite a day. I've been very busy, as you can imagine. Things have been very fraught, to say the least. Anyway, I've been holding discussions with the State Department and Spanish military intelligence on this issue."

"What are they saying?" Lauren asked.

"They have had the opportunity to view surveillance footage from a nearby hotel. It shows clearly that the man we believe to be Adam Ford killed the officers in cold blood. Clear as day."

"Believe to be?" Lauren said.

"There will have to be DNA tests to establish that it's him. The problem is this might very well be degraded after the explosion, so we'll have to rely on DNA from the roots of a tooth. But we're sure this is our guy."

Reznick said nothing.

"Lot of information to process, right, Jon?"

Reznick nodded.

"OK, here's where we are. Your daughter, Lauren, as an FBI employee, was integral, from what I understand, in apprehending Ford. Technically, there might be breaches in protocol. She was armed."

"It was my gun. I was legally carrying overseas."

"I'm sure there are aspects of this that might alarm members of the numerous intelligence oversight committees in Washington, but that's another matter for another day. The Spanish are quite clear that Adam Ford was responsible for the killings. With regards to what happened to Martha Meyerstein and the other deaths, I cannot talk about that. Neither can you." He looked at Lauren, long and hard. "Lauren, many elements of what have happened are now classified, top secret. You don't have the right clearance.

So we're going to trust that this subject will never be broached by you outside these four walls."

"I understand."

"Failure to comply will result in your prosecution in the US. Are we clear?"

Lauren nodded. "Quite clear, sir."

Finsburg sighed. "The State Department is freaking out, not to put too fine a point on it. But they seem satisfied that what happened here in Mallorca will go no further."

Lauren bowed her head. "What about me? What about my career?"

"I've been speaking to the Director about this. The FBI is looking forward to you returning to the field office in Manhattan in six days' time."

Lauren looked up and smiled. "Thank you so much."

"The next time you're on vacation, though, you might want to go without your father."

"I appreciate your advice."

"All part of the job."

"So we're good?"

"It's fine." Finsburg looked at Reznick. "Jon, I can't stress this enough, but I'm going to, one more time, tell you not to discuss this matter. You cannot discuss this matter or anything that has occurred here in Mallorca."

"What if I'm called to give evidence by an oversight committee?"

"You say what you have to say, but remember, this is classified."

"You want me to take the Fifth?"

"Take whatever you like. But nothing happened here."

Reznick nodded.

"Spain's national intelligence center knows what happened. And we have been liaising with them throughout."

"What about Mac? David McCafferty."

"He's alive. He's back on British soil."

"I'm pleased to hear that."

"He'll be held at a secure location in the UK until this blows over, before he's allowed to return to Mallorca."

"What about the body of his sister?"

"Very sad what happened to her. The repatriation is complete. That's all I know. That's a matter for the British."

Reznick leaned back in his chair. "How are they going to explain the killings of the two Civil Guard officers?"

"We have a cover story. Adam Ford, American citizen on holiday, high on drugs, kills a couple of Civil Guards before he flees the scene, losing control of the stolen vehicle. I believe that narrative will hold water."

"You've got it all figured out."

"Not me."

"Then who?"

"You don't need to know that, Jon. One of our red lines I've been discussing over the last few hours is access to you and your daughter."

"So what's the result?"

"The result is the Spanish police and Civil Guard will not be permitted to interview you. Military intelligence is leading on this."

"National security?"

Finsburg nodded. "It's in no one's interests for all this to get out. It's a mess. But it's done. You're both free to go home."

Lauren got up from her chair and hugged Reznick tight, as if she didn't want to let go. "The job is done."

Reznick said nothing.

Finsburg got to his feet and shook Reznick's hand. "I'm glad you're going to finally make it home, Jon. It's been a hell of a week."

"It certainly has. Appreciate you pulling those strings, Lionel. I owe you one."

"You don't owe me a thing. There is one proviso with the deal, though."

"What's that?"

"You're being allowed to leave, but it has to be now."

"How soon is now?"

"Right this second. A private plane is waiting, and it's already been allocated a takeoff slot."

Fifty-Four

It was dark when they landed back on American soil. Reznick knew it was Camp Peary, known as the Farm. It was a military airfield ringed by woods, used by the CIA in rural Virginia, near Williamsburg.

Reznick and Lauren disembarked and were driven by a burly plainclothes officer to an office on the base.

The man behind the desk didn't get up. He just sat, smiling, staring at them both. "Good to have you back, Jon, and you, Lauren."

"Thank you, sir," Reznick said.

"Lauren, would you mind leaving the room for a moment?"

Lauren stared at the man. "Why would I have to leave the room?"

"I've got something to say to your father. It won't take long. There's a female operative outside. Don't be afraid."

"I'm not."

The man smiled. "I like your spirit."

Lauren got up and looked at Reznick. "See you in a little while, Dad."

Reznick touched her hand as she passed. "Sure. I'll join you in a little while."

Lauren left the room, quietly closing the door behind her.

The man sighed long and hard. "I'm sorry about that. Nothing personal."

"Not a problem."

"My name is Jeff Moreles. CIA. Associate Director of Military Affairs. I've been overseeing what's been going on."

Reznick nodded. "And what's your assessment?"

"Wild vacation, Jon. Very, very wild. But I'd expect nothing less."

"It had its moments."

Moreles nodded. "I've spoken to a few people who knew you, back in the day. And I know you're well acquainted with what goes on here. I just want to give you a heads-up, in case Lionel Finsburg didn't fill you in on all the details."

Reznick nodded.

"Adam Ford . . . you took him out. An American citizen, namely you, taking out an American citizen overseas, namely Adam Ford. It's problematic. Especially if the oversight committees, intelligence committees, or whatever bullshit committee is formed to investigate this, come calling. Do you see what I'm saying?"

"You don't have to worry about me. It didn't happen."

"Take the Fifth. Makes it nice and easy for everyone."

"Will it be behind closed doors?"

"One hundred percent. We'll cite national security and classified this, that, and the next thing, and it'll be fine. So you won't be on public display."

Reznick looked at Moreles. "You mind if I ask a question?"

"Sure, fire away."

"Was Adam Ford CIA at one time?"

"I couldn't possibly comment. Let's leave it at that."

"I'll take that as a yes."

"Take it whatever way you want, Jon."

"The operation he was involved in . . . to kill the President?"

Moreles smiled. "I don't know anything about that, Jon."

"You sure?"

Moreles said nothing.

"Are you sure about that?"

"Quite sure. The CIA is this country's foreign intelligence service. We collect information and conduct operations, by and large, abroad. That answer your question?"

"Did you know or work with Adam Ford at any point?"

Moreles stared at him for what seemed like an eternity.

"I'd like to speak to David McCafferty."

"Why?"

"I want to offer my condolences."

Moreles pulled out his cell phone and dialed. He handed the phone to Reznick. "Secure line, don't worry."

Reznick pressed the cell phone tight to his ear.

"McCafferty."

"David, it's Jon Reznick."

"Alright, Jon?"

"I'm OK. Mac, I'm calling to say how sorry I am for the loss of your sister. I wish I could've done more."

"I was told what you did to help her. I'm very grateful. But I would've expected nothing less."

Reznick felt himself smile. "Anyway, I just wanted to speak to you. You back home?"

"I'm in Scotland just now. But I'm hoping to get back to the sunshine in a couple of months. And if you manage to make it across again, we can share a wee dram. How does that sound?"

"I'd like that."

"Until the next time."

"Until the next time. Take care, Mac."

Reznick ended the call. He sighed as he looked at Moreles. "So, are we done here?"

"All good, Jon. Welcome back."

Epilogue

Three months later, the golden leaves falling as temperatures dropped across Maine, Reznick was sitting alone in the Rockland Tavern, nursing a beer, when his cell phone rang.

"Jon?" The raspy voice belonged to Jerry Meyerstein.

"Jerry, how are you?"

"I'm sorry I haven't had the chance to thank you."

"Relax. You have nothing to thank me for."

"That's where you're wrong, Jon. I asked you to go over there. And you risked your life. So did your daughter."

"Well, we had a good outcome."

"It was a great outcome. You took the fucker down. And I owe you so much."

"What's done is done. How's Martha?"

"I thought I had lost her." Jerry sighed, his voice breaking with emotion. "I thought I had lost her."

"She's tough. Like her dad."

"Maybe. I don't know. I haven't got long. But I'm at peace knowing we got her back home. Flesh and blood, Jon. Nothing more valuable. It's all we have."

Reznick took a gulp of his beer. "All there is, Jerry."

The man cleared his throat. "I'm calling, belatedly, just to thank you. My wife was ill when we heard about the explosion. It nearly killed her when we heard. But she's now back to her old self since Martha's return."

"I'm glad."

"I'm at peace now."

"I'm sorry, Jerry. About your prognosis, I mean."

"It comes to us all, Jon. Listen, the next time you're in Chicago, be sure to come around for a drink. Make it soon."

"I hear what you're saying. You got a deal."

"And bring your daughter too. Maybe catch a ball game. I believe in a month's time the Giants are in town playing the Bears. How does that sound?"

"Sounds good."

"Then that's settled."

"How's Martha?"

A sigh. "Martha is . . . Jon, the physical scars are there, but they're healing. The mental scars? That'll take a bit more time. She lost her friend."

"I know. Look, I've been meaning to call her," Reznick said. "But I thought it best to wait until I knew she had fully recovered."

"She's been on a long vacation down in Florida. Boca Raton, I believe. But I know she's been planning to contact you."

"As long as she's recovering, I'm happy."

"Jon, thank God there are people like you. I owe you one. From the bottom of my heart, I thank you."

After the call, Reznick finished his drink and took the long way home to his isolated cabin on the outskirts of Rockland.

The moon illuminated the sodden leaves covering the path. The same path his late father had walked to and from his work at the sardine packing plant. The same path he'd walked down a million times. To the house his father had built with his own hands when he returned from Vietnam.

Up ahead, Reznick's gaze was drawn to a car outside his home. A silhouetted figure was sitting inside the vehicle.

This time of night, it could be a few different people. Maybe Bill Eastland, the former police chief of Rockland, stopping by for a nightcap, which he sometimes did. Reznick's mind flashed back to the surreal conversation with Moreles at Camp Peary when he got back from Mallorca. But as he got closer, Reznick could see it wasn't Eastland or Moreles. The silhouetted figure was a woman.

The car door opened.

Wrapped up in an ankle-length coat and a scarf was Martha Meyerstein. "Hey . . ."

Reznick walked toward her. She was crying. He stood in front of her and smiled.

"Why didn't you call?"

"Had a few things to take care of."

"How are you now?"

"A few aches and pains, but hey, nothing to lose sleep over. Had a long vacation."

"It's great to see you again."

"You too. Sorry to turn up unannounced."

"How long have you been waiting?"

Martha took a handkerchief from her pocket and dabbed her eyes. "Not long. A lifetime, maybe. I don't know."

Reznick smiled. "I was just talking to your dad."

"So I heard. He texted me just before you arrived."

"Did you coordinate this?"

"A little, maybe."

Reznick reached out and held her hand. "You're freezing cold."

Martha gazed at him and smiled.

"You wanna come inside? I'll get some logs on the fire."

Martha handed him a bottle of single malt scotch. "Strictly medicinal purposes, Jon."

"Nice to have you back home."

"Nice to be home."

Acknowledgments

I would like to thank my editor, Jack Butler, and everyone at Amazon Publishing for their enthusiasm, hard work, and belief in the Jon Reznick thriller series. I would also like to thank my loyal readers. Thanks also to Faith Black Ross for her terrific work on this book, and Caitlin Alexander in New York, who looked over an early draft. Special thanks to my agent, Mitch Hoffman, of the Aaron M. Priest Literary Agency, New York.

Last but by no means least, my family and friends for their encouragement and support. None more so than my wife, Susan.

About the Author

J. B. Turner is a former journalist and the author of the Jon Reznick series of action thrillers (*Hard Road, Hard Kill, Hard Wired, Hard Way, Hard Fall, Hard Hit,* and *Hard Shot*), the American Ghost series of black-ops thrillers (*Rogue, Reckoning,* and *Requiem*), and the Deborah Jones political thrillers (*Miami Requiem* and *Dark Waters*). He has a keen interest in geopolitics. He lives in Scotland with his wife and two children.